The Copy Cat

DETECTIVE ANNA JAMES

THE
COPY
CAT

EMMY ELLIS

Joffe Books, London
www.joffebooks.com

First published in Great Britain in 2024

Cover art by Dee Dee Books Covers

ISBN: 978-1-83526-678-6

PROLOGUE

1993

A brood of maggots writhed beneath the discoloured skin, creating an undulating blanket. Some, swollen from greed, spilled out of the stab wounds. They wriggled away, tumbling across the stomach to fall off onto the peat of the moor. Others landed in the boggy ground beneath the dead man's head and shoulders. Newly hatched flies whizzed around, exuberant in their quest for gorging, a cloud of black. Older ones had arrived on Day One to feast as soon as they'd picked up the scent of the corpse, and their bodies were fat now, their buzz sluggish.

They'd probably eaten too much.

Ten-year-old Rory McFadden didn't know why the flies wanted to stick around. The smell was awful, like strong, mouldy cheese and ruined fruit.

"Do you like what you see, my boy?"

Rory nodded at Dad, confused because, oddly, he *did* like it. Just as he'd liked this body when it had been alive in the cellar of Nan's cottage. It wasn't something he should enjoy, all that blood, the stab wounds, the man pleading for Dad to

1

please let him go. And now, the flies, the maggots, the lower arm ripped off to the elbow. Dad had already removed the hand and placed it in a shoebox so he could watch the deterioration "at his leisure".

When Rory had gone down into the cellar and seen Dad with Number Three, he'd hidden in the corner, the shadows cloaking him. Fascination had gripped him hard. Number Three had a suit on, the jacket discarded on the floor, his shirtsleeves rolled up. Blood had seeped through the slits in his white shirt. His hair, swept back, had shone beneath the single bare bulb, as black as Mum's. Three had sweated, his forehead damp with it, and when he'd spoken he'd sounded foreign.

"There's a boy over there," he'd said. "For the love of God, don't let him see this."

Dad had spun round. "Son?"

Blinking the memory away, Rory concentrated on the now.

"Where did that part of his arm go?" he asked, looking around for it.

"Likely a fox," Dad muttered. "They're hungry bastards when they have a mind."

Rory cast his gaze ahead to the vast expanse, the Yorkshire city of Marlford in the distance. No foxes around. Maybe they only came out at night. To the left, Nan's cottage round a bend, and thank goodness for that. The last thing they needed was for her to see them. To the right, a long stretch of moor that butted against farmland about a mile away.

This man, this very dead man, lay beneath a tree, the thick trunk obscuring much of Rory's view. He walked round it, but the chunk of arm wasn't there. Dad must be right. A fox, then.

He returned to stand at Three's shoeless feet — Dad had the man's shoes on, said he liked to walk a mile in someone else's, to see what it was like, whether an expensive pair made him feel different. Richer, the same as Three. He had two other pairs lined up in Nan's cellar, taken from people he'd once known, people he'd thought were his friends.

"See that?" Dad asked.

He pointed to a clump of . . . a clump of something Rory hadn't seen before.

"They're fly eggs," Dad said. "Each patch has about three hundred of the buggers. From the moment the fly lays them, it takes a day for them to hatch into larvae. To begin with, they feed on fluid from the body."

Rory nodded, used to the way Dad preached. "Then what?"

"Then they moult for the first time."

"What's that?"

"Their skin comes off. Similar to that snake we watched on telly, you know? They moult four times, so four days. Then they become what's called pre-pupa. They stop eating, move away from the body. It takes another four days to become a pupa, then ten days for them to become a fly." He gestured to the hovering bluebottles. "So this lot, they were born from this tosser's body."

Rory counted it up. Had all that time really passed since Dad had stabbed Three at Nan's? He supposed it must have. There had been the final week of school, then last week had been the first of the summer holidays.

"Now then, if this bloke's found, there's a person who'll be able to work out when he died because of the maggots and flies. There are a few stages on the go at the minute, flies have been laying eggs ever since we put this bastard here, but anyway, some clever sod will know. Like I do."

"Is that from the books you read in the library?"

"Yeah."

Dad had already told Rory that you had to cover your tracks when you killed someone. Taking a book out could point the finger at him, there'd be a record of it, so that's why he read them *in* the library. There was this new thing that had come out in April, called the World Wide Web. Rory had learned about it at school, and you could look things up. Dad couldn't afford a computer, you needed one of those for it to work, and if he did, he wouldn't use it to find out what he needed. "Too dangerous, kid," he'd said. "I'd be caught in no time."

Rory didn't want Dad to get caught. That would mean he'd go to prison, then Rory would be left with Mum.

He shivered at the thought.

Dad chuckled. "Look at that! His belly's all bloated. Makes him seem pregnant."

Rory stared at it. The bloat had stretched the shirt and knife slits, and the buttons strained against the fabric. How had the tummy grown? Was it full of maggots?

"Putrid gas formation," Dad said, as if reading his mind. "Makes the belly distend." He seemed proud he'd remembered all that information. "See those veins? Think, boy. Were they here last time I brought you?"

Dad liked to test him.

"No."

The skin had a marbled effect like Nan's worktop in her kitchen. Some of it sagged, on the face and neck, as if it wanted to fall off. Now Rory came to study Three better, there were more changes since last time. Liquid came out of the eye sockets, the nostrils and the mouth, tinged with the colour of blood. It glistened in the sunlight.

"Urgh, what's that watery stuff?" he asked.

"A purge of putrid fluid."

That didn't really explain it to him properly, but Rory didn't fancy listening to all the ins and outs today. "Where's his eyes gone?"

"Birds pecked them out on Day Two. I came for a quick gander and they were gone."

Rory had been here on Day One, when they'd dumped Three here, and this was his second time back. Day Eighteen? Nineteen? Twenty? He gave up trying to work it out. "How come you haven't brought me every day?"

"Because I like to watch the changes on my own. Maybe I'll let you join me on the next one. Besides, your mum will start asking questions if we keep going off together. We've got to play it careful, like. Go off on our own more often, build it up so she doesn't notice you're hardly at home."

Mum ran her pet shop all day, so she wouldn't know if Rory was at home anyway. But he didn't want her being nosy. She was bad enough as it was.

Dad wrote something in his notebook. "In a month, you might get lucky and see some corpse wax."

"What's that?"

"It's like soap, formed when bacteria decays the body fat. That'll happen because his head and shoulders are in the wet boggy bit. That's why I put him here. Wanted to see what it was all about, didn't I?" Dad sighed and batted away a cluster of flies that had chosen to zoom at him. He glanced around, a frown forming. "Bugger. We'd better go."

Rory looked to where Dad was staring. The tiny specks of two people and a dog in the distance.

Dad grunted. "Doubt they'd venture over here, not with the bogs this far out, but you never know. Come on. Walk in front of me."

Rory marched ahead, back the way they'd come. He reckoned, if those people stared this way, they'd think Dad was on his own. That made sense, why he'd said for Rory to go first. He didn't want him getting into trouble, and being seen meant trouble.

"What will Three be like tomorrow?" Rory called over his shoulder.

"Maybe that fox will come back and eat the rest of his arm."

"But he looks bad, like he's gone off. Why would a fox eat off meat?"

"I was just testing you, son. Whatever bit into that arm did it on Day Two, when the meat was fresh enough."

"Why hasn't anyone found him yet?"

5

"Dunno."

"But you said you want them found. If you do, you shouldn't put them so far away." Rory had a feeling Dad had lied and that he *didn't* want them found. He liked watching them rot too much, he'd said so.

"I don't want them discovered until I've finished watching the decay. Now then, remember what I said. This is our secret."

"I know."

Rory didn't want to tell anyone. He loved keeping this from people. Something only he and Dad shared. It was naughty, killing people, but Dad had been so happy since he'd started his plan, Rory never wanted it to stop. There were things he didn't understand, reasons that confused him, but one day it would all make sense, Dad had told him.

They walked for ages, round the bend, then came to the hedge border that separated the moors from the main road. Rory kept to the moor side, using the hedge as a shield so any passing drivers didn't see him. He glanced back. Dad had his head bent, making sure he wasn't spotted either.

Nan's cottage came into view, and Rory had the urge to run there, get a drink. Although it had been a cool summer, he was still thirsty. He could get a can of pop from her fridge and sit in the shade of her trees out the back. Nan would say he should have some squash, not pop, but Dad always brought Cokes to hers if they were going to be there. A treat. Another secret they kept from Mum, who'd say the sugar would wreck their teeth.

Rory smiled. One day, when he was big enough, he'd do what Dad did. He'd kill someone. Put a severed hand in a shoebox and watch the decay every day. And he'd put the body where it could be found. After all, what was the point if no one knew what he'd done? That was the part of Dad's plan he didn't understand. If he wanted to make a point, which he claimed he did, then he wasn't doing it right.

Rory would think about that another day.

Nan came out and waved to them. Rory didn't bother calling out, she wouldn't know what he'd said. She was getting deafer by the day but didn't want hearing aids. Reckoned they'd make her feel old. Besides, she liked the silence.

"I saw you coming," she shouted, "so I made you an ice cream wafer. Hurry up before it melts."

Rory raced into the house and found the wafer in a bowl on the worktop. A flash of the veiny skin popped into his mind, but he pushed it out.

It was time to be a normal boy now.

CHAPTER ONE

No maggots this time. No undulating blanket. Rory supposed the time of year had something to do with it. Flies hibernated in winter, preferring to annoy everyone in the summer months with their buzzing, their futile butting against windows, their incessant swoops at faces, drawn by sweat.

He didn't like flies.

Returning to the places where the bodies had been dumped was an indulgence, a risk, so he wouldn't come back, but he'd done it many times with his father. If he'd wanted to completely follow in Dad's footsteps, he'd return every day, take notes. The draw to do that tugged at him. It would be better than twiddling his thumbs or staying at Mum's — but no, he *had* to stick to his way of doing things.

Mum didn't want him "hanging around", as she put it. She'd also said no self-respecting forty-year-old should be living with his mother. "You're getting under my feet," she'd say. "Go back to your own place, for God's sake!"

He didn't like his mother.

He glanced around, the light from his head torch ploughing through the dark. The empty warehouse that used to be the storage area for a pottery business had been empty for years, a stagnant imperfection on the deserted ghost street it stood on, its surroundings festooned with knee-high grass that encroached on the footpath by the back door. Old Dobson had snuffed it almost a decade ago, and his family were still arguing about what to do with the properties, in a stubborn stalemate. Seemed some people preferred to dig their heels in rather than give in to the opposing side. What about all that money? Wasn't it better to just sell it?

Not that Rory was complaining. This was somewhere to put his first kill, Martin Lowe, where the body would eat itself from the inside out. Every day corpses looked different, even if at first there was only a slight change. That was if a body was outside. Rory had never experienced a whole one decaying indoors before. By tomorrow, the rats would have feasted, wouldn't they? On their haunches afterwards, licking their scarlet front paws, cleaning their bearded faces.

They'd scattered upon seeing him dragging Martin in here, alarmed by his presence, his bright head torch, when they'd previously had the place to themselves. He could wipe them out if he felt like it. But he didn't feel like it. He *wanted* them to eat Martin.

Rory contemplated what he'd done to this man.

His torch beam shone on the body. Martin lay on his back, as had all the ones Dad had killed; better to stick to tradition, he would have said. The criss-cross slashes on the face showed how sharp the knife was — nice clean cuts, the skin partially peeled apart to expose the gore beneath. That pattern reminded Rory of Mum, scoring the pork rind for the Sunday roast. Crackling was one of her favourite things, top of the list next to berating her son. He'd even poured salt on them like she did and rubbed it in.

While Martin had been alive.

Extra pain. Suffering.

His torn clothes bore the beautiful pigments of blood. So much blood. Martin had suffered, as was only right. The grey suit didn't look so expensive anymore, nor did the stiff-collared white shirt, although it was barely that colour now. The emerald-green tie — now askew, a winding country road on the ravaged chest — appeared tie-dyed where blood had dripped from the stump of Martin's severed hand, which Rory had held over him while he'd lain on the grey floor tiles in the kitchen, pleading for his life.

Funny how words came out differently when the lips were split and swollen.

They sound daft in the head when they're shitting bricks, don't they, son?

That's what Dad would have said.

Rory's mind reversed in time, going back to the moment this had all started for him. Ten years old was no age to see such atrocities, and he should have been frightened. Instead, wonder and curiosity had taken him by the hand and pulled. Hard. Drawing him out of the shadowed corner in Nan's cellar and into the light, towards what Dad had done. Liking it.

Would they all be found eventually, those men Dad had chosen? If they were, someone would join the dots, make the connection to what Rory was doing now. *Eureka*, the coppers would say, *those men all had something in common*. Dad had tried to fulfil the plan, but he'd died before he'd seen the fruits of his many knife-wielding labours. Rory was now in the right frame of mind to continue it. He'd just proved that, hadn't he? Killing Martin?

Despite the heavy bulk of his extra-large army fatigues — all the better to hide in the dark, my dear — he threw his arms out to the sides and spun round, the dance of the victor, the unflappable murderer. "She's going to miss you, I think."

Martin, one hand and both eyes missing, had received what he should have. Pain. Rory had wanted to have more of a chat with him before he'd died, so he could discuss the man's life choices, but as this was his first foray into actually committing murder, he'd thought it best to get a shift on.

So many emotions had barrelled into him at the moment the knife point had met that once-unsullied skin — not counting the freckles across the bridge of the nose. A mini marble of blood had sprouted, trickling into an ear, and a wail of utter despair had barged out of Martin's mouth. It had startled Rory, but only for a split second, then he'd drawn the blade across the face, temple to opposite jaw, bypassing the nose with its recognisable bump in the middle.

"Will she cry?" he asked, spinning, spinning, imagining Dad was swinging him round and round, his meaty hands beneath Rory's armpits. "Like, proper cry? Maybe she'll need to be sedated. Maybe she won't be able to face you being dead."

Rory was supposed to have experienced that. Sobs, a pain in his chest, his lungs refusing to allow air in, his whole *self* asphyxiated by grief. Instead, he'd stared into space. News of Dad's death had hit him like a bag of bricks; he was simply unable to consider a life without him. A shell, that's what he'd become, a body with no emotion in it, for a long, long time.

That's why Kirsty had left him. Kirsty, who'd kept his last name even though they'd divorced. That name didn't belong to her anymore, like McFadden didn't belong to Mum. Mum's excuse had been that she'd wanted the same surname as Rory, but what was Kirsty's? They didn't have any kids. Was it too much hassle to change all her documents?

Probably. She's always been a lazy cow.

"She didn't love me like your missus loves you." Rory twirled some more, throwing himself around, thrashing his arms, dipping his head then hoisting it up, back, staring at a ceiling of steel rafters. Strip lights hung between them on dull silver chains, their long, dusty tubes grey and vacant of the glow that would, if switched on, illuminate this cavernous space and pick out all its faults. "If she did, she'd never have walked out on me."

He stopped abruptly. Heaved in big breaths. He wasn't fit enough to be dancing. Wasn't fit enough to hoist a dead body over his shoulder and wade through that high grass. Yet he'd done both, albeit in a staggering fashion.

He faced the body, his head torch shining a tunnel of light towards it. Dust motes, brought on by his manic movement, eddied in the air. A brown rat, poised mid-scuttle, stared his way at the edge of the lit-up area, its eyes glinting red.

"Eat him while I watch," he whispered. "Go on."

Rory stood stock-still, slowing his breathing. He went into that mind space Dad had showed him, where he became one with his surroundings, as stiff and unyielding as a girder, something that belonged here. The rat observed him for a while, still stuck in its rigid pose, a statue of furriness and quivering whiskers. Perhaps a minute or two passed, then it crept towards Martin.

No, not towards Martin but the little bundle at his side. An easier target? The rat nibbled at the exposed flesh of the smaller body. Rory forgot his state of being and almost sagged. How disappointing that the vermin had ignored the bigger meal. As if the rat had thought the same thing, it scurried closer to the stump of Martin's arm.

That's it. He'll taste better.

The rat seemed to agree.

More of them came, migrating out of the darkness, until a swarm clambered over the body. If Rory squinted, he could almost convince himself the rats had taken the place of the maggots. Writhing. Undulant. A mass of the living upon the dead. The brown multitude attacked with a viciousness he hadn't expected, a few of them fighting among themselves, even though there was plenty to eat.

No table manners, this lot.

Fascinated by their behaviour, he watched until the furry congregation had lumbered off and only two rats remained, then he stepped forward. They bolted away, bellies distended, into the darkness, likely to clean themselves and sleep.

Something Rory should do.

He stared at Martin, whose face was less like pork rind now, more a stew of flesh. "Good job your wallet's in your pocket, else no one would know who you are to begin with."

He chortled. "I wonder how long it'll be before someone finds you, eh? Anyway, I'd best be off."

He walked backwards to the rear door that hung slightly wonky on its rusted hinges, the frame rotted, pocked with woodworm. Gaining access yesterday had been easy when he'd come to scope the place out in the early hours of the morning. Squatters or the homeless had already done the hard work of breaking the lock for him. Would anyone come back? See Martin?

He switched his head torch off and left, yanking the door closed — it put up a fight, sticking a bit — and marched down the abandoned road, one-two, one-two. The December weather bit at his cheeks, and his eyes watered from the cold.

Other buildings either side of the warehouse also belonged to the Dobsons, joined by one-storey corridors in pale brick that didn't match the original red. One had been used for creating the pottery, the other for glazing, the warehouse for storage. Dobsons had once been a bustling enterprise, pumping out plate after plate, cup after cup, tea sets, dining sets, vases, all sorts. Now, the trio of bricks and mortar that had housed busy-bee workers had been left to crumble. None of Dobson Senior's offspring had wanted to continue to trade, to pay managers to oversee things. They hadn't even discussed selling the business; the only thing each warring side could agree on was that they didn't want the hassle. That was what it said in the papers anyway.

So many jobs lost. Such a waste of property. Money.

A bit like my house.

Unless I move back into it.

Rory took his torch off, doused it and slid it into his pocket. He kept the black beanie hat on, though, and the gloves. His clothes, bought in an army surplus shop a couple of years ago, and the dark-green face paint would be sufficient to mask his identity. He'd looked at himself in the bathroom mirror earlier, and even *he* didn't recognise himself. Not with the camouflage cream colouring his white-blond eyebrows and the hat covering his fair hair. His size might give him away, though. Tall and wide, he was.

Wide. Another reason why Kirsty had left.

He thought of Martin's car, parked among others at the train station at the edge of the scrubland behind Dobsons. It was one of those places where you paid when you got back from your journey, so it'd be a good couple of weeks before anyone noticed the Mondeo had been there a fair old while. There were cameras, so he'd parked in a corner, close to the diamond-wire fence that bordered the scrubland. He'd cut the wire in readiness, a rectangular doorway big enough for him to get through, and he'd fixed it again with twists of steel wire to hide that it had been tampered with.

He made it to the street behind his cul-de-sac and jogged down the alley behind the four-bed house he'd shared with Kirsty. The empty one he still paid the council tax on — and the electric, and the gas — although now he was staying at Mum's, the outlay was minimal. He'd move back one day, once he'd redecorated, once he'd got over being discarded for being too in his head, too "fat" — Kirsty had actually said that word, the nasty woman.

"One day" might be soon. By killing Martin, he'd already climbed out of his cocoon and flown, so perhaps he was ready.

He entered the rear garden and checked the house next to his. There were only two at the bottom of the horseshoe, his and Bob's, and there was ample space between them. Bob was as deaf as a post, going on ninety, and only lived on the ground floor now. He found the stairs difficult, found *life* difficult since his wife had passed on, and regularly said he didn't want to be here.

Rory turned the key in the lock and stepped inside. The other neighbours out the front wouldn't take any notice. He'd told them he'd be nipping back to do the rooms up, and since the back of his place had tall evergreen trees standing guard along the alley, and with Bob not going upstairs, Rory had been able to bring Martin here without being spotted. And anyway, if anyone *had* noticed them going into the garden, a valid excuse had sat on the tip of Rory's tongue.

"I'm selling up, and he's come to view it."

Martin had gone into the house willingly in that grey suit of his, that white shirt and green tie, a brown briefcase swinging with his stride, giving the impression of importance. It had been dark, and Rory had closed the curtains prior to the visit. Martin had only managed to see the kitchen before Rory had struck, and now the white island, the glossy cupboard doors and the floor all boasted specks of blood, smears of it, puddles of it. Rory thanked God the dark-grey floor tiles had black grouting. It would have been the devil to get the blood out otherwise.

Kirsty had stripped the place bare apart from Rory's personal items, the integrated washing machine, dishwasher, fridge and cooker. Oh, and she'd left the kettle, and a random golden teaspoon in the cutlery drawer, the one he'd chosen every time over a sea of silver counterparts. All the food and drink had gone bar a dribble of milk in a four-pint flagon.

She'd said she'd taken everything as payment for putting up with him the last two years of their marriage. The house had belonged to him before she'd come on the scene and, as she hadn't worked during their relationship, and therefore hadn't contributed to the household bills, she knew she didn't have a leg to stand on if she'd asked for half the equity. Or her solicitor knew and had passed that snippet on to her. Rory could have argued that it was theft — she'd taken the sofa, the beds, the cabinets, all things he'd bought, selling what wouldn't fit in her new flat — but he was just glad to be rid of her. She received benefits these days, and the last he'd heard she was on her uppers.

Serves her right. If she'd have just stuck by Rory through his two-year patch of mourning and overeating, she could have still had money in the bank. He'd given her four hundred a month to do whatever she wanted with. Dad had left him a chunk of money in his will, not to mention the cottage on the moors where he'd lived after Mum had chucked him out. Martin rented that out to a nice couple, and he'd paid off the mortgage on this place.

Weird how life repeated itself. Rory had gone to live with *his* mother, too, when the woman in his life had turned mean.

He got on with cleaning up, working until the early hours, doing four rounds of wiping and mopping with bleach water. He left the knife until last. Hot and sweaty despite the heating not being on, he stripped off his army clothes and stuffed them in the machine, using a detergent pod from a box he'd brought here last week. He'd also purchased teabags and the like, a towel and soap for his shower, milk and a snack or two. A blow-up bed, a quilt and pillow. Basics he could get by with for now.

He turned the light off and went upstairs, switched the shower on, and got on with the business of washing away all traces of blood and camouflage cream. He stayed there for a few minutes, imagining the rats going back to Martin for a second course. He laughed as he stepped out of the shower, his skin sprouting goosebumps, and dried off quickly. In the spare bedroom — he'd never sleep in the one he'd shared with Kirsty again — he stuck the light on, slipped on some pyjamas and sat on the bed. Pulled the briefcase towards him.

The locks sprang open without him having to fiddle with the combination. Inside was Martin's phone, which he'd switched off when they met at the park earlier — he'd said he wasn't sure he could lie to his wife if she asked why he wasn't home yet. He'd wanted to buy Martin's place, then present it to her as part of some big surprise.

Rory scanned the rest of the contents. A few pieces of A4 paper. Letters addressed to clients. Martin was a financial advisor. The correspondence was nothing for Rory to worry about.

Rory had used a burner phone to contact Martin at first, standing in an alley a couple of miles away so the masts close to his house or Mum's didn't pick him up. He'd told Martin, via text, that he didn't want to give out the house address until he'd met him in person, adding that Martin could be a weirdo for all he knew. The park was mainly empty, and they'd shaken hands and traded a few words at the bandstand, apparently getting on well enough that Martin deemed it OK to go with him. If he'd been a woman, he likely wouldn't have agreed to it. Martin had driven them here and parked in the street behind. He'd swallowed the story that Rory was a sergeant major. The camouflage gear and Rory's research into soldiering at the library had stood him in good stead. He'd pretended he'd come straight from training, hence still having on his gear and the face paint. They'd had a good laugh about it.

He shoved the briefcase away and got under the covers. Closed his eyes. Reckoned Mum would think he'd moved out because he hadn't been there for three nights, this being the fourth. He hadn't even told her where he was going, and she hadn't rung him to check if he was all right. Mind you, he'd left a lot of his stuff there, so she'd expect him back. But being here, in this house that had once been filled with his and his wife's laughter, wasn't so bad now he really came to think about it. With his marital bedroom door shut, he *could* live here.

He could.

He would.

He'd go and collect his things tomorrow.

As he was drifting off, he fully woke again, to set an alarm so he could go and post a note to Martin's wife. Dad would expect him to do that.

The image of the man's hand floated into his mind. It currently lay in a shoebox in the corner, a keepsake he could watch putrefy.

Dad had taught him well.

CHAPTER TWO

DI Anna James sat in her office, putting her hair into a pony-tail. DCI Ron Placket stood against the closed door, and DCs Sally Wiggins and Warren Yates sat opposite Anna. DS Lenny Baldwin was perched beside Anna on a foldout chair. All of them felt nervous in case DC Peter Dove came to work early and caught them in the weekly conflab.

About him.

Anna glanced at the clock: 7.15 a.m. "OK, has anyone got anything new to report? He'll be rolling in at half eight, so we need to get this chat over and done with by then. I've got a lot to say, so let's get a move on."

Sally lifted her tea from the desk. "Is it just me, or does he look ill?"

Placket snorted and moved closer. He rested against a tall filing cabinet. "Wouldn't *you* look ill if you were worrying your arse off?"

Sally blushed. Anna made a mental note to ask her later, in private, if it was because Placket had seemed to reprimand her or whether it was over something else — like her vile ex-husband, Richard.

"Well, yes," Sally said, "but he's only been *really* off since Jamal Jenkins was killed. If you remember, he got a bunch of phone calls and messages that day."

"Are you saying he's involved?" Anna wasn't sure if Peter was *that* bad, *that* in with the Northern Kings, the gang a specialised team were working to bring down. "Can you see him killing anyone? Really?"

"Who knows? When your back's against the wall . . ." Warren said. "Ordinarily, I wouldn't have him down as a killer, but he was in with the Kings from the start as a kid. That's got to have an effect on you, surely. Like, they have rules. OK, he supposedly left them to join the police, but those rules might be ingrained in him."

"Enough that he'd kill a sixteen-year-old lad?" Placket asked. "Come on, he promised me, and my seniors, that he was done with the Kings. He left before they got into anything nefarious — and he hadn't done anything bad with them. Anyway, Kevin Clough has said they're not looking at the Kings for Jamal's death."

He glanced at Anna. In truth, DI Clough's team *were* considering the Kings for it, but that information was on a need-to-know basis.

"Have you changed your stance on Peter, sir?" Anna asked Placket. "Sounds like you're sticking up for him."

"God no, I just don't see him as someone who'd stab a boy. So, Sally?"

"I'm just stating a fact," she said. "He *was* iffy that day, and he has been ever since. Just because *we* don't think he'd have it in him to kill someone doesn't mean he wouldn't. He could have been acting all this time, making us believe he's a good person. People *do* change for the worse, you know. My ex-husband is proof of that."

Warren nodded. "That's true. Peter's not as competitive when we play squash. Like his heart's not in it. He's lost his *oomph*. Then there's that tattoo . . ."

19

Anna had once thought she'd seen a Kings crown tattooed on Peter's arm. He'd used to cover it with long sleeves, but recently he'd been showing it off — but it wasn't what she remembered.

"I think he had the eagle tattooed over the crown," Anna said. "I tried to tell myself I'd seen it wrong the first time, because the feathers on the wings *do* look like the tips of a crown."

"No," Sally said. "It was obviously a crown. Otherwise, why would we be spying on him?"

"Because he was a King as a kid," Warren said. "Add that to the crown tattoo and his shifty behaviour . . . and Trigger just *happened* to offer him intel about that former King, that Smithy bloke."

Trigger Mike, the leader of the Kings, was a scary bastard.

Warren continued. "Yeah, it came good, Smithy's now in the nick, but was he given up as a sacrificial lamb because Peter was seen getting into Trigger's car? Maybe they cooked up an excuse for it?"

Lenny rubbed a hand over his bald head. "We've been through all this before. We're justifying ourselves because he's part of our team and someone we trusted. The bottom line is, if he *is* still a King and he *did* have something to do with Jamal, he's a criminal, not our buddy."

Warren seemed to relax at that, content that his point had been understood. "D'you know what *really* dogs me off? I thought we were friends, not just colleagues. All that squash and going to the pub together. We've chatted about all sorts. It's going to sound mad, but this has been like a bereavement, except he's still alive."

Anna nodded. "I agree. We thought we knew him, that he was being honest, leaving the Kings behind him. Sadly, too many things point to that not being the case. As Lenny said, we have to stop thinking of him as the Peter we knew and accept he might be someone else entirely. OK, anything else?"

No one offered anything more.

Anna took a deep breath. "So, last night . . ."

"Wait." Placket walked even closer, planted his hands on her desk and leaned over. "First, is everything all right on that score?"

Anna couldn't very well say she enjoyed going out with the man she was investigating undercover, so she just said, "Yes."

"Good. First, I need to say something. I'm getting panicky that Peter's going to show up unexpectedly early. Got a weird feeling about it. If he *does* turn up, we'll say Sally and Warren are thinking about taking their exams and stepping up to the DS role." He reversed to his spot against the door. "Positions in other teams, something like that."

Lenny chuckled. "Other teams. I was going to say . . . I thought you were turfing me out for a minute there."

"Not a chance," Anna said. "Right. I've been on several dates with Parole now, and, much as I dislike having to play the undercover role to such a degree, I can't palm him off anymore. Last night, I had to kiss him, otherwise he'd have got suspicious."

Parole, aka Joshua Cribbins, was a high-level King who'd made his intentions quite clear to Anna. She hated the fact that she fancied him, too. In order to wheedle out information about Peter, she'd agreed to go out with Parole and insinuate herself in the gang. She would never be a bent copper, but, if he put a word in with Trigger about letting her enter the fold, then she could be a proper mole. Bring the Kings down from the inside.

"This role has been challenging." She glanced at Placket, who'd been the one to push her into doing it. "I've never admitted this to anyone before, but I find myself actually liking him. I mean, he's a nice bloke. Yes, I know, he's been in and out of the nick and does whatever Trigger wants, but if you take the Kings out of the equation he's all right. Before anyone says it, no, I'm not on the verge of jumping over to the other side. I want him in prison as much as any of you do.

All the Kings. So, back to last night. We slipped into an alley and kissed, then he said something odd."

"What was it?" Lenny asked.

Anna took a deep breath. "That he wished he could make me a queen. Is that a thing? Women in the Kings are called Queens? *Are* there any women in the gang?"

"Could just be a term of endearment," Warren said. "Like princess. Either way, it sounds like he wants to progress things. How far are you prepared to go?"

"I'm not having sex with him if that's what you mean." Anna's face grew hot. She'd thought about it, of course she had. It was hard not to when Parole was so magnetic, years her junior and fit as anything. His tattoo sleeves did something to her, as did his eyes, and the sooner she got away from him the better.

"So, how will you evade that?" Placket asked. "A man like him, he's bound to want to go farther."

"I'll think about it when I have to. So, moving on. After the alley, we went to a pub in York. I was driving so didn't drink." She never drank in his presence. Couldn't trust herself under the influence when it came to him. "He had a few vodkas. Next thing I know, yet again the conversation turned from your everyday stuff to him suggesting I poke into the database for him. This is the third time he's asked me. He wants me to look at the Northgate area, specifically the Plough, to see if there'll be any police presence there today. I made the call off my own bat to say I'd do it." She looked at Placket. "You said I had to act as if I was fit for turning, right?"

"Within reason, yes, but I'd prefer it if you'd run it past me. Did you at least find out why he wanted to know?"

She resisted rolling her eyes. He was teaching her to suck eggs. "Yes. I told him I wouldn't do anything unless I was aware of what's going on because, given my position here, I have to be more careful. Apparently, Trigger wants to give Harry Wells, the landlord, a talking-to. I double-checked if that's all it is, and he assured me nothing else will go down.

22

Wheels, the landlord of the Kite, will be going with Trigger, as will Parole. We need to keep eyes on Peter at all times today, please, in case they contact him."

She sighed and held up a hand to stop anyone from butting in.

"Yes, I'm well aware that having all those gang members in the Plough could mean they need an alibi. That they think I'm stupid enough not to realise. This tells me something else will be going down in another part of the city. So, is this a test? Does Parole expect me to come and tell you about it, sir, so you can put the word out? Is he checking whether he can trust me?"

Placket nodded. "I suspect that's what this is, but if something else is going to happen elsewhere we can't exactly ignore it, can we?"

"Hardly anyone knows what we're doing, though," Lenny said. "Like, we're working covertly here, so if we alert anyone that the Kings might be up to something, and they find out, Anna could be in danger the next time she meets Parole."

Warren blew out a long breath. "But can you have it on your conscience if someone gets hurt because we stood back and did nothing?"

Anna thought for a moment. "What about Karen? She's trustworthy."

The daytime station sergeant would be the best bet as she'd be overseeing all patrols. She'd have her eye on the ball, and no one would think anything of it if she sent a message out that there might be unrest in the city.

Anna stared at Placket. "What if you whisper in Clough's ear, and he tells Karen he has intel that something's going to go off today? Make out it's to do with one of the other gangs, the Chiefs or the Loops, seeing as he's the lead street crime officer? Would that work?"

Placket pulled at his earlobe. "It'll have to do. We can't sit by on this one. At least this way you'll be in the clear, Anna. Actually, next time you go out with Parole, slip something in about the SCT. Say the heat has been turned up because of Jamal Jenkins' death. Actually, ring him in a minute. Say you've had a look at the system and the only thing that came up for that area today is SCT visiting a member of the Loops, but the name's redacted so you can't pass on who it is."

Anna swallowed. "OK."

Placket checked his watch. "Was there anything else?"

No one responded.

"Right," he said. "Off to work as normal."

He walked out, followed by Lenny and Warren, leaving Sally, who appeared to have something on her mind.

"I'm glad you stayed back," Anna said. "Close the door for me, will you?"

Sally got up and shut it. She remained standing.

Anna eyed her. "Everything all right? Only, you seem a bit off."

"It's Richard."

Anna drew in a long breath at the mention of Sally's ex. "What's he done now?"

"He's getting worse. I'm not sure whether to bring the police into it or not."

"He hasn't hurt you, has he?"

"No, but I'm worried he might."

Movement out in the incident room caught Anna's eye through the partition window wall that separated her office from the main space. "Peter's here. Bloody hell, we've cut it fine today. Maybe we should do our weekly meeting after work in future. Why has he come in early?"

"Maybe he was asked to do the same thing you were. For the Kings."

Anna returned her attention to Sally. "Probably. Listen to me, the minute you think Richard is going to go down a darker path, you phone it in, got it?"

Sally nodded. "OK. I'd better get on."

24

She walked out. Anna stared after her. She shouldn't think it but, if she were the kind to ask Parole to get rid of someone for her, it'd be Richard.

God, don't say Parole's got to me in that way. Just don't.

She shouldn't be thinking along those lines.

She prepared herself to call him. This undercover lark wasn't easy. Other officers not in the know might see her with him, think she was skating the thin line and report her. Yes, they always had their dates in York, but they met up in Marlford first.

We'll cross that bridge if we come to it.

She prayed they didn't.

CHAPTER THREE

Only a handful of times in her adult life had Prudence McFadden not lived up to her name. Ever since she'd realised her mistake in marrying Eric, she'd ensured she took care and used the sense the good Lord had given her when it came to making decisions. She may have been overly fastidious, checking and double-checking each crossroads she came to, thinking things through until all the pitfalls had been inspected, but that was better than stumbling down an avenue she couldn't find her way out of. It was better than being married to a monster.

God, he'd been such a strange, frightening man come the last knockings of their relationship, when her suspicions had become too great. Their son wasn't any better. Rory was an enigma, always had been, and she'd never bonded with him. It wasn't any wonder Kirsty had left him. What did he expect, acting all moody and insular? A marriage wouldn't survive if you didn't take care of your spouse, and it certainly wouldn't have any longevity if you didn't buck up and smile once in a while.

Or in Eric's case, if you kept severed hands in shoeboxes.

Rory had been out of her house for four nights now, and the peace was bliss. She could do without his irritating presence, thank you very much. She'd thought about asking Sid Baxter over. A widower, Sid was a pleasant sort who didn't expect any how's-your-father, just a bit of company. Watching a film and drinking hot chocolate. But Rory hadn't given her any indication of where he was or how long he'd be gone, so she'd told herself not to risk it. He wouldn't like it if she announced she was seeing someone. But if she wasn't careful, Sid might turn to his next-door neighbour for company instead.

I'll have to pop over and see him. Tell him I'll try to get Rory to go home.

"Selfish boy, isn't he, Patch? Too much like Eric, that one."

The guinea pig twitched his nose in response, although he was more than likely just waiting expectantly for the treat she had pinched between slim finger and thumb. She held out the slice of raw carrot, and Patch took it gently.

"Good boy."

Prudence's Pets had been open since 1958. Her father had named the shop after her and handed it to her when he'd retired. He was long gone now, may he rest in peace. She'd inherited his animal whisperer tendencies, though, and the joy she got from sending pets to their forever homes could never be beaten.

She closed the cage and moved to the next one.

"Oh." She frowned.

Copper was usually at her door by now, sniffing. Prudence had only had the guinea pigs for a month; they weren't old enough to be sold yet, but they'd trained well. She opened the cage and shifted the hay bedding aside, hoping her fingertips brushed warm fur.

They didn't.

"Copper?"

She made kissing noises, like she would for a cat, but the guinea pig wasn't there. She searched the whole shop but couldn't find her.

She swallowed, a crest of dread rising inside her. "Not again. Please, not again."

She closed the door and checked the rest of the cages, relieved to find that the other ones were OK. She handed out the carrot snacks, then rushed to the little staffroom she'd created out the back. She hadn't opened up yet, but Cuddy would be here in a minute, so she'd better be quick.

She launched herself into the toilet and threw up, memories bubbling up in her mind. She had previous with guinea pigs, when she'd been married to Eric. When all those men had gone missing. She'd never forget it. Each moment was embedded in her brain.

It had been such an awful few weeks; one man after the other, gone, just like that. Thirty years ago, it was, in the first flush of the 1990s, hanging on to the eighties in some respects yet creeping towards the middle of the decade. She'd been so innocent then. So blinded to what her husband had really been like. Eric had yet to show his real face beneath that mask, and she'd yet to find those weird shoebox hands, and . . . and she'd struggled so hard to find common ground with a son who'd never once wanted to spend time with her.

Why, then, had he come home after Kirsty had left?

Prudence wiped her lips with a tissue. She flushed the loo, swilled her mouth at the sink. In her handbag, hanging on a hook in a row of five in the staffroom, she found a mint, and crunched on it as she steadied herself against the wall.

Rory had been ten when all that business had gone on. There'd been those times he and Eric had snuck off together to God knew where for hours on end, with no explanation when they came back as to where they'd pissed off to, just secret glances and sly smiles, which had looked weird on a child's face. Their time together had increased more and more over those weeks.

In Eric's absence, Prudence had begun to wonder if he was having an affair, and the thought, the wicked, wicked thought that he might leave her and take Rory with him had been wonderful. Her husband taking a mistress was better than convincing herself he'd had something to do with those men disappearing. They'd been his friends, after all.

But it hadn't been an affair. He'd posted guinea pig fur to the men's wives, tufts of it in envelopes, brown and white and copper and black, and she'd known.

She'd *known*.

Rory had a key to the pet shop for emergencies. If Prudence was ill and she couldn't open up, he had to come and feed the animals — he had no job, didn't need one, so it would hardly mess with his life. Maybe she ought to get it back off him and give it to Cuddy instead. That young lad was as trustworthy as they come, and then it would mean Patch and all the others would be safe.

But if another man had gone missing, what then? Could she hide it a second time round? She wasn't as frightened of Rory as she had been of his father, and the shame wouldn't bother her now. She was older, wiser, and people would understand if she grassed her own son up.

Wouldn't they?

But will I be in trouble for not telling the police about Eric?

A tap at the back door had her jumping, letting out a stupid little scream, and she glanced that way. Cuddy pressed his face to the glass in the door to make her laugh, and she did, glad to release the tension. A wisp of his brown hair poked out from beneath the hem of his navy-blue woolly hat, the rib pattern pressed flat against the pane.

"Silly sod." She hid her unease regarding Copper and went to open the door. She pulled it back, smiling. "You're a daft apeth, you are, Jacky Cud. Get in here out of the cold."

Cuddy grinned and stepped inside. "Did you have a good Christmas?"

"I did, lad." She didn't, not with Rory there. Sid never came for his customary glass of eggnog. "What about you?"

"Ah, it were right grand. Our mum bought us all a new phone each."

Prudence shut out the cold weather and twisted the key in the lock. "At those prices? What did she do, win the lottery?"

He took his coat and scarf off and hung them on a hook. "Nah, she got her yearly bonus."

"Ah yes, she's management at the factory, that's right."

The Cribbins chocolate factory had enjoyed a stellar reputation until the owner, Bruce Cribbins, had had an affair with some woman called Maureen from Upton-cum-Studley. Bruce treated his employees well — a little too well in Maureen's case — and a bonus for line managers was part of his generosity.

Prudence smiled. "Ah, she's a good woman, your mum. Want a cuppa?"

"Please. I'll get on with cleaning the cages out."

Her face fell. "Oh, sad news there, I'm afraid."

"Oh no. Have we lost one? Was it Harold the hamster? He was looking a bit poorly yesterday."

"No, Copper."

Cuddy shook his head. "Sorry you had to deal with that on your own. Do you want me to bury her? It'll save you getting upset."

"No, because then *you'll* be upset. I'll do it in a minute. Let me just make that brew for you. I've already wrapped her up nicely, so all you need to do is sort her cage out. Give it a good scrub."

Cuddy sloped off into the shop, his shoulders slumped. Prudence gazed after him. She hated lying to the lad, but she couldn't have him suspecting anything if history was repeating itself, not until she'd got to the truth, at any rate. She'd have to have a word with Rory, feel him out, see if he confessed to anything — his old self, the one he'd been before his precious father had kicked the bucket, would have boasted about it. With no security cameras in here, she didn't even have the proof to confront him with.

I'll get some CCTV sorted later.

30

She made the tea, took a cup through to Cuddy and placed it on the till counter. He turned his red face to her, his eyes watering, then got on with scrubbing Copper's cage. Prudence felt so guilty for the poor kid thinking the creature was dead, but it was better than the alternative.

Look, Cuddy, I think my son's up to no good.

"Right, I'll be back shortly, so can you open up for me?" Before he could question her, she bustled out the back and closed the door that shut the staffroom off from the shop. Coat and gloves on, she went into the yard, sucking in a quick breath at the ferocious cold. She found the shovel in the shed and moved to the bottom, to the rockery where they buried all the pets that didn't make it to a sale. She dug a hole, bent as if placing a dead bundle in it — Cuddy could have come to watch through the window in the door — then filled it back up again. Cuddy smoked rollies, so, if he came out on his break for a puff or two, he'd spot the disturbed earth. Her lie would become a truth in his eyes.

Wretched subterfuge over, she returned to the warmth of indoors. Coat on a hook, she washed her hands, made herself a cuppa, then entered the now-open shop. Cuddy was chatting to a couple of little boys with a woman who Prudence assumed was their mother, discussing which habitat was best for gerbils. Cuddy said a glass one, like an aquarium, with lots of sawdust and some small logs for climbing and gnawing.

Prudence shifted her attention to outside. Although Christmas had come and gone, there was still the New Year celebrations to go, and plenty of people were out in Marlford, shopping in the frosty High Street. She caught sight of Rory thundering along, his cheeks red from the chill and the unaccustomed exercise, and, although they didn't get on, she worried about the state of his mind if Copper's disappearance was what she thought it was.

He pushed on the door, huffing in, walking past Copper's empty cage without a second glance. He came up to the counter,

31

spotted her steaming tea and picked it up. "Cheers. You must have known I was coming."

She shouldn't be surprised at what he'd done, yet she was. "Err, that's mine, actually."

He shrugged. "So? Make another, then."

Not for the first time, Prudence had sympathy for Kirsty.

Angered by his complete lack of respect, she strutted through to the staffroom. Alarmingly, her son followed. He closed the door and flopped down on the old sofa she used to have at home.

"We've lost a guinea pig," she said, studying his face for a reaction.

His features remained impassive. "And? It'll be around somewhere. It probably got out in the night."

"How can it get out of a locked cage, then relock it once it's got out?"

Rory shrugged. "Ask Cuddy."

"What do you mean?"

"Maybe he came in and nicked it. I bet it's for that whiny sister of his."

"He hasn't got a key. Which reminds me, I want yours back."

Now he was bothered. He blinked up at her, his mouth contracting, probably in an effort to hold in his usual sour words, and said instead, "What for?"

"You don't need it. Cuddy's going to be my emergency contact now, seeing as he actually works here."

To her surprise, he fished in his coat pocket and took out a bunch of keys. He held them out and Prudence took them, recognising the one for the shop as she'd put one of those silicone identifiers on it. She took it off and handed the rest of the bunch back. He stared at her as though he'd like to punch her lights out, the same look Eric used to have, and she shuddered, hating herself for disliking her son, for seeing so much of his father in him.

"Now you've brought up keys . . ." He took the one for her house off the ring and passed it to her. "You can have that back an' all because I'm going home. I packed my stuff this morning. Holdall's in the car."

Oh, thank God. "Right." She wouldn't say it was a pleasure having him because it wasn't. "New year, new start, is it?"

"Something like that." He slurped some tea.

She slipped the keys into her trouser pocket. "Are you going to be getting other parts of your life in order, too?"

"Yep, going on a diet."

"What about a job?" she prodded. "Surely you must get bored."

"Don't need one, don't want one."

Of course he didn't. He probably still had a lot of the money Eric had left him. Then there was the rent coming in from the cottage. She'd often wondered why he hadn't offered his tenants the house if he disliked it so much, then he could have hidden himself away in that cottage to lick his wounds. And, if he'd have been a kinder person, he could have asked Kirsty if she wanted to stay in the house, but he wasn't. He'd taken their split badly.

Kirsty had tried, the poor woman, she really had.

I must nip round and see her. Take her a bunch of flowers. It's been a while.

"Haven't you got work to do?" Rory asked, a sneer on his top lip.

"That's why I employ Cuddy, so I can take it easy."

Rory narrowed his eyes at her. "That Sid bloke came over while I was packing."

Her heart leaped, and she feigned confusion. "Why would he do that? He knows I open the shop between Christmas and New Year so I wouldn't be home."

"Dunno. Maybe he wants a hamster."

His chuckle grated on her nerves. She swiped the half-empty cup off him and poured the contents down the sink.

"Oi! I was drinking that."

"Not anymore. Best you be getting on and redecorating like you said you would," she sniped at his shocked stare. "I've got the books to do in my office, and I can't have you nattering to me while I'm doing them."

With effort, he pushed himself to standing. He walked out, leaving the door wide open, and she watched him go to make sure he didn't stop and say anything spiteful to Cuddy. But Rory barged outside, stomping past the window.

Prudence shrank with relief.

He was gone, from her shop and her house, and if she was lucky she wouldn't see him for weeks, maybe months. Then she wouldn't have to question him more about Copper. Wouldn't have to face it.

Coward.

CHAPTER FOUR

Rory stood in the shadows of Nan's cellar, hidden from the man Dad had taken down there. It was Friday, late, and they were staying over-night. Dad had told Mum they were off to a farmer's market early tomorrow with Nan, and, as Mum didn't want to come, it had been so easy for Rory to leave with a little bag packed. No fuss. No mother having a rant about being excluded. Excitement had fizzed through him at the thought of being so included in what his father was doing. He anticipated lots of blood.

Blood didn't scare him, it never had, not like some of the kids at school when someone fell over and grazed their knee. They probably thought he was weird, but he loved to stare at it, see it dribbling down people's shins.

While Dad had gone to collect Number Four, Rory had eaten his tea with Nan — fishcake, chips and mushy peas. The obligatory orange squash. A blackcurrant jam tart for pudding. When Dad had come back, Rory had asked Nan to run him a bath, like Dad had told him to. It kept her out of the way while Dad lured the man into the cellar with some excuse or other. Dad said he was going to tie him up and stuff a rag in his mouth, then they'd wait for Nan to go to bed. She was tucked up there now, snoring.

The single dusty bulb splashed light into the centre of the cellar, basting Number Four, who sat on the floor, his arms bound behind his back with rope, the rag discarded. He snorted, eyes wide, and they darted about in their red-rimmed sockets, snot shooting out of one nostril.

Dad paced in front of him, back and forth, back and forth, the knife in his gloved hand glinting every so often, his attention on the wooden rafters in the ceiling. "Not so cocksure now, are you?"

Four's lips wiggled, like he was really scared. Or maybe he thought this was a joke and was on the verge of laughing. "Come on, Eric, what's all this about?"

Dad paused and stared at him. "Like you don't know. You humiliated me in front of the whole pub, laughing at me, mocking me for needing money. All of you did."

"Jesus, that was ages ago!" Four seemed to think of something. His face paled. "Fucking hell, it was you, wasn't it?"

Dad smirked. "Me, what?"

"Who took the others."

Dad chuckled. "Fuck me, you've only just twigged? How thick are you? I mean, you're tied up in a cellar, for Pete's sake. I couldn't get more clichéd if I tried, bringing you down here. How the hell do you run your company if it takes you this long to work shit out?"

Four got a smug look about him. Maybe hope had come for a visit. "The police are going to cotton on. Someone will have seen you with me in the Plough. I stand out a mile in there these days."

"What, with your fancy suits and shoes? Yeah, you stand out, and that's why I asked you for a loan. Not just because of that but because I thought we were friends and that's what friends do. They help each other out."

"We haven't hung around together for years. I thought it was weird that you asked to meet me there. Out of the blue." Four narrowed his eyes. "You met the others, too, didn't you?"

"So what if I did? That was a year ago, and I've waited all this time before getting my own back on the lot of you. Who the fuck's going to remember me meeting you one by one back then? Nobody, that's who."

Four seemed struck by the gravity of the situation. "W-what are you going to do to me?"

Dad shrugged as though it wasn't a big deal. "Slice you up a bit. Get you to feel the same as I did. That useless feeling when you're trying to get yourself out of the shit and no one will help you — because no one will help you here."

"Look, the reason I said no to that cash was because of your circumstances. You owed a fucking loan shark, Eric. I can't afford to be associated with people like that. You're a gambler, and you'd have come back to me for more. Your sort always do."

"I'm packing that in soon."

Dad crouched, pressing the tip of the knife into Four's cheek. A bead of blood swelled, then dripped down his face. Rory's willy felt funny, and he squeezed it over his shorts. He wasn't sure if he needed a wee or if it was something else.

Four's eyelashes fluttered. "That's enough now, pal. You've made your point."

"Pal? So we're pals now, when the shit's really hit the fan? Bloody typical."

Dad pushed the knife into his cheek; a few centimetres disappeared into the slit. Four screamed, and Dad laughed. He removed the blade, then slashed and slashed, carving criss-cross patterns all over the face. Four hefted his top half to one side, forcing himself downwards until the side of his head hit the floor. Dad fell back on his bum with the movement, and he glared at Four, like he glared at Mum when he was going to hit her.

Dad stood, took a deep breath to calm himself. He withdrew himself and put the knife on a piece of greaseproof paper on the workbench, pressing both hands onto the wood, his head bent, eyes closed. While his back was turned, Four rolled onto his front, drawing his knees up to balance on them, and, planting one foot on the floor, he pushed himself to standing.

"Dad!"

Rory's father spun round and, at the sight of Four shuffling towards the stone steps, he grabbed the knife and chased him. He rammed the blade into Four's back, the suit jacket slicing open, blood staining the grey material. Four grunted, let out a weird, deep scream and fell to his knees.

Dad kept hacking, each punch of metal into Four's back laced with terrible screeches from the frantic man. Rory wet himself, hot liquid coasting down his legs, and bit into the side of his fist. Scared but at the same time happy, he didn't know what to make of his emotions, so just watched, didn't feel.

Slumped on his front, Four reached a hand towards the steps as if he believed that would save him, that if he could just touch the bottom one he'd be able to get away. Dad flipped him over, one boot either side of his shins, and sat on them. He brought the knife down over and over, cutting into the white shirt, into the skin beneath, into the thighs. More blood, so red, so bright, seeping into the fabric, the silver tie lapping it up on the arrowhead end.

"Fucking die, you bastard!" Dad shouted. "Die!" He got up and bent over near Four's head. Swiped the knife across the man's throat. "That'll do it."

Four stared up at him for a split second, shocked, then so much blood gushed that it puddled on the floor. Rory squeezed his willy again, confused as to why it tingled. He wanted to run away yet stay. To cry yet laugh.

Dad stepped back. "Shouldn't take long for him to cark it now. Did you like that, son?"

Rory nodded, then remembered Dad couldn't see him. "Yes." His whisper floated out of the darkness and into the light, towards the one man who could do no wrong in his eyes, even though this was wrong.

"Good." Dad breathed heavily. "Good. You can come with me to dump him if you like."

"OK."

"This is our little secret, isn't it?"

"Yes."

Dad took the knife to the workbench. Placed it on the greaseproof paper. Red dripped from it. He glanced across at Four, who lay still, staring, and somehow Rory knew he was dead already. Something was different about the man now, a weird thing he couldn't explain. Maybe it was his stillness. The way he was so silent as blood slowly oozed from his neck wound.

"Will he stop bleeding soon?" Rory asked.

"Hmm. The blood will start clotting. Want me to explain?"

"Yeah."

"See, when we're alive, blood circulates all the time because the heart is pumping it. Now he's snuffed it, it's stopped, and the blood moves with gravity. Like, he's on his back, so all the blood will go downwards eventually, in about four hours. It'll settle, leaving dark marks. So those special people I told you about before, they'll know, if we leave him here long enough, that he died on his back. Anyway, we'll take him out of here now. Once we've popped him in his special place, I've got to clean the cellar then have a shower. After that, you can go to bed, because I need to post a note."

Rory imagined all those dark marks. He wanted to see them, watch them grow, but Dad was in charge.

"Go on up and open the door for me, son. You need to hold it wide, all right? Keep out of my way, because I'll have to run through the kitchen so the blood doesn't drip on the floor up there."

Rory did as he was told. Each step upwards was a climb to the next exciting stage. He called down, "Shall I make sure Nan's still in bed first?"

Dad smiled up at him. "That's my boy."

Happy he'd pleased his father, Rory turned to go into the kitchen. The sound of something hitting concrete had him peering back down the steps. Dad placed an axe on Four's chest, then stooped to pick up a severed hand. He held it up and examined it. Sniffed it.

Licked it.

Rory thought that was a bit too weird and scampered off. He checked on Nan, then changed his wet pants and shorts for clean ones. He shrugged on a sweatshirt, too, because there was a long walk ahead, and it might be nippy now the sun had gone down. That was OK, he didn't mind. At last, he'd be involved in this from start to finish.

He smiled.

CHAPTER FIVE

Damon and Owen Kent tromped over the long grass. Damon, fifteen, had been given a vape kit for Christmas off his best mate, Shorty, so he and his thirteen-year-old brother were off to smoke it and drink the alcopops they'd been stealing from the drinks cupboard one by one since Christmas had begun. Mum and Dad wouldn't have noticed — they'd had two parties so far, with all the neighbours there, and everyone had been too rat-arsed to clock the bottles going missing. They clinked against his leg inside the Tesco carrier bag he gripped in his freezing hand.

Should have put gloves on like Mum said.

This bit between Christmas and New Year's Eve was crap. Boring. All his mates were busy, what with family staying, and even his girlfriend had said no to coming out today, so that meant he only had Owen. That wasn't so bad, not really. Owen was one of his best friends, even if he *was* two years younger and a bit of a div sometimes.

They'd been congregating at the Dobson warehouse for ages now, getting drunk and having a good time in the pale light of their phone torches, what with there being no electricity. Shorty usually brought his Bluetooth speaker and he was the only one with Spotify, so he got to choose the music. Robin provided drinks because his parents were alkies and always had umpteen bottles of voddy on hand. No music or vodka today though.

Even though it was ten in the morning, Damon still wanted an alcopop. It'd brighten his sour mood, bring his tired body to life. They'd stayed up late last night, him and Owen, whispering in the darkness of their bedroom about getting pissed, smoking and chilling out, then sobering up before it was time to go home. In his rucksack, Owen carried Mum's yoga mat for them to park their bums on. The warehouse floor was too cold at the minute, and it saved sitting on bobbles of rat shit. Damon hated the rats, although they usually minded their business and stayed in the shadows when people were around.

He stared at the faded foot tracks in the grass. They began at the warehouse back door and ended over by the train station car park. Someone else must have been here recently and not said anything in the WhatsApp chat. Maybe Jamal and — no, Jamal Jenkins *wouldn't* have been here with Sasha for a snog because he was dead. Stabbed in the leg. Weird how Damon sometimes forgot that, or maybe his mind was doing it on purpose so he didn't get upset. Jamal had stopped hanging around with them because he'd got caught up in selling drugs, something no one else wanted to be involved in.

It had scared Damon, Jamal being killed. His murder had been all over the news, and the papers reckoned he'd belonged to either the Chiefs or the Loops, two rival gangs. One article had suggested he'd been in with the Northern Kings, a completely different kind of gang full of older people who weren't fussed about territories and all that shit. The Chiefs and Loops were younger, kids really, who should be fucking around being teens like Damon and his friends instead of stabbing or shooting each other.

Speaking to the police about Jamal had brought home how serious gang life was. How final it could be. All of Jamal's friends had been questioned separately, but DI Kevin Clough — "Call me Kev, son" — had been nice enough, and Damon had felt all right with him in that little room at the police station. Damon's mum and dad had sat at the table with him, and he'd worried about whether the gangs would come for them afterwards for speaking out. Not that they'd said anything people didn't already know, that Jamal was selling coke and weed. Once it was obvious they didn't know anything about the Chiefs or the Loops, Kev had left them alone.

Still, it was a worry.

"Someone's been here," he said and pointed at the grass tracks.

Owen stared over. "Might be a pisshead or some homeless bloke."

Damon nodded. They *had* disturbed a sleeping man once, so yeah, that could be it.

They reached the door, and he shoulder-barged it open — the damn thing was always sticking — and they entered their dark hideaway. The sound of rats scurrying and squeaking brought on a shiver, and Damon turned his phone torch on, tracking their path. A load of them ran in a swarm towards the other side of the warehouse, which was unusual. Normally, there were only a few of them, but this time a horde of them had scattered in the same direction, safety in numbers.

"What the fuck?" Owen muttered. "Bloody weird, they are."

Damon panned the torch beam over to where the rats had come from. "What the bloody hell's *that*?"

Owen stared. "Fucking hell . . . We should go."

Damon crept closer, his heartbeat thumping. The nearer he got, the more the . . . the whatever it was became clear. Dark patches, so much of it in places, and clothes. A suit. A green tie.

A man.

"Shit. Shit!" He turned to Owen, his light pasting him. "There's a . . . there's a body."

42

"Pack it in."

"I'm not kidding."

Owen stepped up to him. "It's got to be a joke. The others, they'll have left it here because they knew we were coming. Like, they'd have made it *look* like a body, that's all, it won't be a real one."

"None of them are allowed out."

"They might have just said that when they're here really, hiding." Owen smiled. "Guys? Where are you? Come on, the gag's over."

Damon swung round to face the man again, and the beam picked out an arm lying on the floor. Without a hand. And beside it, fur the colour of pennies. He stepped closer still, blinking, trying to equate what he was seeing with what his mind wanted it to be — a joke, like Owen had said.

Damon swallowed bile.

The man's black hair framed a pulped face. It was like one of the horror films Damon had seen, where all the skin had been ripped off, the flesh exposed, the lips gone, teeth bared. The man's clothes were ripped to shreds. He thought of Jamal, how he'd only had one knife wound in his trackie bottoms, but this bloke . . . God, whoever had killed him must have been angry. So many slices in the shirt and the suit jacket, the tops of the trousers, all soaked with blood that had gone brown.

The rats must have been eating him.

Damon pleaded with himself not to be sick.

Owen retched behind him, groaning.

"Don't puke," Damon warned. "The police, it'll muck it up for them." He spun round and rushed to his brother, the alcopop bottles clanking in the bag he'd forgotten he held. "We need to get out. Phone them."

He grabbed Owen's arm and steered him towards the door. It opened before they'd got there, and Damon screeched, too frightened now to care whether it made him look a dickhead. He stopped, as did Owen, and Damon stared

43

at a super-bright light, high up, as if someone held a torch above their head. Winter daylight turned whoever it was into a chunky silhouette standing in the frame, and Damon couldn't see any features. But the shape was tall, wide.

"What are you doing in here?" the man asked.

"We came for a smoke an' that," Owen blabbed. "But there's a body, this bloke, and—"

Damon nudged him to keep quiet. Something told him this fella had something to do with the dead one. He wasn't the owner of the warehouse. "We were just going."

He'll be able to see our faces. Might know who we are.

"Leave," the silhouette said. "And never come back."

"But we need to phone the police," Owen said.

"No. No police." Heavy breathing. "Did you like it? What I did?"

Damon wasn't sure how to answer, and a horrible chill flickered through him.

More breathing. "I liked it when I saw a dead man for the first time," the silhouette said. "I want *you* to like it."

Again, something inside Damon piped up, telling him to agree. "Yes, we liked it."

"Good. Good. Now go. And remember: no police, all right?" The man cleared his throat. "Anyway, enough chat. I've only come for the guinea pig. I need it for next time. Now piss off."

Guinea pig?

The silhouette moved from the doorway, into the pocket of darkness beside it. Damon guided Owen to the opening, desperate to get him out of there, to protect him. He kept himself closest to the man in case he lashed out. At least then Damon would be hurt and not Owen. He pushed his brother over the threshold and out into the fresh air, glancing across at the man. Enough light from outside meant he caught a glimpse of army clothes, and what was that on the shadow man's face? Green paint?

He didn't stay to find out for sure. He gripped Owen's hand, and together they pelted across the scrubland to the left, Damon's lungs screaming from the effort, his legs aching. Owen sobbed, and Damon wanted to cry, too, but he wouldn't. He'd stay strong, be there for Owen, and they'd get through this, they would.

At the edge of the scrubland, they squeezed through a border of prickly bushes, coming out at the end of the street the warehouse stood on. The area was so quiet, no cars or people around, and they'd have to go a few hundred metres yet to see anyone on the nearby trading estate.

The booze bottles bashed against each other as they ran. Damon would never forget that sound, he'd forever associate it with this day. He might never drink one again. Or vape.

At last, they reached the estate and stopped beside the Home Bargains distribution centre to catch their breath. This was so surreal, and it took a moment for Damon to get his thoughts in some kind of rational order. The scene at the warehouse flashed through his mind, and he just knew he'd have nightmares about this. He'd be waking up screaming for weeks now, he was sure of it.

Think. Think what to do.

If they did what that bloke had said and kept it secret, Damon wouldn't be able to cope, so there was only one option.

He let go of Owen's hand and moved to the line of wheelie bins. He dumped the alcopops, took the vape from his pocket and put that in there, too — still worried about getting caught for boozing and smoking, even now when something much more important was going on.

He returned to Owen, who swiped at his eyes with the sleeve of his puffa jacket — orange, which would make him easily recognisable.

"Don't wear that anymore," Damon said. "Not until that bloke's been caught."

Owen stared down at it. "Fuck, man . . ."

45

In an unusual show of affection, Damon grabbed hold of him and held him tight. He wanted to comfort his brother, but really he needed comfort, too.

"What are we going to do?" Owen asked, his voice muffled against Damon's chest. "What if he knows who we are? Like, he's someone *we* know? Do we do what he said and keep it a secret?"

"No, fuck that. We'll get someone else to do it."

"Who? And what will we say we were doing there?"

"Hanging out."

"Right." Owen drew back, stared at Damon, his eyes red, his lips trembling. "Fucking hell, bruv, this is massive. It was a *body*."

"I know, pal, I know. He . . ." *Should I tell him what the man looked like?* "He had camo clothes on, and his face was green."

Owen chuffed out a wobbly laugh. "You what?"

"I'm not messing about. He didn't want anyone recognising him." Damon straightened his spine. "Come on."

He led them round the front to a set of open roller doors. Inside, men and women drove forklift trucks, cardboard boxes piled on the fronts.

A grey-haired man lounging against the wall beside one of the doors looked up from his phone. He waved them off. "You can't be around here, lads. Go on, sod off."

"There's a dead man in the Dobson warehouse," Owen blurted. "And this other man, he came and said he was collecting a guinea pig, told us to piss off."

The worker chuckled. "A guinea pig? I've heard it all now. Are you taking the mick?"

Damon shook his head. "There *is* a dead man, and he's got no skin on his face."

Their would-be saviour paled. "Fucking hell . . ." He gestured at them. "You'd better come inside with me, then."

CHAPTER SIX

Anna had opted to speak to the kids at the distribution centre before seeing the body. SOCO were busy setting up at the Dobson warehouse, and Herman Kuiper, the pathologist, hadn't arrived yet, so she thought it best to deal with the brothers so their ordeal didn't drag on any longer than necessary. Fifteen and thirteen were no ages to have gone through what they had, and she imagined they just wanted to go home.

Lenny sat beside her at one of the tables in the staffroom, Damon and Owen Kent bookended by their parents on the other side. Both boys appeared frightened, pale, and Anna's heart went out to them. According to Steven Timpson, the lead SOCO, what these lads had seen wasn't for the faint-hearted.

With Lenny recording the chat on his device, Anna mentioned the date, time and location, then introduced herself for the tape. She asked everyone else present to say their names. This included Oliver Watson, Anna's favourite PC, standing over in the kitchen area. One of the workers at the distribution centre had made the call on the boys' behalf, and Watson had been the first to respond to the call.

"OK, can you take me through what happened, starting from before you entered the warehouse?" she asked.

Owen glanced at Damon as if to beg him to take charge. Damon launched into the story, and by the time he'd finished his hands were shaking.

Anna was alarmed that the suspect Damon and Owen had encountered had returned to the scene, but at least she knew who to look for — a male, not a female.

"So you didn't manage to see his face because of the light in your eyes — a torch above his head, you think it was."

"Not at first," Damon said, "but as we were leaving, he stood to the side of the door, in the dark bit, and the light from outside made it easier to see, maybe a quarter of him? He had army gear on, camouflage, and his face was green, like soldiers have on them."

"Right, that's really helpful. Did you pick out any features?"

"Not properly, just part of his cheek by his ear, the edge of an eye and nose. Oh, and the corner of his mouth. Nothing where I'd recognise him. But he was tall and big, like."

"How tall?" Anna asked.

"About the same as Dad."

Anna turned her attention to his father. "How tall are you?"

"Six-one."

"Thank you." She smiled at Owen. "Do you have anything to add to what your brother has told us? We all see things through a different lens, notice what someone else might not."

Owen told her his side of events. "He told us he could kill us if he wanted but we were too young."

Anna frowned. What killer, returning to the scene, would so freely leave witnesses? Maybe he hadn't planned on staying there for long. But why were they too young? What did that mean? That he wouldn't hurt kids? Or was it something more specific?

"And he said he was only there for the guinea pig."

Guinea pig. Oh fuck.

Owen's face flushed red. He appeared bewildered more than anything.

48

"OK . . . Did you see a guinea pig?"

"I saw something furry," Damon said. "Next to an arm that didn't have a hand on it. It was ginger."

Oh. These poor kids . . . "Owen, you said he told you not to phone the police. Did he say anything else about that?"

"I can't remember, but he said he needed the guinea pig for next time, dunno what that means, and he told us to leave and never come back."

Anna's whole body turned cold. She remembered that a few men had gone missing years ago, all around the same time. She'd been a child, and it had scared her that her dad might fall prey to whoever had snatched those blokes. Someone had posted guinea pig fur to their wives with ominous notes, she'd overheard her mother saying. Placket would have been a copper by then, so maybe he'd know more. This could just be a coincidence, but Anna would rather look the case up and familiarise herself with it than let it fall to the wayside. In Anna's experience with murder cases, the past played a large part in the present. Lately, she'd wondered if she ought to be on the cold case team rather than violent crime.

Damon threaded his fingers together on the table. "He said he liked it when he saw a dead man for the first time and wanted *us* to like it. I got this feeling, like it was telling me to say we liked it, too, so I did. But I didn't like it at all."

"I don't suppose you did. Are you OK to continue?"

"Yeah." Damon scrunched his eyebrows, clearly pulling at his thoughts to dislodge something. "There were tracks in the grass, I saw them before we went in, as if someone had walked through it. Because it's long, it gets trampled down. They led to the wire fence at the train station car park. I wish I'd checked when we ran off whether there were any more, but I was too bothered about getting Owen away from the bloke."

Owen seemed surprised at that, as though he hadn't thought his brother cared about him. Maybe that was the way with teenage siblings — they pretended they weren't bothered about you and it took an extreme situation to show they did. Anna wouldn't know; she was an only child.

"That's good you remembered that, it'll help us a lot."

If there were still only the two tracks, it meant the man had left the same way as he'd come or he'd followed the boys' tracks — a tad disturbing if he'd gone after them. If there were three . . . that could mean the ones towards the station were nothing to do with him, or he'd chosen a different route of escape.

To gauge what was what, she asked, "Which direction did you approach the warehouse from?"

"We came and went the same way, so, as you're leaving the warehouse at the back, go left over the grass. There's a gap in the hedge where we went through."

A gap in the hedge. Anna's mind went straight to the last murder case. The killer had escaped through a gap in a hedgerow. It might not be significant in this case, but it always fascinated her how her brain threw up links, as if it played its own game of word association, except with images and incidents.

"Is there anything else you can recall?"

The boys shook their heads.

Their father, a beefy sort who probably loved the gym, glanced over his sons' heads to his wife, and his shaved scalp caught the lights. The woman, blonde, petite and pretty in a doll-like way, gave him a look as if to tell him she'd deal with whatever he had on his mind. Maybe she had more tact.

She stretched an arm out to lay it across her boys' backs. "What were you doing there in the first place? You won't be in any trouble — we were all kids once, so we know how it goes. I'm just a bit worried that you went to a warehouse that's been abandoned for years; it could be dangerous."

"We hang out there, that's all," Owen said. "Like a den."

The mum glanced at a backpack on the floor near the table, a rolled-up yoga mat poking out of the top. She pointed to it. "And you were going to sit on that?"

"Yeah."

"You'll get piles," Mr Kent said, "sitting on a cold floor."

Owen frowned at him, clearly confused. "What?"

"That's what your gran told me, anyroad." Mr Kent shrugged and looked across at Anna. "Is that it, then? Can we go?"

Anna nodded. "Yes, we have all we need for now, although the interview will be typed up and someone will come to yours for it to be signed." She switched her gaze to Damon and Owen. "If you want to talk about this with anyone, I can give your parents a card for a therapist."

They dipped their heads.

"We'll sort that," Mrs Kent said. "But thanks anyway."

Anna checked her watch. "Interview ended at 11.33 a.m."

Lenny stopped the recording, and everyone stood.

Anna held out her card to Mrs Kent. "If your sons think of anything else, just give me a ring."

The woman fussed with her mittened hands. "What about their safety? The man saw their faces."

"Just lay low for the time being, and if they go out, better to have an adult with them, or at least be with a group of friends."

"Maybe we could put on face masks? We have a few of them from the pandemic," Owen suggested.

Again, Anna's mind made associations. Jamal Jenkins had been found wearing a black mask covered in neon skulls.

"I think we threw a box of those out," Mrs Kent said.

"I don't mean the paper type ones but material. Loads of kids still use them."

"If they're in the Chiefs or the Loops," Mr Kent muttered. "*You're* not involved with anything like that, are you?" He sighed. "Still, better than having that mad bastard recognise you. As if it wasn't bad enough you got called in about Jamal, now this. People are going to think my boys are wrong 'uns."

Anna's interest piqued. "Oh. What was that about Jamal?"

"Him being stabbed. Damon and Owen were mates with him before he went off on his own, selling those bloody drugs."

"By called in, do you mean interviewed by the police?"

51

"Yeah."

Anna made a mental note to dig out the file. For now, she sensed the lads had had enough. "Let's call it a day here."

The family filed out and Mr Kent closed the door behind them. Ollie puffed out his cheeks and pushed off the cupboard unit he'd been leaning on. He sat where Damon had and rubbed his eyes. Anna and Lenny retook their seats.

"What was your take on them when you first got here?" Lenny asked Ollie.

"Shit-scared, hiding something."

Anna nodded. "Probably the real reason they were at the warehouse. I got the idea Mr Kent sees his boys through rose-coloured specs. You know, *my precious boys wouldn't do anything wrong*. I didn't get up to anything at their ages, but so many people I knew did, it's part of growing up, but I don't think they were hiding anything more than that. Do either of you?"

"No," Lenny said.

"I doubt they're anything to do with it," Ollie added. "I mean, did you see their faces when they were talking about the camo bloke? They weren't frightened as such, more confused."

"I saw that, too." Anna sighed. "*I'd* be confused if a man in green face paint told me he'd come back for a guinea pig. I mean, come on, it's weird."

"For 'next time', though." Lenny picked at a hangnail. "Which tells me he's going to kill someone else. And why leave the animal there if he only had to go back for it? Did he forget it? Was he disturbed?"

Anna let that percolate. "No idea. OK, here's what we'll do. Nip to the warehouse to see the body and chat to Herman — he should be there by now and might have something to pass on to us. I'm hoping for ID. I need to get the team poking into the missing men case in the meantime."

"What one was that?" Lenny asked. "I can read your mind a lot of the time, but you've got me stumped here."

"Sorry, I sometimes forget I only *thought* something and didn't actually say it." Anna explained her idea about the guinea pig. "So you can see why I want to cover our arses here — look how the last case turned out, digging up all those other crimes we hadn't known about. This could be the same."

"When did all this go on?" Lenny asked. "The missing men, I mean."

"It happened in the nineties, as far as I can remember."

Ollie leaned back, a finger resting on his chin. "So, say there was a bloke — I'm assuming it's a bloke — taking men during that time, and he was, what, thirty for argument's sake? That would mean he's sixty now. Why have a thirty-year gap between abductions, if that's what it even was?"

"Maybe he was in the nick all that time for something else," Lenny said.

"It'd have to be serious for that length of time." Anna pinched her bottom lip as she thought. "Or he moved away and men have been going missing elsewhere ever since. Although 'guinea pig' would have been flagged on the nation-wide system in that case. I'm going to ring the team and get them cracking on this."

She took her phone out of her pocket and jabbed the screen for Sally's number, as she was the one who excelled in research. Anna explained what she needed her to do, then stood, slipping her mobile away.

"We'd better go and see the body," she said.

Lenny groaned.

"I know, it's not my favourite thing to do either, but there you go."

They all walked out, and the man who'd met them at the roller door spotted them from where he leaned on the wall down the corridor. He escorted them down the side of the loading bay and out into the cold.

"Come with us, Ollie," Anna said. "I expect another pair of eyes will come in handy. Steven will likely use you for checking the grass. Actually, now we know the tracks went to the train station car park, you can go and ask for the CCTV

53

footage. It'll save Peter or Warren coming out to do it. The old case might take up a lot of their time."

They parted ways and Anna drove towards the warehouse, her mind skipping to the missing hand.

Had Steven and his team found it yet, or had the killer taken it as a trophy?

CHAPTER SEVEN

Suited up, Anna and Lenny stood at the victim's feet. He had no skin on his face except at the hairline, and the flesh was uneven, as if it had been gnawed at. Hopefully he'd have passed out or died long before all that skin had been stripped away.

These days, many fellas wore suits even if they weren't classed as businessmen, so his clothing didn't necessarily mean he was a high-flyer. His shoes were missing, and the socks still on his feet spoke of someone with a sense of humour. They were green to match his tie and had cartoon cats on them, white with googly eyes.

Most of the wounds were localised around the torso and thigh areas. There were no slashes to the material over the lower legs. Drips of blood marred it, though. Anna had learned a lot during her time at scenes with pathologists and attending post-mortems, which she preferred other officers to do now if she could get away with it. Going by the direction of the blood flow on the trousers, he'd been standing when attacked. This location wasn't the attack site, she knew that much, so where the hell was it?

In the vast space that had once bustled with noisy employees, SOCO worked quietly, reverently, as if making any sound would be wrong somehow. The stark difference between what the place had been like in the past and how it was now was creepy. The whole warehouse had a chilling feel to it, despite the police halogen lights brightening the place up. Rats lurked in every corner, loads of them, watching with their marble eyes. Some had scampered outside when Anna and Lenny had arrived, off to find their Pied Piper. PCs were currently questioning people on the trading estate, looking for any witnesses who may have seen the man arrive, and Ollie had gone to the train station.

Herman bent over and inspected the victim's face using a magnifying device. "The rats have been at him."

Anna's stomach churned. "Free food, that's all he is to them."

How awful to die and have animals eating you. Not something a regular person would ever dream could happen to them.

"Can't you shoo them all out of here?" she asked the nearby officers in white suits.

One of them shrugged and swivelled his eyes towards Steven.

"We already had a go when we arrived," Steven said. "We're not bloody collie dogs, Anna. The little gits scattered everywhere. Better to have them in the corners than near the body. So long as they stay out of the way, we can make do. Besides, them trotting all over the floor would disturb any evidence. Those lads coming in have already compromised it."

Anna thought it best to keep her mouth shut on the subject. Steven wasn't in the best of moods. He was usually pretty laid-back, so maybe someone or something had upset him. Or he'd woken up in a shitty frame of mind, as she sometimes did, for no reason.

I bloody hate that.

Thankfully, Wayne the photographer approached, which signalled the end of the conversation nicely and cleared the air a bit. "Ready for me to take any more pictures yet?"

Herman nodded. "Some close-ups of that arm, the one without the hand. Specifically the blood on the floor beside it. I don't think it came from the arm. It looks like something else was placed there that bled. See the clean shape left on the concrete?"

"The hand?" Anna asked. *Or a guinea pig?*

"Maybe. There isn't enough blood for him to have been killed here, and any spatter present appears thicker than it would have had the wounds been fresh, as if the blood had coagulated before the body was placed. That patch there . . . whatever it came from bled *here*, not elsewhere."

Steven stepped closer. "I agree. And it's a small amount, so perhaps he killed a rat and took it with him?"

"The lads who found him mentioned a guinea pig," Anna said. "Could it be that?"

Steven seemed to calculate the amount of blood such an animal would lose if it was killed there and bled out. "Hmm. I'll make a note of it for the lab techs."

Herman knelt on an evidence step and gently pressed the stomach. "Rigor's present." He peered at the blood patch. "Can I have a tech over here, please? There's hair in and around this blood that isn't the same colour as our man's here."

"What colour is it?" Anna asked.

An officer came over and, using tweezers, picked up hair from beside the small puddle that had congealed on top. "Ginger."

Lenny readjusted his face mask. "That's what the boys said."

Anna didn't know whether to prompt Steven to make another note, seeing as he was being so dour, but if she didn't she wasn't doing her duty. "It could be a guinea pig, then, Steven. It'll save the lab some time in working out what it is."

"Right." He took a device out and tapped on the keypad, then stopped. Sighed. Stared at the steel rafters. "Look, I've got to say something. It's not fair on you lot for me not to." He called out to his team and asked them to gather round.

Anna stared at him. What the hell was up with him?

Steven cleared his throat. "It'll come out sooner or later, but I'm prickly because I caught the wife at it last night." He paused. "To clarify, with someone else." His face flushed red.

"Jesus," Lenny said. "Sorry to hear that, pal."

Steven nodded his thanks. "So if I go over the line, pull me up on it. You can't be expected to put up with me like that."

"Aren't you better off going home?" Herman asked.

"No, work will take my mind off it."

"What's the score now?" Anna asked, then regretted it immediately. A bad habit of hers, blurting. "Sorry, that was tactless of me, but what I was *trying* to say is it might help to talk."

"What, when we've got that poor bastard down there on the floor?"

"He's not going to get any deader," Herman muttered. "And five minutes of chatting won't make a difference."

Steven sighed again. "She's moving out today. The bloke she's been seeing, she's going to his place. Guess what her excuse was?"

Anna rolled her eyes. "You're never home, you're married to the job, you love your work more than her."

"Yep." Steven shook his head. "She knew this when she started going out with me. I warned her the hours can be nuts. And it's my calling, for fuck's sake. How can she expect me to give that up?"

"Is that what she wanted?" Anna asked.

"Of course it bloody was. Not a chance, and now she's been playing away . . . I told her at the beginning that was a dealbreaker for me, so she did it *knowing* I wouldn't stay with her once I found out."

"Maybe that was her plan." Anna said what everyone else was likely thinking, but maybe she should have kept it to herself.

"Already thought of that." Steven took a deep breath. Let it out. "Right, back to work."

As if nothing had happened, the techs wandered away, Steven returned to his device, and Herman rose. He stepped over to the other side of the body. Checked the trouser pockets. Nothing. He peeled back one side of the suit jacket, hardened with dried blood, and dipped a gloved hand into the pocket there, bringing out a wallet.

Anna tensed, hoping it contained something that would tell them who the victim was. For all they knew, the killer could have robbed him of his cards to either have a contactless spending spree or conceal his identity.

"Driver's licence," Herman said, "and cards that match the name on it. "Martin Lowe, fifteen Pembrooke Avenue."

"Westgate," Anna said. "So he had a bit of money, or he lived on the council estate there."

Anna had grown up in Westgate, an area of Marlford that rarely suffered from crime-related issues. People there just wanted to get on with their lives, and, if truth be told, they thought themselves a cut above the likes of folks in Northgate, say, which gave the city a bad name, specifically the Rowan estate. Drug dealers, addicts, and what some thought of as the dregs of society regularly aired their differences in the streets.

Anna sighed. "I'll get on to Karen." She walked away to a quiet area, rang the station and requested the name of Martin's other half, if he had one, or his parents, so she and Lenny could go and inform the next of kin.

"That would be his wife," Karen said. "She's listed as living at that address. Donetta Lowe. That name rings a loud bell. Hang on." The tapping of a keyboard filtered down the line. "Thought so. She's a supermodel."

"Not on my radar."

59

"She's Spanish but lives here permanently. Google's thrown up pictures of her on a catwalk in what appears to be a dress made of carrier bags. Good Lord. I could make one of those with the number of bags under my sink. She's thirty-two, and I can even give you her measurements."

"Um, no."

Karen laughed.

That gave Anna an age bracket to go on for Martin, whose face had been ruined so they couldn't tell his age — but then again he could be older or younger than Donetta. She chastised herself for assuming they'd be of a similar age. "Thanks. How old is Martin?"

"Two secs . . . Thirty-eight. He runs a company called Lowe Financials."

"Ta."

"Donetta reported him missing last night. Is it bad?" Karen asked.

"Um, yes. Martin was possibly known to whoever murdered him. Lots of knife wounds, so it looks personal."

"I've never been completely in agreement with that theory."

"Which part?"

"That they might have known each other. Sorry, but you could be arsey with someone for a number of reasons. Even those who choose a victim at random can knife someone more than once."

"I agree, but all those studies do have a point. Violent attacks usually have some emotional cause."

"I know, but it's not true all the time. Anyway, I need to go. Looks like I've got to book in yet another spice-head."

"Rather you than me."

Whoever supplied spice in Marlford had done so without detection. The drug squad had been trying to pinpoint the source for a good couple of years now, and no number of undercover officers posing as buyers had been able to get any solid leads. It was like all those involved knew not to give out any information. Maybe Anna should ask Parole about that, see if the Kings were the ones supplying.

She said goodbye to Karen, then mulled over her phone conversation with Parole earlier. He'd seemed extremely happy that she'd done what he'd asked, but her lie about the gang member's name being redacted in the file had brought on a rash of questions. *Why would it be redacted? Is it because it's a minor? Is there an ongoing case? Is it the kid who stabbed Jamal Jenkins?* She'd rebuffed him, saying she had no idea about any of it because certain sentences had been blacked out.

"I can't tell you what I don't bloody know," she'd said.

"Oi, daydreamer," Lenny called.

She returned to stand beside him. "I've got the NOK details, so we'd better go."

They left the warehouse, and Anna felt relieved not to have the rats' beady eyes on her anymore. They took off their protectives, popped them in a designated bag and signed out on the log. She scanned the grass. Foot tracks from the gap in the hedge to the path by the door. Another set from the door to the train station fence. That didn't mean the weird camo man had made any of them when he'd left the area, though. A concrete pavement ran along the back of all three buildings, leading to the car park at the front, so he could have used that.

Yellow markers sat beside speckles of blood, but not many, so the blood must have done what Herman had said and coagulated prior to the body being brought here. With the amount on the clothing, it must have soaked the material and dripped onto the path. Whoever had carried him would have been covered in it, as would any vehicle he'd used.

Round the front, in the car, she put the victim's address into the satnav and prepared to drive away, but Ollie's patrol car drew up, so she waited.

They lowered their windows.

"Anything?" Anna asked him.

"CCTV for the car park isn't anything to do with the train station. It's a private area owned by a company called PS

61

— Parking Solutions. I've requested the train station footage to be sent in, just in case the killer used a train at any point."

"Thanks. I'll let the team know about PS."

"What I *did* notice, where the tracks stop, was the wire fencing has been snipped in a door shape and held back together with metal twists. I was just about to tell Steven so he can send someone over there. I've also got a list of all cars currently parked there. Want me to send it to you?"

"Please. We're just on our way to see the victim's wife. He's called Martin Lowe, and she's Donetta. Ever come across them on your travels? Any domestics? They live on Westgate, Pembrooke Avenue."

Ollie stared out of the windscreen, then back at Anna. "Not that I recall."

Ollie isn't up on supermodels either, then. "Cheers."

Anna raised the window and nudged Lenny. "Do *you* know who Donetta Lowe is?"

"A supermodel. Super bloody hot an' all. Is that the wife?"

Anna tsked at him. "You really don't want to come across as a perv, pal."

"What? I'm just saying she's pretty."

"Hmm. But being pretty isn't the currency women should have to pay to be worthy of your attention."

"I see what you mean. Sorry."

Anna let it drop. "Can you get hold of Karen for me to see what kind of car Martin drove?"

"Yep."

While Lenny made the call, Anna's phone bleeped. Ollie must have sent the registration numbers after he'd parked. She opened the email and scanned the makes and numbers. Lenny finished speaking to Karen and read out a licence plate.

"Ford Mondeo," Anna said. She'd matched it to one on the list. "Silver. So was he abducted after he parked his car?"

"But that doesn't make sense if the wire fence was snipped. That's premeditated."

"Yes, but the killer could have made it to the doorway and then waited for Martin. He might have known his patterns and stood there until he turned up. We'll know more when we get to view that CCTV. In the meantime, the team can search ANPR for where Martin's car was prior to this. Oh, and we need to request information from PS. If it's one of those car parks where it takes a picture of the number plate as you drive in, it'll be easy for them to tell us when his vehicle entered. And we might get lucky and see who was driving. It may not necessarily have been Martin." Anna set off in the direction of Westgate. "Ring Warren and get that organised for me, please. We don't even know how long Martin's been away from home. Once we do, you can fire off another message so Warren can narrow down the timeframe."

Ollie was telling Steven about the car, so that was one thing off her list. She breathed deeply to combat that feeling she sometimes got when there was so much to check, so much to *do*, that it threatened to overwhelm her. She was an introvert by nature, forcing herself to play a different role at work, and every so often she wanted to go home and crawl into her safe space, hiding from it all.

Not today, love.

Lenny got back on the phone and, to stop her mind from spinning in all directions, Anna pondered what could have gone on. Had Martin used the car park regularly? Was he a commuter, despite owning a business here? Had the killer been watching the area recently and chosen Martin off the cuff? Or was there something more sinister at play?

She entered Westgate. The satnav bypassed her old estate and took her to the new-build properties that had sold for over half a million each. Pembrooke Avenue, each home standing in its own grounds, was for the more affluent types. Oak trees stood along the road, the foliage finally surrendering to gravity now it was December. Not one mulchy leaf littered the ground. Did the residents pay for someone to maintain the street? Expensive cars sat on driveways, not at the kerbs, as if there was some unspoken rule about it.

Anna swerved into the Lowes' driveway and parked behind a black Range Rover Evoque, something she was aware would have cost a packet.

The perks of being a supermodel.

"Everything sorted at the station?" she asked.

Lenny nodded and unclipped his seat belt. "Yep. Warren was in the loo, so I spoke to Sally. She said she'd go with Peter to the PS place. Head office is based in the city, who knew?"

"OK, let's get this horrible bit out of the way, then we can go back to the station for a debrief."

Lenny glanced at his watch. "With a stop at Brunch along the way?"

Anna smiled. "Yep, I could do with a decent coffee, not to mention one of their sausage rolls."

CHAPTER EIGHT

Anna and Lenny got out of the car and approached the house. A silver plaque on the wall had *Casa Perfecta* etched into it. Anna wasn't au fait with the Spanish language, but she felt confident she could translate that. She shook herself out of the introspection. Now wasn't the time to think about such inane things.

But it isn't inane. It could tell us a bit about Martin. That he liked everything to be just so.

She rang the bell and waited.

A woman answered. Anna guessed her to be late fifties, or life had been especially kind to her, as she didn't have many wrinkles — or was that the miracle of surgery? Black hair reached the shoulders of her pale-pink fitted jumper; black leather trousers and ballerina shoes completed the ensemble. She screamed money but in an understated way. Classy.

I'd never be able to pull that look off.

Anna held up her ID and introduced them. "Is Donetta Lowe in?"

"Yes, I'm her mother, Ines. I assume you're here about Martin. Do come in." A slight Spanish accent coloured her words, as if she'd lived in the UK for more years than she had Spain.

They followed her through a large foyer, their shoes tapping on the shiny white floor tiles. The woodwork and banister rails were done in a tasteful mid-grey, the walls in a lighter shade. Artwork, the modern kind, hung on the long wall to the right, splashes of colour as if a child had created them. One of them was a scribble of lines. Anna entered a kitchen that belonged in a magazine, all reflective white surfaces with grey accents.

Ines seemed to glide over the floor. She sat at a huge island in the centre beside a woman who Anna assumed was Donetta.

"The police are here to see you, *querida*."

Anna smiled, although it felt cruel in the circumstances, so she hoped it had come across as sympathetic. "I'm DI Anna James, and this is DS Lenny Baldwin. I understand you reported your husband missing yesterday, Mrs Lowe."

Donetta nodded. She was red-eyed, her cheeks ruddy from crying and smeared with mascara. Her sleek black bob swung with the movement, the ends cut bluntly, her fringe severe. It suited her. She had the air of the rich about her, too, what with that beige cashmere jumper dress, cinched at the waist with a thick brown belt. She held herself with a poise Anna could never emulate even if she tried. The smell of perfume wafted over, and she recognised it as Dune by Dior, a scent her mum loved. It brought on a pang of longing. She wanted to see her, speak to her, but her parents lived down on the south coast. Maybe she should take some time off for a visit. Their weekly catch-up calls suddenly didn't seem like enough.

She studied Donetta.

Is that yesterday's make-up? Was she so upset last night she didn't bother to wash it off?

Anna returned her attention to her surroundings. Everything here pointed to a household that didn't have to worry about money. Was that a factor in this case, though?

Had Martin been chosen because of his wife's status? Her fame?

"He didn't arrive at his usual time," Donetta said, her accent tinged with Yorkshire. "I waited for an hour, then messaged him to see if he was running late. Do you want to see what I sent him?"

"Lenny will have a look," Anna said.

Donetta held her phone out. "You'll see in the call log how many times I rang him."

Lenny took the phone and sat at the far end of the island to look.

Anna preferred to remain standing for now. She glanced at Ines. "What time did you get here?"

Ines gripped Donetta's hand, their sparkly nails glimmering together. "It was about eight, wasn't it, when you rang me last night?"

Donetta nodded. "You got here about half past."

"What time should Martin have arrived home?" Anna asked.

"Six at the latest," Donetta said. "He doesn't like to hang around at work unless it's absolutely necessary. He says work and home life need a line drawn in the sand between them. They mustn't cross over. I'm away a lot, so he also likes to spend as much time with me as possible before I fly off again."

"For the modelling," Anna checked.

"Yes." Donetta didn't seem fazed by that, as if she *expected* Anna to know who she was, although it didn't come across as arrogant.

"So you must have been considerably worried by eight o'clock when you rang your mother."

"I was worried by half past six. It's not like him at all. He would have messaged or phoned if he was going to be late. We sat here until eleven — I'd been ringing him on and off until then — and at that point I phoned the police to report him missing."

"I'm sorry to have to ask this, but was everything OK in your marriage? No reason for him not to come home?"

Ines snorted. "That man is too honest and loyal to worry my daughter like this. He's devoted to her."

While Anna appreciated Ines answering, she didn't want to hear it from her. Donetta may not want to say anything about a rocky marriage in front of her mother, so maybe Anna should offer her a chat somewhere more private.

Instead, she prompted, "Donetta?"

"I'm his world. He'd never do this to me. Something's wrong, I can feel it."

Anna believed her, but before she dropped the bombshell on them she wanted to be sure they were at the right house with the right wife. Just because the cards in the wallet had belonged to Martin, and yes, he hadn't come home, it still might not be him. What if the killer was playing silly buggers and had put someone else's wallet in that suit pocket? She had to ensure she told them they *suspected* it was Martin, not that they had proof it was.

"What was he wearing yesterday?"

Donetta thought for a second or two. "Grey suit, white shirt and a green tie. Black shoes, the ones with the red soles. Christian Louboutin."

Had they been taken along with the hand? That brand cost a pretty penny, and maybe the killer knew that. He could probably get a fair whack for them if he listed them on Vinted and the like.

"Excuse me for a second." Anna turned to Lenny. "Can you do the usual about the shoes, please?"

"What about them?" Ines asked.

Anna held back a sigh. She'd mucked up. These women didn't know the shoes were missing. "I've asked Lenny to message our team to look at whether any shoes of that description have been put up for sale online."

"Why would he need to do *that*?" Ines asked.

Anna was going to have to come clean sooner than she wanted. "I'm concerned because earlier today, a person wearing the clothes you've described was found, but he didn't have any shoes on."

Ines stood, letting go of Donetta's hand. "Why the *hell* didn't you say so from the start instead of all this talking?"

Anna understood the woman's anger. She would have to explain so Ines's fury came down a notch or two. "An investigation into a missing person isn't an uncommon occurrence, sadly, so the person I mentioned could be one of many. We have to ascertain whether the person is who we suspect them to be, hence the *talking* first. I prefer to ask questions beforehand, rather than delivering distressing news right away, as it might not be necessary. As we couldn't identify the person visually, we only had a wallet to go by, and now the clothing you've described."

"What do you mean, *visually?*" Ines demanded.

Anna chose to ignore that for now. "I'm sorry to have to tell you that the man has passed away."

Ines dropped down onto her seat, and Donetta blinked, perhaps in an attempt to hold back tears. It didn't work. They fell over her cheeks, reaching her chin and hanging there for a moment, then plopping onto her dress, glass baubles that soaked into the wool.

Anna softened her tone. "Please bear in mind this may not be Martin. We won't know until a DNA test has been done."

"But you're sure, aren't you?" Ines said. "*You* personally, gut instinct, whatever you want to call it, you *know*. I can tell you think it's him."

"I do, but until we have definitive proof we can only suspect. Unfortunately, that may give you hope, but in this case I don't feel there is any." There, she'd said it, but only because Ines seemed the type to want the truth.

"Did he have an emerald ring on his right hand?" Donetta whispered, staring at the top of the island as though in a state of limbo, detached from the conversation yet hearing it all the same.

"Not that we saw," Anna said.

She could hardly tell them the right hand was missing. Not yet. Herman would likely be the one to pass on that nasty snippet.

"How did he pass away?" Donetta asked. "He was healthy, we never ate rubbish, and he kept fit."

"I'm afraid he was murdered." Anna disliked having to watch people for signs of deception at a time like this, but the man who'd come for the guinea pig may not have anything to do with it, although it was highly unlikely. Still, she had to check whether next of kins reacted in a way that pointed the guilty finger at them.

Donetta's face scrunched up, but, as if by strength of will, she composed herself. Her features hardened, and she sat up straighter. Was that a touch of anger Anna detected?

Donetta looked at Anna. "I'll cry for him later. At the minute, I want the person who did this caught."

Ines patted her hand. "I knew you'd say that. Stiff upper lip. The breaking dam can wait, we know that from before."

"Before?" Anna frowned.

"We've already had tragedy in our past. So, what do you know?" Ines asked Anna. "And we want to hear *all* of it."

"He was stabbed." Anna wasn't prepared to say *several times*. "He was found by two teenage boys. Brothers."

"Oh, how *dreadful* for them," Ines said. "Are they OK?"

"Coping as best they can. Forgive me if this sounds strange, which it will, but did Martin have anything to do with guinea pigs?"

Donetta froze, her face draining of colour. She shot her gaze to Ines, snatched at her mother's hands and held them tight. "Mum?"

Ines stared at her, eyes wide. "Guinea pigs. Oh God. Oh God, no."

"So they *are* relevant?" Anna pressed.

Ines blew out a long breath, her eyes filling with tears. "Thirty years ago, those men who went missing."

"I remember my parents talking about it," Anna said. "And as the guinea pig angle rang a bell with me, I've already asked the rest of my team to look into it."

Ines swiped at a falling tear. "Why did you ask about them?"

"The teenagers were leaving the location to phone the police when a man came in. He told them he'd come to collect a guinea pig."

"It's happening again," Donetta whispered.

"What is?" Anna asked gently.

Ines stiffened her spine. "My husband went missing, and someone sent me guinea pig fur and a nasty letter in the post. His body has never been found — and I say body because, like Martin, Toro would never have walked out on us. Whoever did this thirty years ago has started again."

She stood and rushed out into the foyer, returning with a small stack of post. She sifted through it and stopped at a cream envelope.

"Oh God. It's the same type."

Before Anna could tell her to put it down, that they'd need to pop it in an evidence bag, Ines had already ripped it open. She pulled out a piece of cream card, stared at it, then threw it on the island.

"It's . . . no, this can't be happening again."

Donetta's cheeks sprouted circles of pink. Anger? Fear?

Anna looked at the card. The words. A few strands of copper-coloured fur that had been taped to one corner.

Anna stared at the envelope. No stamp.

"Do you have CCTV?" she asked.

Donetta shook her head. "The cameras are dummies."

Someone else in the street might have them, though.

Anna got on the phone to arrange for PCs to come and question all the neighbours. The street was too long for Anna and Lenny to do it alone. If that card had been hand-delivered, they stood a good chance of seeing who'd posted it through the letterbox.

She then sent a message to the team chat, asking them to get hold of Martin's mobile provider and request the data. That could take some time, but it was the only route available while Martin's phone was missing.

She eyed the note. It read: WHERE *is the body in the* HOUSE?

She shook her head, held in a wry chuckle. He *wanted* the body to be found? It was obvious what he was saying by using capital letters — *warehouse* — but would she have thought the same if she didn't know Martin's location? Probably not. She'd be trying to think of all the houses where he might be. And it didn't make sense. Why did he want Martin to be discovered?

She sighed. This case was already doing her head in, and it was only day one.

CHAPTER NINE

Once he'd cut off enough of its fur, Rory put the guinea pig in a shoebox, then placed the strands in a sandwich bag and zipped it shut. He'd already dropped one tuft round to Martin's wife. She would have opened the envelope by now. Seen the note. He'd been a bit more obvious with the clue than Dad had been.

How cool it had been to discover Donetta had married a rich man. Rory had done his homework regarding all the men Dad had killed, and his list was full of sons or sons-in-law he planned to murder. Maybe this time round the police would do their jobs better and discover the first batch of bodies from the nineties. The clues Dad had left in those notes — what a waste of time. The police hadn't worked them out. Hadn't spotted the locations hidden in the words.

Rory still had the articles in the loft, ones he'd taken from the cottage after Dad had died. Maybe he should make one of those murder walls like the police did so he could keep everything straight in his head. Which son or son-in-law belonged to which missing man from the past.

Which one was next.

"Got no preference," he muttered. "Makes no odds to me so long as they're all dead."

He sat on the floor in the kitchen, sipping a cup of tea, pondering those lads who'd found Martin. Of all the luck, eh? Rory wasn't bothered about them. He knew they'd tell the coppers, but it wouldn't do any harm.

Those boys were scared of you, son. Did you see that? Feel the power?

Rory had, although he'd felt sorry for them, to be fair. He'd heard bottles clanking in the carrier bag one of them held, and he reckoned they'd gone there to get pissed up, something he'd done a time or two with his old mate Billy, who just so happened to be on Rory's list.

That had been a shock during his research phase, using the internet on his burner phone in different parts of the city. He'd found out his pal from his younger years had landed on his feet by marriage plus hard work. Having money was the crux of this thing, Dad had said so. Men who lorded it about, showing off their wealth, bragging — they naffed him off something chronic. The fact that he'd become rich later in life, putting him on a par with others, was beside the point. At the time Dad had killed them all, he hadn't known how much cash Nan had in the bank, inherited from an aunt who'd had more money than she'd known what to do with. Nan had acted thrifty still, as if she didn't have a pot to piss in.

Dad was Yorkshire born and bred, of the mould that helped others out when they hit hard times. The men he'd killed, they'd knocked him back, laughed at him when he'd approached them for a loan, yet he'd been to school with them, they'd been buddies.

And they could have afforded it.

It brought Rory's mind back to Billy. They'd promised to be friends for life, yet, as soon as college had come and gone, Billy had married and then buggered off abroad to make his millions, starting a company, raking it in. He'd recently come back to Marlford to live, and Rory had seen him swanning around in his swanky sports car or strutting through town

74

with his wife draped on his arm, a large diamond sparkling on her finger.

Rory was rich now — by most measures anyway. He wouldn't have to go to work for years to come. So wasn't he the same as the men Dad had killed? The same as Martin, Billy, all the others on the new list? Wasn't he the same as Dad, who'd eventually coined it in?

No, he and Dad didn't gad about as if they were better than other people. That was the difference. Dad hadn't changed after landing all that money off Nan. Look at how Rory had let Kirsty sod off with all the furniture.

Besides, being rich wasn't the reason Rory was doing this, although it *had* been his father's reason. Rory only wanted to finish what Dad had started, tie off that loose end. He imagined his father wouldn't rest properly until it was done, the bodies found. That man had always put a full stop at the end of everything he'd been involved in, but he'd gone to his grave with the pen still poised to make that final dot on the notepad in his mind.

He'd bloody hate that. It's probably why he still talks to me in my head. He can't pass over.

Did that mean Martin might not? Did his soul have unfinished business, too? Rory didn't know one way or the other. His list had been determined by Dad's, and he couldn't exactly follow Martin around to get a feel for his life, he might have got picked up on CCTV. Mind you, a lot of Martin's life was displayed online — his wife was famous in fashion circles, after all. He'd have a lavish funeral, what with the amount of money she must earn.

Rory had to resist going to it. He'd stand out too much. He couldn't completely walk in his father's footsteps. Dad had gone to his friends' memorial service — well, they hadn't been true friends in the end, had they, because they'd sent him packing, the cruel bastards. After seven years had passed with no sightings of the men, no proof of life, the wives had got together and held a joint service for all of their husbands.

Dad had said he'd had to stop himself from laughing as he'd sung a hymn or two, knowing exactly where their loved ones were while they were all clueless.

Rory knew, too.

After Kirsty had left him, he'd often gone to the moors and visited each grave. Dad had finally buried them all. Rory had spat on the ground and cursed the men beneath the earth. Wankers, all of them. While hurting them, Dad had made sure to tell them what they'd done, why they had a knife to their throats, and all of them had said sorry. They hadn't meant it, though, just like Martin hadn't.

Would Billy?

Will knowing him skew my emotions?

Dad had been so cold to his victims, as if they'd never shared their youth, their secrets. He'd locked his feelings away in the moment as Rory watched from the corner of the cellar. After Toro's death, he'd been allowed to see everything from beginning to end. Nan had no clue what her son was up to in her home, deaf as she was.

Like Mum didn't know what her husband had been up to.

Or her son.

"I bet that fucking bitch won't let it go about that guinea pig," Rory said. "Maybe she'll even twig what's going on." He thought back to that morning. "And what the fuck did that Sid bloke want?"

Mum had seemed confused about the old boy asking after her, so there couldn't be anything going on between them. Mum hadn't had a fella in all the years since Dad had left her. She said she'd rather be alone than with "someone like him".

Rory had often wondered what she'd meant by that. *Did* she know what Dad had really been like? She'd always looked at him funny, and Rory, as if she couldn't comprehend how she'd ended up with them in her life. And what was all that about, taking the shop key off him? Did she suspect he'd nicked the guinea pig?

"She must do. She isn't stupid."

Rory pushed up off the floor and stood by the sink to drink the rest of his tea. He consoled himself with the fact that no more pigs would go missing, so maybe she'd forget about Copper. That Cuddy kid might be an issue, though. He was as batty as her about the animals, so he might keep bringing up Copper's disappearance.

Rory didn't like Cuddy. Mum mothered the kid more than she ever did Rory, and, while it didn't hurt exactly, it still bugged him. Why didn't she love him like Dad had?

His time spent living with her after the split with Kirsty was still a puzzle to him. He didn't understand why he'd run to the one person who'd made it clear she wasn't fond of him. Did he *want* her to care? Had he thought that, with something so big, so life-changing happening to him, she'd finally, *finally* play at being the good mother? Or was he desperate for her to play Dad's role now? Dad being gone had messed Rory up, and without his steadying influence, their secret looks and smiles, he'd felt adrift. He'd only had Kirsty, who, now he thought about it, he shouldn't have married at all.

He gulped the last of his tea and swilled the cup out, then went upstairs to change out of his second set of camo gear. The washed lot from last night was drying on an airer in the living room. He cleaned the green cream off his face, put on his joggers and a hoodie, and trundled off to the smallest bedroom to inspect Martin's hand.

A faint scent came off it, so mild the average person wouldn't detect it, but over the coming days the stench would get stronger. Old cheese mixed with out-of-date chicken. He couldn't wait to sniff that.

Bored, because he had to wait for tonight before he went after the next bloke, he walked round to Bob's next door to see if he needed anything from town. It would give Rory an excuse to go there, see if any gossip had reached his mother about Martin. If those lads had phoned the police, the news would spread pretty fast.

Plus, he could see whether Mum mentioned Copper again. If she did, he might need to have a think about what he'd do with her.

She wasn't allowed to ruin this.

CHAPTER TEN

Number One looked and smelled so disgusting now. Rory and Dad were visiting all the men, five so far, so Dad could note the various stages of decomposition in his little book. The spaces between each body meant there was a fair old walk, and they stayed with each one for at least an hour, but Rory didn't mind so long as he got to spend time with his father. It was better than being at home with Mum, who was acting weird lately. Jumpy, like she thought the house was filled with ghosts who hid round every corner.

They'd set off early this morning, stopping to have a picnic halfway through the checks, and now, at Number Five, Rory was tired. While Dad jotted in his notebook, he sat and picked at the scrubby grass and poked at the thick patch of moss nearby.

"Why the fuck haven't they been found yet?" Dad muttered. "Don't the police have a brain cell between them?"

Rory had read the paper with Dad last night while Mum was at bingo. The notes Dad sent to the wives had all been published, and Rory had pretended he didn't know where the bodies were so he could see the words like a policeman would. He wouldn't be able to work out where the men were from the notes, so no wonder the police hadn't either.

"The notes don't tell them nothing," Rory said now. "It's like a secret code or something. Too secret."

"Yeah, well, they need to up their game. Those women will be wanting to bury their husbands, I'll be bound. They can't do that with the bodies out here."

"Why don't you send more notes and just say where they are, then?"

"Because I want to watch them rot right until the end, I told you that."

Once again, confusion swaddled Rory. Dad wanted them found, then he didn't. Then he did. God.

"When I'm a man and I kill someone, I'll be clearer about where he is."

Dad glanced over from his stooped position over Five. "You're going to kill someone, are you?"

"Yeah."

"How come you don't want to watch them rot?"

"Because I know what it looks like now, don't I? Anyway, I'd take his hand like you do. Watch that rot instead."

"You need to learn a lot more before you go down that road," Dad said. "But we have time. I'll teach you." He grinned. "You're a right chip off the old block, aren't you?"

CHAPTER ELEVEN

Sally had passed on that they needed to visit PS to view the CCTV footage, and Peter had asked Warren if he wanted to come with him, as if what Sally wanted didn't matter. After this morning's secret conflab, she wanted to put some feelers out, so she'd stood up from her desk and announced she'd go with him, using the excuse that she was sick of staring at a computer screen. Just because she was the best at research, it didn't mean she had to do it all the time. Warren knew the score, and she'd given him a look to let him know she had something up her sleeve. And anyway, she really did need to leave the office. The words had been blurring in front of her, not taking her mind off her own problems at all. Maybe being out in the field would help with that.

Richard had been worse than usual lately. Since they'd split up, he'd changed more than ever and started being awkward about having their son, Ben, for the weekend. Snide comments at pick-up and drop-off times. Side-eye looks. Accusations. A general feeling of him *owning* her. But he'd been ultra-odd recently, sitting outside her house in his car in the evenings when he should be at home. And their son, Ben, came back from his nights away asking strange questions about men, wanting to know if she had a boyfriend. Richard was obviously using him as a vessel to get information out of her. The fact that Richard had had a stream of women since they'd gone their separate ways didn't matter, but Sally having a bloke — no, he wouldn't like that. That wouldn't be "allowed".

Cheeky shit.

She was so sick of him, she wished he was dead. Not a nice thing to think, and she'd never act on it, but God, why couldn't he just let go? Move away? Leave her alone? Why did he still have to control everything? That was one of the reasons they'd split. Sally felt stifled, her light dimmed, with Richard orchestrating every little thing. She'd cottoned on to his gaslighting and manipulative ways just in time, before he'd taken her over completely. She'd thought being a single parent was the best way to go, but every Friday evening, without fail, he said something to her to put her down in the hope that it would ruin her weekend.

She spent the time when Ben was away to catch up on the washing, housework and sleep, not a man in sight, unless you counted those she watched on the telly. Richard insinuated that she was having the time of her life in bed for the two nights a week he had Ben — not that it was any of *his* business if she was — and it riled her up that he could still have such an effect on her.

She glanced across at Peter in the driver's seat. It seemed he was thinking, too. About his old life with the Kings? His life now? He really didn't look well, and, no matter what anyone else said, he *didn't* seem the same lately. He seemed downtrodden, vacant, as if he had a million and one things on his mind.

Is that how I come across, too?

Did everyone think they were concealing their pain when, in fact, it was plain as day?

On the day Jamal Jenkins had died, Peter had acted weirdly. His phone had kept ringing, and he'd gone off each time, looking shifty. Since then, he'd seemed on edge. She wanted to prod him to see how he reacted.

She reached into her handbag and pressed record on her portable recorder. Naughty of her, but . . .

"Are you all right?" she asked.

"Why?" he snapped, a bit too quickly.

"You haven't seemed yourself lately, that's all. Neither have I, which is why I wanted to reach out. It's no fun keeping everything locked up inside, I should know."

"Why, what's going on with you?"

Clever. He's deflecting. "The usual with Richard, except worse."

"In what way?"

"He's taken to sitting outside my house in his car on weeknights."

He frowned. "Err, stalker much?"

"Hmm. I won't go out there and ask him to leave because he'll know he's bothered me. He lives for doing that, and I don't want to give him the satisfaction." Although after the chat with Anna this morning, Sally was leaning more towards getting Richard in the shit for his behaviour.

Peter gripped the steering wheel hard. "Twat. So you're just going to leave it?"

"Yes."

"But that's sending him a message that he can do whatever he wants to you and you can't do anything about it."

Can't? Is that how he feels with the Kings? "I might move away from Marlford. I mean, if the situation won't go away by itself and I don't want to do anything about it, then it's best to remove myself, right? If I'm not here, he can't hurt me."

Peter glanced over at her, then back to the road. She got the sense she'd struck gold with that comment. Was *he* thinking of removing himself?

"Are you serious?" he asked.

She'd expected him to be relieved to hear she was leaving. Seemed he actually felt sad, though, which surprised her.

83

"I wouldn't have said it if I wasn't," she said.

"Blimey. Anna will be gutted."

Sally shrugged, faking nonchalance. "She'll find someone else to fill my role, easy."

"It'd be weird without you. We've all been a team for so long."

Do it. Say it. "I wonder if that's how the Kings felt when you left them to join the police. A part of their team was missing."

He bristled at that. "No clue, and I don't care."

She'd hit a nerve, but would carry on regardless, as if she hadn't noticed. "I'm curious. What was it like being with them? I mean, they're suspected of doing some really bad stuff, and you don't seem the type."

"I'm not. I left as soon as it looked like they were going down a dodgy path. I want to do good in the world, not bad."

It sounded like he meant it. Had they all got it wrong and he wasn't a bent copper? Or was he a master at playing both roles? She hated the idea of him going off to Kings meetings and laughing at his colleagues, saying they were dumb because they didn't have a clue what he was up to.

She chanced her arm. "So when you applied to become a police officer, they didn't say anything? They didn't think it was weird that a gang member was joining the force?"

"Why would they? You're thinking of the Kings as they are now. Back then, all they did was nick a few things. I passed that on, obviously, I was open and honest about my role, which was fuck all really, and that was that. Just a kid who wanted to belong."

"I s'pose if you walked away before they got into the proper bad shit, you can't be held accountable for what they did after."

"And what they do is only speculation."

"Sounds like you're sticking up for them."

"Nope. I was a young lad who hung out with a group of boys, which was all we were. I didn't *do* anything. I didn't want that life, so I joined up."

84

It all sounded plausible.

"So that rumoured rule they have — once a King, always a King — that didn't apply to you?"

"They must have brought that in after I'd left."

"Trigger and all that lot, did you just cut them off? I mean, you were friends for a long time, at school and whatever. It must have been hard to walk away."

"Not really." Peter reached up to scratch his head. The new tattoo on his inner wrist was visible as his sleeve moved up.

"Nice tatt," she said. "Do they hurt when you get them done?"

"On that thin skin, yes. Not so much on the top of your arm."

"Oh, have you got one there, too?"

"Yeah."

"What is it?"

"Broken chains."

"Any reason for that?"

He inhaled through his nose. Released the air, his nostrils flaring. "No."

"Why an eagle?"

"Why not?" The muscles in the side of his face, near his jaw, flickered.

I'm pissing him right off. She'd best pull back a bit. "I was thinking of getting one."

"What sort?" Peter slowed and came to a stop behind a line of vehicles.

"Don't know yet. Probably something to do with Ben. His date of birth maybe." She stared out of the windscreen at the backed-up traffic ahead in Warner Road. "What's going on up there, can you see?" *Shit, is this the reason Parole asked Anna to check the database?*

Peter's face flushed, and he craned his neck. "Err, looks like someone's been knocked over. There's an ambulance."

Knocked over or mown down? "Poor sod. I hope they're all right."

"I doubt it." His cheeks flared red again; he'd said too much, didn't disguise it in time.

He didn't mean to blurt that. She frowned at him. "What makes you say that?"

"Nothing, it's just . . . doesn't matter."

"No, go on."

Peter glared at her. "Can you just shut up? You've done nothing but peck at me for the past few minutes."

Pleased she'd got under his skin, she continued to play her game. *Richard's* game — gaslighting. "Peck? It was a normal conversation as far as I'm concerned. If you think it's something more than that, then that's on you, not me. Maybe you've got a lot on your mind, but Jesus, pal, wind your neck in. You sounded like Richard then, and I don't need another dickhead in my life."

"I'm sorry, OK? Yes, I've got a lot going on, and you chattering was doing my head in. Not your fault, you weren't to know."

"Want to talk about it?"

"No amount of wise words from you will fix what's going on with me."

"Maybe give it a try?"

He swallowed. Shook his head. "Please, just give it a rest."

Out of spite, she was dying to spill everything to him, say everyone was watching him, that they knew he was up to no good. That'd shut *him* up. But as he'd only been under surveillance for a short while and nothing untoward had come of it, they had no proof he was dodgy. And Anna, not to mention Placket, would go through the roof if she did that. Still, the urge was there, especially as he'd spoken to her the way he had.

Did she want control in this situation because she didn't have any with Richard?

Peter glanced in the rear-view mirror, then U-turned out of the queue. Belatedly, Sally realised she hadn't once thought of going to help any uniforms at the scene ahead, but she smothered her guilt by telling herself the situation would already be in hand and they had a murder case to deal with.

"Listen, ignore me," Peter said. "I get that you've clocked I'm not myself, but honestly, there's nothing you can do. It's best I don't involve you."

"That doesn't sound ominous . . ."

"Let's just get to the parking place and see what's going on with the victim's car, all right?"

"Fair enough," she said begrudgingly. Really, she wanted to tell him arseholes like Richard weren't welcome in her life, so if Peter had turned into a version of him he could fuck off an' all.

Rage at her ex stomped through her mind in big, heavy boots. Why the hell should she put up with him sitting outside her house like a weirdo? What did it *matter* whether he knew it had annoyed her? He'd crossed a line, and loitering wasn't on.

She took her phone out and rang Karen. Peter was speeding now, looking like he was dealing with some angry boots of his own.

"What can I do for you, my lovely?" Karen asked.

"First off. Warner Road. We've just left a traffic queue there. Me and Peter. What's going on?"

"Fatal stabbing."

Oh God. "Does Anna know?"

"No. Clough's on it."

So Anna was right. Something is going down.

Karen cleared her throat. "What did you want me for?"

"Can you make a note to send a patrol car down my street this evening so the next shift know it needs doing? About seven will be fine."

"What for? Are you having trouble or something?"

Sally explained, and the more she spoke the more she became indignant on her own behalf. "If the officers could ask him what he's doing, he might stop coming."

"Bloody exes. By the time they've rinsed you dry of any warm feelings towards them, it makes you wonder what the hell you saw in them in the first place."

"That's pretty much what I've been thinking."

"Did I ever tell you about one of mine? George, his name was. Total mind-bender. He had me thinking I was going mad."

"I know the feeling."

"I binned him, obviously. OK, that's in the system. If he comes back again after tonight, ring it in. I've popped a note in that says a neighbour called it in, that he's been seen there most weeknights. He'll probably still blame you if he's anything like that George fella, but sod him. He's being creepy, so he has to pay the price."

"Thanks, Karen."

"Not a problem."

Sally said goodbye and cut the call.

Peter drew up in the PS car park and stopped. Clicked off his seat belt. "Sounds like you mean business."

"I do. I'm sick of men thinking they know it all, that they can do whatever they want without repercussions." She smiled at him. "Not on my bloody watch, they won't."

His eyebrows betrayed him with a slight twitch.

What she'd said had bothered him.

Good.

CHAPTER TWELVE

Peter's mind had gone into overdrive. Was Sally interrogating him? He had to stop being so paranoid, but, since he'd been forced to stab Jamal Jenkins, he hadn't been himself.

Who would be?

He hadn't lied to Sally. Times *had* changed since he'd first joined the Kings. Shoplifting, swiping stuff off market stalls, basic bad teen behaviour. Peter had known it was wrong so had wormed his way out of it, making out to Trigger that his old dear would go spare if he ever got caught.

Peter had joined the police force to filter information to the Kings when they stepped up a good few rungs of the criminal ladder. Drugs, protection rackets, robberies. The intel he'd had as a PC had been invaluable, and when he'd taken the detective exam, without telling Trigger, then announced he'd earned a spot on Anna's team, Trigger had been livid. He'd wanted Peter's boots on the ground, not holed up in an incident room.

But Peter had wanted to distance himself from the Kings by then, and that was the only way he could think of to do it.

His plan had gone to shit, though, and Trigger still expected him to leak information on police presence when the Kings were about to conduct big business. And to tip them off if it looked like the pigs were getting too close.

The only way out now was to change his name and move away. Start again, below the radar. Peter had already looked into it, yet he was still here, hadn't taken that important step into a new life. Why? He didn't even know. Something was keeping him here, some sense of belonging, and starting anew was scary.

But wasn't staying scarier?

He was supposed to be on a six-month sabbatical from the Kings, so if anyone was watching they wouldn't see sod all, but Trigger had moved the goalposts with Jamal. His murder was a loyalty test, and now the street crime team were upping the ante to find the killer. The Chiefs and the Loops were in the frame at the minute, but what if the focus switched to the Kings?

What if Peter got caught?

Trigger had videoed the stabbing, though Peter had tried to hide his face. That wouldn't save him, though. Trigger had taken the clothes Peter had worn. His DNA would be on them. And Jamal's blood.

And what the fuck was Anna doing, seeing Parole on the quiet? She didn't know he knew — and he couldn't say anything because she'd ask how he'd found out. He couldn't exactly tell her a King had told him, could he? Parole had been bragging to Trigger that he was turning a new copper, bringing another into the Kings fold. The thing was, it wasn't just that. Parole really liked Anna, and it seemed his charm had worked on her, if she'd agreed to date him.

Peter never would have expected it. Strait-laced Anna, always putting the job first, always on the right side of the law, going out for dinner with a man who'd been in and out of prison more than she'd had hot dinners. Maybe she had a hidden, sneaky side to her — and why should Peter even care?

He wanted out of it all, didn't he? Who gave a toss if she took his place as the Kings' mole?

Except it hurt.

God, he needed to get his head sorted. All these seesawing emotions could land him in trouble. Especially because he'd just been on the cusp of telling Sally what was going on, including that Anna was dating Parole.

Last night, Peter had got home from work to find Trigger sitting on his sofa again, the same as the night Jamal had been killed. Trigger had crowed about Anna, saying Parole was working hard to talk her round and she had no clue what he was up to.

"She's putty in his hands," he'd said.

Anna? Putty? Fuck off!

Trigger had to be messing with him. Or worryingly, Anna had taken it upon herself to use Parole's attraction to her to coax information out of him. About Peter? Or the Kings in general?

"What if she's undercover?" Peter had asked. "Are you thick or what?"

"We're enjoying playing the game either way."

"It's a *dangerous* game. What if Parole's dick ends up doing all the talking and he falls for her, lets stuff slip? About *me*?"

"Nah, Parole's too savvy for that." Trigger had smirked. "Anyway, there's going to be a fatality or two on Warner Road tomorrow. Let me know if any coppers are going to be around."

Peter had clenched his fists behind his back, wanting to end Trigger, kill the bastard so all this would stop. "I'm not meant to be doing that. We agreed, six months off, yet you made me kill Jamal and then spy on the team dealing with it. This isn't fair, you turning up here, telling me about a job you lot are doing — a murder — and dumping it on me that Anna's seeing Parole. Next you'll be asking me to watch her at work, see if she's up to anything."

"You read my mind. Go to work early tomorrow and get the info I need." Trigger had left, ending his burst of laughter with, "And you had no clue, did you, that your DI's getting her oats from one of us. Fucking classic."

Trigger's gloating and Sally's questions had only served to tell Peter he had to be careful. Yes, he and Sally had chatted on the way to jobs before, and maybe he'd taken today's pecking session the wrong way, but what if he was right? What if Anna *was* undercover and Sally was in on it? Lenny most certainly would be. Was Warren, too? They played squash together regularly, and the idea that someone he thought of as a pal was duping him . . .

Fucking hell. I've been duping him. *Hypocrite.*

He swallowed down his need to bolt, to run home and grab his packed bag, get the hell out of Marlford, but those men would see him, the ones who'd been watching him. At first he'd thought they were the police, that someone had discovered he'd been using other people's login details to access the police database. Then, he'd entertained the idea that Trigger might have sent them to mess with his head, that they were Kings, and now — now he didn't know *what* to think. His mind was stuffed with too many questions, the main one being: *Why haven't you run away yet?*

"You look like you're going to be sick," Sally said, unclipping her seat belt.

"Must have eaten something bad last night."

He got out and walked towards Parking Solutions, a tall glass building that reflected the scudding clouds, their bellies heavy and grey. He caught sight of Sally in the reflection, trotting behind him to keep up. He needed to watch himself around her. She'd fired so many questions at him that he'd almost panicked. Punched her to shut her up. Screamed in her face to leave him the fuck alone. He liked her too much to ever hurt her, but the need had been strong.

There was only so much he could take, especially with the nightmares about Jamal's death keeping him up at night.

Maybe I should end it all. Just die and be done with it.

The double doors slid open at his approach, and he entered the reception area. His gaze went directly to the glass-and-chrome desk. A man sat behind it, all posh suit and quiffed hair, and Peter mourned the loss of his own. He'd taken to shaving it like Lenny's as a bald spot had appeared.

When I run, I'll wear a wig. Grow a beard.

And when's that likely to be, eh?

Soon. I just . . . just need more time.

What, time to get caught? Dickhead.

He stuffed his warring thoughts away and smiled at the man, whose nametag identified him as Sajid. Peter held up his ID and introduced himself and Sally.

"Who would you like to speak to?" Sajid asked.

"Whoever runs the place."

"That will be Mr Davis. I'll just let him know you're here." Sajid picked up a phone.

Peter turned away to study the artwork on the walls. Several aerial views of full car parks, likely in various parts of the country. Sally hovered by his side, an irritating presence.

Please, Sally, just back off.

"Um, Mr Dove?" Sajid said.

It was nice being called plain Mr, not DC. Mr Normal sounded so good. No one with the mountain of troubles he had. But that feeling didn't last long. Peter spun round and gave the receptionist a smile, a fake one. Wooden.

"Mr Davis will see you now." Sajid returned the smile. "Top floor. His office is right there when you step off." He gestured towards the lift standing between two car park canvases.

"Thank you."

Peter led the way and called the lift. If only he could enter it and be transported elsewhere, the decision to actually leave Marlford taken away from him, governed by something other than himself. A decision taken out of his hands.

The doors opened, and he entered, Sally too close behind him.

Is she deliberately trying to wind me up?

93

He didn't bother making small talk while they ascended.

As promised, the office was right there when the doors slid across. The open-plan office, too big for one person, was sectioned off into three areas. A desk straight ahead, all those windows behind it, a view to the outside world. To the left, a seating area, black leather sofas and a glass coffee table, and to the right a bizarre assortment of fake greenery surrounding a massive tropical fish tank, the inhabitants aimlessly swimming around.

"Ah, what can I do for you?" Mr Davis stood and extended a hand. Portly and around the sixty mark, he gave off an air of excitement at the prospect of having something to do other than dealing with the two stacks of papers on his desk, and his black suit brought to mind funeral attire.

Peter shook his hand, as did Sally, and they took a seat.

"So," Davis said, "has there been a car theft or something? Someone stealing from inside a vehicle?" He rubbed his hands. The sound was grating.

"A murder," Peter said.

Davis widened his eyes. "Oh, bloody hell, I wasn't expecting that. What has this got to do with PS?"

"A Ford Mondeo belonging to the victim is currently in one of your car parks at the train station. Do you have CCTV there?"

Davis puffed up. "I have the most up-to-date technology. Each car is recorded entering and leaving. I even have a system where I can put in the number plate and all the relevant information comes up on one page. If you give it to me, we'll have the file in front of us in no time."

Davis's overly jovial mood got on Peter's nerves. Murder wasn't something he found exciting, especially not after Jamal, so this man's demeanour had him wanting to say something cutting. However, he remembered he was at work and had to act accordingly.

Sally checked her phone and recited the licence plate.

Davis tapped away at the keyboard of a particularly sleek-looking computer and beamed. He swung the large monitor round to face them. "There you go. It entered last night." He prodded a line of text indicating the time. "Do you want to see the CCTV to go with it?"

"Please."

Davis clicked his mouse, and a window popped up. A black-and-white image. Clear, not the usual fuzzy mess. Only the lower half of the driver's face was visible, and it had something on it. The camouflage cream Lenny had mentioned to them. The Mondeo had been captured driving beneath a metal frame at the entrance. Another camera showed it taking a parking space in the corner.

"Oh, look at that."

On the screen, a tall person got out of the driver's side and moved to the diamond-wire fence.

"That little sod!" Davis said. "He's breaking my property!"

The suspect gradually twisted the metal wires Lenny had told them about, then pushed open what amounted to a door in the fence. He bent to wedge it against the grass, ensuring it would stay open, then moved to the rear of the car, opened the door and dragged something out. Owing to the position of the vehicle, part of the Mondeo was bathed in shadow from the scrubland. Peter squinted, trying to clearly make out what the man had flopped over his shoulder, but, knowing what he did, it was obvious.

The man tossed it through the door in the fence, then stepped onto the grass.

"Shall I forward it?" Davis asked.

Peter nodded. "Please."

Davis did that, and clicked again as the bloke wired the door back up.

So he didn't leave the same way? Or does he go back later and walk through the car park?

95

He became a murky silhouette, only the edge of the lighting infiltrating beyond the boundary. He appeared to bend again, scooped the body up, then disappeared from sight.

"Can you fast-forward so we can see if he comes back?" Sally asked.

Davis obeyed, and three hours of manic footage skipped by. "Doesn't look like he did, but I can keep watching if you like." He stopped the recording. "Well, I never. A man getting rid of a body. I expect you'll want a copy of this."

Peter handed over one of his cards with the team's email address on it. "If you could just send it there. All of it."

"It'll be a link and a password. I'll give those to you, obviously." Davis got on with that, the gleam in his eye now gone. "Done."

"That's brilliant." Sally stood and shook the man's hand. "If you could keep this to yourself."

"Of course." Davis appeared sheepish. "I don't want to sound uncaring, but I suppose the car park will be overrun with police?"

"It will, yes." Sally smiled. "We'll do our best to create minimal disruption, but, as you can imagine, the area will have to be gone over by crime scene technicians."

Davis grumbled wordlessly.

Peter stood. "Someone will give you a ring and let you know when business can resume as normal. Thanks for being so understanding."

Goodbyes said, Peter strode to the lift. Inside, Sally beside him on the smooth descent, he thought about another CCTV camera. One that would have captured the murder in Warner Road. Trigger would have sent whichever Kings in with balaclavas to get the job done, but the whole scene would be recorded. It was daylight, for God's sake, and Peter didn't have a clue why Trigger was allowing a murder to go ahead where so many witnesses would have been present.

What is he up to?

CHAPTER THIRTEEN

The team had gathered in the incident room for a catch-up. Anna needed it. There were so many strands of information going on that her mind had become cloudy. She forced herself to shrug off the need to go into her office and sit by herself for a minute. To breathe. She couldn't afford the luxury.

She'd picked up baguettes for everyone from Brunch, sausage rolls as extras, plus a proper coffee each in insulated takeaway cups. Maybe the latter would help to clear her head. Placket had said to take the money out of "the pot" as expenses — as if she'd do it any other way.

She stood in front of the whiteboard, which she preferred as she could use a marker pen as and when. While Sally and Peter had gone to PS, Warren had sorted the newer interactive board for those who favoured that. Grateful that he'd dug in and found as much as he could in the little time he'd had, Anna flashed him a smile of thanks.

"So, what have we got?" Placket sat at the spare desk and stretched his legs out. Flakes of sausage roll pastry decorated the front of his suit jacket. "Start with Parking Solutions."

Peter explained what had gone on and how helpful Mr Davis had been. "Nice chap. Gave us a link and a password to access the CCTV. I've asked a couple of PCs to go through the footage. One to see when the door in the fence was created, the other to see if the suspect returned that way after he'd taken the body."

"So the suspect was driving," Anna confirmed.

"Yes. Martin was dead by this point or at least unconscious. Only the lower half of the face was visible, and he had paint on it, like the Kent lads said. He's done his homework in how to disguise himself. The murderer could be hiding in plain sight." Peter winced.

"Everything all right?" Anna asked.

"Err, yes."

She didn't believe him, but now wasn't the time to poke at him. The others would have clocked it too, but they weren't meant to make it obvious that they were noting each and every one of his mannerisms. "OK, the Mondeo was last spotted" — she glanced at Warren's information board — "in the region of Catherine of Aragon Park in Northgate. Interesting location. Is our man from there? Or was he trying to throw us off?"

She wrote that down on her board. Warren added it to the interactive one.

"The victim drove from his place of business on Landmere Road towards Aragon, a straight route on Mile Street," she said to get it cemented in her head. "He enters Gene Road, where Aragon is, then CCTV ends. After that, no more sightings, so the journey to the train station was done on roads without cameras. Sheer luck?"

"Half the bloody cameras have been purposely broken in that area," Placket grumbled. "Drug pushers and whatnot at the park. They're not going to want the authorities seeing them or their customers."

"Could he have had a drug problem?" Lenny wondered.

Anna scratched her cheek. "The toxicology report will answer that."

"So was he meeting someone to buy?" Sally said. "If not, why else was he at the park? And why didn't he tell Donetta where he was going?"

Anna couldn't answer that. "Was he keeping secrets from his wife, even though she said they didn't? While we're waiting for the lab reports, we'll put it to her — gently — to see if she knew if he took drugs. As for who he was meeting and why, without his phone data we can't check for any calls or messages."

Placket harrumphed. "What did his phone provider say, Sally?"

"They'll *try* to get it to us as quickly as possible." She sighed. "Which could mean tomorrow or a few days. It's *that* company. The one where they like to drag their heels."

"Bloody great." Anna huffed in frustration. She wrote on her board: *Contact Donetta — phone data backed up to cloud? Drug use?* "Someone do this for me after our chat, will you?"

"I'll do it now." Peter stood eagerly, as if to leave the room.

Anna was quick to shut him down. "No, afterwards, please, and there's no need to go out into the corridor to do it either."

He sat, clearly on edge. "I was only going out there because of all the talking in here."

"Then we'll make sure to keep it down, won't we?" *Why is he so desperate to go? Are the Kings trying to contact him?* "Back to the debrief." She checked the interactive board for the next item on the list. "Operation Everest. The missing men in ninety-three. Can you click to that page, please, Warren?"

He did that, and the screen switched to a new one, a list of men's names at the top. "As you can see, the Toro you mentioned, Donetta's father, is there."

"That's a bit concerning, don't you think?" Anna asked no one in particular. "I mean, has our man decided to go after the next generation, thirty years later?"

Warren clicked to another page. "This is a list of the sons and sons-in-law of all the missing men from ninety-three. I need to dig in and collect info on what they do, where they live et cetera, but for now we at least know who might be next

— that's if this is what's going on here. Best to be on the safe side and warn them all to be careful, yes?"

Anna nodded. "Most definitely." She wrote that action on the board beneath the one Peter would be dealing with. "Do you remember Everest, sir?" She turned to Placket.

"Yes, but I didn't have anything to do with it. Obviously it was big news, six men going missing in a short space of time, none of them ever found, but I wasn't on that team." He paused as Warren brought up a new page. "All well-off men, look, as was Martin. Another link?"

"Also, not including Martin, they were all friends with two blokes in particular," Warren said. "Eric McFadden and Lewis Winch, both of whom were questioned at the time. They all used to go to the same secondary school and college together. McFadden is now deceased, and Winch is currently sleeping and eating on His Majesty's dime and has been for the past six years, so neither of them could have killed Martin."

"A copycat, then?" Lenny suggested.

"Bloody hell," Anna muttered. "When did they go missing in ninety-three?"

"Summer," Warren said.

Anna tapped the end of the marker pen against her chin. "So the time of year has changed."

Warren switched to another page. "You'll see here that guinea pig fur was sent to each wife back then, along with notes on cream cards. As you said, Donetta received fur and a note as well. Going by hers, it's obvious the killer was giving away the location of the body. He used capital letters for 'where' and 'house'. What if the old notes did the same thing? All right, I had a quick squiz and couldn't make head nor tail of them, but Sally's good with puzzles, so maybe she can work them out." He clicked again.

Anna studied the page of scanned notes. "The writing isn't the same as on Donetta's." Something leaped out at her. "Is there anything in the file about the word 'more'?"

100

Anna wrote another query on her board about whether *more* meant *moor*, like *where* and *house* meant *warehouse*. "See that? It seems bloody obvious to me. Deliberate spelling errors. I mean, that fifth one: 'How many more times do I have to tell you where they are?' If I'm right, we might be able to do something about it — find those men's bodies."

Placket closed his eyes and sighed. He opened them and looked Anna right in the eye. "Those moors are vast."

"I know, but a few cadaver dogs over a couple of days, they might pick something up. They can scent decomposition years down the line, we all know that. It'll cost, but if we send the K9 team to the parts that aren't that boggy first, closest to the outer edges . . ."

Placket sighed. "Do you really think, based on what we have, the powers that be are going to agree to the expense? I'll put it to the super later, see what he has to say. We might get lucky and he gives us the go-ahead, but we need more, I'm afraid." He smiled at Sally. "Is anything else jumping out at you other than 'more'?"

Anna turned to read all of the notes at the same time as Sally.

> To find number one, what more could you ask for? Coxcombry and folly.

> Number two is more to the right of number one. A couple of metres, or maybe I'm lying.

> Man three, another body, more for you to discover farther afield. To roam is to find.

> Four is also more. Pince-nez, radical.

> How many more times do I have to tell you where they are? Shaky legs.

The last one is much more of a pompous twat than the others.
The car lags.

"I'd need to study it," Sally said.

Anna wrote that down as an action. "What the bloody hell does 'coxcombry' mean? Anyone know?"

"I'll look it up," Lenny said.

Anna waited while he searched on his phone.

"Collins has it down as 'conceited arrogance or foppishness'." Lenny frowned. "Hang on." He pressed his screen again. "Foppishness is excessive concern with fashion and elegance. Maybe that's how he perceived that particular man."

"It links in with the men being rich, I suppose," Placket said. "Like, you've got to have money to be at the height of fashion?"

"So did victim four use pince-nez?" Warren wondered. "Aren't they a bit old-fashioned? He wasn't ancient or anything."

"God knows," Anna said, "but we can find out from his family members, or maybe that's in his file." She perused the list again. "'Shaky legs'. Err, anyone got any opinions on that other than the poor man was frightened when he died?"

No one answered.

"And what about 'the car lags'?"

Sally sighed. "I'll have a proper look once this meeting's finished."

Anna's phone rang, and she glanced at the screen. "It's Steven." She popped the marker pen on the lip of the board and swiped to answer. "Afternoon."

"Hi. Sorry I didn't ring sooner, I got engrossed. The Mondeo has blood in it. In the back, as if Martin was placed on the seat and he either bled onto it while alive or blood transferred from his clothing after death. I'm saying the latter as the seat material wasn't drenched. And we have those ginger hairs — or fur — on the passenger seat. So, he was transported in his own car, along with what we think is a guinea pig."

"Thanks. I visited the NOK. She received a note with the fur taped to one corner on a piece of card." Anna gave him a quick rundown of Operation Everest.

"Bloody hell, what the hell's going on around here? All our recent cases seem to be heavily linked to the past."

"It's just a coincidence. Mind you, we could argue that *every* case is linked to the past — most killers become warped because of what happened to them years ago."

"True. OK, I'll let you get on. The car's being taken in now."

"Cheers for the update. Hope you're feeling better."

"Yep, I had a private chat with Herman. He always helps me get some clarity. Speak soon."

The line went dead, and she tucked her phone into her pocket and related what Steven had said. "So does this mean our killer doesn't have his own car? Or that he does and didn't want to get it dirty or risk it being caught on camera?"

"And did he leave Martin's near the warehouse on purpose?" Lenny added. "That makes it even more obvious where to look for the body. If we disregard the word 'more' in the old notes, as if it isn't pointing to the moors, the wording just comes across as nonsense, as if the killer *didn't* want the bodies found, even though it appears in the notes that he did. Why is *our* killer being more transparent about the location?"

Anna thought of something and had to get it out before she forgot. "CCTV on the route from Landmere Road needs going over again. If our killer used the Mondeo after Martin had arrived at the park, how did *he* get to Aragon? Did he walk? Use another vehicle that he picked up later? Did he get on the bus or call a taxi?"

"And *when* did he put the face paint on?" Peter asked. "Getting a bus or taxi with that on his mush is going to stand out."

"Good point." Anna's phone rang again. "I need to take this." She answered. "Ollie, you're on speaker. What have you got for us?"

"I've been to Pembrooke Avenue. The house opposite Donetta's has a Ring doorbell, and it caught someone posting the note in the early hours of the morning — quarter past four. Unidentifiable, apart from their height and build. Tall, wide. Lumbered more than walked. Just looked like a silhouette. Walked down towards number fifteen from the top end, then returned that way. No moving vehicles in the street after 11 p.m., and the first one to appear after he'd gone was at 7 a.m. The homeowner said it belongs to one of her neighbours at number two, and he goes to work at that time every day. No one down that street saw or heard anything during the night."

"At least the build and height match the man in the warehouse. Thanks for passing that on."

"I'm going back to the station now to follow up on CCTV in the surrounding area. Unless you'd prefer one of your team to do it."

"Nope, if you're happy, I'm happy. We need all the help we can get. Catch you later." Anna slid her phone away, then wrote the information on the board. "Hopefully we can start to close in on him now. What struck me during that phone call was, if Donetta and Ines were so worried about Martin, wouldn't they have been on alert and heard the letterbox rattling when the note was posted? Or was it done silently?" She glanced at Placket. "Is anyone searching through CCTV around the warehouse?"

"Yes. I sorted a few PCs for that. I figured you'd have enough to do."

"Thank you." Anna double-checked the actions. "OK, Peter, you get hold of Donetta — also ask her if something woke her at quarter past four. Sally, you study the note. Warren, me and Lenny will help you go through the case history. We need to alert those sons and sons-in-law, and find out about 'pince-nez'. And 'shaky legs' — victim five might have had a medical condition or something."

Placket stood. "I'll put in a visiting order to go and see Lewis Winch in the nick. See if his memory is still up to snuff regarding his alibi back then. For all we know, it could have been him. He could have got pally with a cellmate and convinced them to kill Martin for him. In the meantime, I'll find out who Eric McFadden's family are and speak to a wife if he had one. She might still recall what her husband was doing around the time the men went missing."

"OK, everyone get to it, then." Anna wandered over to the kitchenette. "I'll make the cuppas."

CHAPTER FOURTEEN

As the shop wasn't busy, Prudence left it in Cuddy's capable hands and walked to Kirsty's flat. Maybe she could glean some information about Eric and Rory. She felt bad using her, but consoled herself by thinking that she was being kind by keeping her company. They'd always got along, so Kirsty wouldn't think anything of the surprise visit.

The house converted into flats wasn't in the best shape. Prudence tapped on the scruffy door, feeling glad she had gloves on. Kirsty answered, frowning at first, then smiling. Seeing the decline in her was somewhat alarming. Yes, she'd chosen to leave Rory and divorce him — with his depressive, self-indulgent attitude, as well as his general lack of togetherness, who could blame her — but the sight of her was difficult for Prudence to get her head around. Gone was the vivacious woman with a spark for life, in her place a shell. As if she was existing, not living. Having money helped your mood, Prudence was well aware of that, and, when Kirsty and Rory had been a couple, Kirsty had always looked nice. Hair, nails, make-up. Now, she'd lost a lot of weight, to the point of near emaciation, her skin with a greyish hue, her hair lacklustre, all the shine gone. All her *light* gone.

"I came to see you," Prudence said. "Um, daft thing to say because that's obvious. Fancy making me a cuppa?"

"Does Rory know you're here?"

"No, it's none of his business what I do."

Prudence followed her down a hallway. The walls were grubby, the skirting board chipped in places. Some of these landlords ought to be ashamed of themselves. At least Rory had done the cottage up before the Euston couple had moved in.

Did he put a new layer of concrete on the cellar floor? He must have done, surely.

Prudence shuddered as she sat with Kirsty in the kitchen while the other woman made tea. They sat at the table, chatting like old times for a while. Prudence should have come here sooner. She hadn't realised how much she'd missed her.

"Sorry to ask something so personal," she said, putting her empty cup down, "but are you depressed? You don't seem yourself."

"It's harder than I thought." Kirsty sighed and leaned back on the sofa. "Being on benefits — I can't seem to get a job interview, let alone a bloody job. And while I felt alone with Rory come the end, I didn't understand the true meaning of alone. I barely see anyone these days. You're the first visitor I've had in a long time."

"But what about Christmas? Surely you went to your mother's."

"She's in Spain with her latest fella. Sunshine Christmas break. Dad's living in Portsmouth now and didn't want the 'hassle' of me going down there."

"Your friends? I recall you had a few."

"All buggered off once I didn't have enough cash to be in their clique. Don't forget, Rory gave me money every month so I was able to do lunches and whatever with them. God, I didn't know how good I had it until I had to exist on the shitty amount the government gives me. I can't afford to eat much."

Prudence had brought a bunch of flowers with her — a fat lot of good *they'd* do in Kirsty's circumstances. "Come on, we'll go to that little Tesco at the end of the road."

Kirsty's eyes watered and her mouth quivered. "It's not up to you to help me, Pru. You're not my mother-in-law anymore."

"So? We can still be friends, can't we? I can't stand the thought of you going hungry. Listen, Rory's been staying with me since you two split up — far too long in my opinion, you know how me and him don't get on — but he's moved back to the house now, so you can come to mine for dinner some nights, all right? And what about a job in the pet shop? I could do with handing the reins over a bit more. You like Cuddy, don't you?"

Kirsty's tears fell. "But what about Rory? He won't like me working there."

Prudence stiffened her spine. "What about him? It's none of his bloody concern. If he'd been a decent husband, you'd still be together, but he wasn't. He wallowed in the aftermath of Eric's death, and Lord knows that man didn't deserve the godlike status Rory gave him."

"He was weird." Kirsty blanched, as if regretting what she'd said. "Sorry, but he was."

"Eric? I happen to agree with you. Both of them fit that mould. Rory is . . . Oh, I don't know, I just don't like my own son. I've battled with the guilt of that for years, but I've come to the conclusion that some people just don't have a connection, whether they're related or not." Out of curiosity, she asked, "Why did you think Eric was weird?"

Kirsty shuddered. "There was something about him. Whenever he was with Rory, it was like I didn't exist. They had this strange thing between them, as though they were speaking without words. I can't explain it."

"You don't need to. The sly looks, the creepy smiles."

"Yes!" Kirsty seemed relieved to have her observations confirmed. "I didn't want to say this to him at the time, but his grief when Eric died wasn't . . . well, it seemed excessive to me."

She bit her lip. "I feel bad for saying that, because who am I to understand what he went through — I still have both my parents — but . . . I don't even know what I'm trying to say."

"I think I do. Their relationship was odd when I was with Eric, so God knows what it turned into after we divorced. Eric had almost thirty years to manipulate him. Rory was over at the cottage more than he was home most of the time up until he met you. I'll admit I was glad — dealing with Rory has never been my forte. What did you see in him? What made you pick him?"

"He was charming, believe it or not. Totally different to how he was after we'd married. While he was mourning, I had time to look back on things, and it's obvious he was on his best behaviour until he got a ring on my finger. I didn't notice the change at first, it was subtle, but, by the time Eric died, Rory wasn't the same man. I stuck around for the two years to see if he would get better, but he got worse."

Prudence smiled at a stray thought that wandered into her head. "I'll admit I laughed when you took all the furniture. You deserved that after putting up with him."

"I was angry, I shouldn't have done it. It wasn't mine to take."

"Sod him." Prudence sensed an opportunity. "Did you ever hear any conversations he had with Eric? Private ones?"

"A couple, although they didn't make sense."

"Maybe they will to me."

"One that stands out was about them going for a walk on the moors 'for old times' sake' to see whether they could 'find them from memory'. No clue what that was about. Eric said he'd bought a metal detector and reckoned it would 'pick up their rings'. They'd laughed at that."

"Rings? I wonder what that meant?" But Prudence knew. Oh God, she knew. It had to be the men's wedding rings, didn't it?

Kirsty shrugged. "No idea. I walked into the kitchen, and they soon shut up. I wanted to ask what they were on about, but something told me not to."

Prudence's stomach contracted with unease. "Anything else?"

"The other one that stands out is the 'claret' in the cellar in the cottage. I thought it was wine, like Eric had got into collecting it or something. Rory said Eric ought to get his arse into gear and add a layer of concrete because there was no way they were getting it out of the floor, and he said, 'If we haven't managed it yet, we never will.'"

They were talking about the blood. Christ. "What did you put that down to?"

"Eric had mentioned hunting a few times, about starting it up again, so I assumed it was blood from rabbits or whatever." Kirsty paused, her face draining of colour. "Jesus, you don't think it was from something else, do you?"

"God, no," Prudence lied. "Eric *was* mad about hunting. Right, get your coat and shoes on. We'll nip to Tesco, fill your fridge and cupboards, then I need to get back. Come to the shop when we reopen on the second of January, and we'll discuss your wages and whatever."

Kirsty stood and hugged Prudence. "I don't know why Rory always said you were a cow. We've always liked each other, haven't we?"

A cow. Lovely. But I can't moan. He doesn't like me, I don't like him. "We have. You're the daughter I never had." *The child I wish I'd had instead of that creepy bastard.*

Prudence walked into the small hallway and waited for Kirsty to get ready. She'd do her bit to make up for the shitshow her son had made for this woman. Help her to forget the years she'd been married to him. Yes, Kirsty had been lazy, taking cash off Rory every month and not working, but that was what he'd wanted, no matter how much he bitched about it to the contrary now. He'd *wanted* Kirsty at home, the good little wife, and she'd gladly done it.

Besides, helping Kirsty would give Prudence a new purpose, along with finding out if her son was up to no good.

Would she shop him to the police if he'd done something horrible?

Damn bloody right I would.

* * *

Back in High Street, Prudence walked into the shop and plastered on a smile for Cuddy who, with no customers to serve, was weighing out hamster food and putting price stickers on the outside of the transparent bags.

"Everything OK?" she asked on her way to the staffroom.

"Yep, sold a gerbil and a guinea pig, plus all the bits to go with them."

She paused, anxiety slithering through her. "Who bought the guinea pig?"

"Err, a woman with her daughter. They live by me. Why?"

She relaxed. "No reason. Want a cuppa?"

Cuddy nodded. "Please."

"I'll make it, then you can go and have a break."

She pushed the door open and went into the back room, hanging up her coat and bag. Kettle on, she leaned on the doorframe and watched the shoppers through the front window. Mrs Towles approached, a posh sort. Prudence always thought of *towels* whenever she saw her. She debated whether she could handle dealing with her today or if she should leave her to Cuddy.

The kettle clicked off and, at the tinkle of the bell at the front, she moved to the kitchenette to make Cuddy a coffee.

"Morning," she heard him say. "What can I do for you?"

"I need some parrot feed for my Yuri, please." Mrs Towles had several exotic pets, including a bearded dragon. "Have you heard the news?"

Prudence jolted, sploshing milk mid-pour. She mopped up the spill with a dishrag, then added sugar, her hand shaking, and stirred the brew. What did the woman mean?

Oh God, please don't say another man's gone missing.

111

"What news?" Cuddy asked.

"It's like the nineties all over again," Mrs Towles said on a sigh. "Although you wouldn't know about that, seeing as you're young."

Prudence's legs almost gave out from under her. She left the coffee on the worktop and joined Cuddy behind the counter. "Go on now, I'll deal with this."

Cuddy sloped off and closed the door behind him.

"I was just saying," Mrs Towles said, "about the nineties." She gave Prudence a knowing stare, likely because most people knew that, at the time, the police had spoken to Eric about the men. "A man's gone missing, and his wife's received one of those dreadful notes. History's repeating itself."

How Prudence didn't collapse, she didn't know. "Oh, how awful. Who's missing, do you know?"

"Martin Lowe, that famous model's husband. They live opposite me. I've had the police at mine this morning. My doorbell camera caught someone posting the note." She puffed up, feeling incredibly important, no doubt.

Rory hadn't been at Prudence's the past few nights, so she couldn't even provide an alibi for him. Not that she would. She'd let his father get away with it, but she'd be damned if she'd let Rory.

"Oh, that's not good." She hoped she'd sounded upset enough, and she was, although not really for the missing man but for herself. Selfish of her to be more bothered about her own part in this, but what if the truth came out about Eric and she was done for not phoning the police the first time around?

"He was found in the Dobson warehouse," Mrs Towles went on. "Dead."

Bloody hell. "How do you know?"

"I popped over to see if Donetta was all right."

To get information out of her, more like. "That's kind of you. When was he killed?"

"I assume last night as he didn't come home from work. Do you know the most curious thing about it? His shoes were missing."

112

A row of shoes lit up in Prudence's head, as if a camera flash had gone off, then they were gone. But the emotions produced by seeing them remained. Sickness. Fear. Worry. "What sort of shoes?"

"Louboutins. I don't expect you know what they are, you're not the type to be able to afford them, but they have red soles. I have several pairs."

Bully for you. Prudence placed a box of parrot feed in a carrier bag. "Contrary to the rumours that went round back then, Eric can hardly have killed that poor man."

"No. I thought the same thing, which is why I didn't mention it to the policeman." Mrs Towles glanced over at the guinea pig cages, then back to Prudence. "Although Donetta mentioned some fur was taped to the corner of the note. A piece of card — again, the same as in the past."

"What did the note say?" Prudence had read in the news what the others had said. Eric, playing with the police, like he'd played with her mind.

"Something about where the body was in a house. I can't remember the exact words. But it was a single sentence, I know that, unlike the strange ones from before. And it's odd, because Martin wasn't found in a house, so maybe the killer is still as weird as he was last time."

"What colour was the fur? If I remember rightly, it was all different for the others."

"Ginger."

Prudence had heard enough. It had to be Copper's, didn't it? This was too big a coincidence. "That'll be four ninety-nine, please."

She rang the purchase up, and Mrs Towles tapped her gold card against the reader.

"Have a lovely day," Prudence said, needing to be rid of her so she could think.

"Hardly, with all that police presence in my street. Still, it's a bit of excitement in the boring few days between Christmas and New Year, isn't it?" Mrs Towles picked up the carrier bag and breezed out.

Prudence leaned her hands on the counter and took a couple of deep breaths. *Was* it possible that Rory had taken over from Eric? Why now, so many years later? Had Eric's death done something to his mind? All that time he'd stayed at Prudence's, had he been plotting? Under *her* roof? Like father, like son?

Had Eric been teaching Rory how to kill all those years ago?

She was about to go and get Cuddy so she could sit out the back and mull things over, but the devil himself walked in. Prudence immediately glanced at Rory's shoes. They weren't anything he'd normally wear. Too expensive-looking. She couldn't see the soles, so she'd have to invite him out the back and offer him some tea. See if he crossed his legs at the ankles so she could get a good view of them. If they were red, what would she do?

"Back again?" she said.

Rory stuck his hands in his pockets. "Hmm. I've nipped in to get Bob's dog some treats."

"That's unlike you to be neighbourly."

Rory's eyebrows scrunched. "Why do you always have to be so snarky with me? Christ, it's no wonder you haven't had a bloke coming near you since you turfed Dad out. Who'd want to saddle themselves with a spiteful old cow like you?"

She brushed that aside, went to the dog treat bin and used the scoop to pour some biscuits into a bag. At the counter, she secured the top with blue sticky tape. "That's two pounds."

Rory glared. "Are you having a laugh? You expect me to fork out for it?"

"Of course I do. The bills don't pay themselves."

They stared at each other, Prudence refusing to look away first. She wanted this . . . this layabout to know she wasn't scared of him. Not like she'd been scared of his father.

The shop bell jangled and Rory broke their connection and turned towards the door.

"Can I help you?" Prudence asked the man.

He held up some form of ID. "DCI Ron Placket. Are you Prudence McFadden?"

"Yes . . ."

"Can I have a quick word?"

Rory hotfooted it out the back, which told Prudence all she needed to know. She'd ignore him for now, but she'd question him about it at some point. Why had he bolted because a copper was here?

Isn't it obvious?

"What about?" she asked.

The policeman walked closer. "Your ex-husband. Eric."

Prudence smiled through the alarm that bolted along her veins.

Here we go.

CHAPTER FIFTEEN

Prudence stared at the line of men's shoes in Ida's cellar. And the dark stains on the concrete floor. On a wooden workbench that spanned the whole of the right-hand side sat a knife, the blade long, extra-wide at the end closest to the handle. She'd come down here to collect Ida's washing from the machine beneath the bench so she could hang it outside for her. Eric had taken Rory to a theme park for the day, as a treat for being good, so Prudence had grabbed the chance to quiz her mother-in-law. She didn't for one minute think Ida suspected her son of anything, but the woman might have overheard or seen something that would cement what Prudence had come to believe.

That her husband had a hand in those men going missing.

She wasn't sure whether to collect the washing or not. To do so meant walking over the dark patches, which could be evidence. What if the police twigged that Eric was a killer and she was accused of having something to do with it because of her presence down here?

But you don't even know if it's him.

Prudence had listened through the door as the police had questioned him about how he knew the missing men. His answers had sounded plausible — until he'd been asked where he was on the nights the men hadn't come home from work. He'd said he was with Ida, yet he'd told Prudence he'd been down the bookies. Why had he lied to the police if he had nothing to hide? His alibi would so easily be proved if the coppers went and questioned the people who worked there. Or was it the other scenario she'd thought about? He was having an affair and didn't want the other woman to get into trouble. Was she married, too? Did she have a husband who'd beat her up for cheating on him?

From then on, Prudence had been suspicious, keeping track of each time he'd gone out and for how long. But he'd also had Rory with him sometimes, so surely he hadn't abducted the men with their son there, nor could she imagine him taking the lad to some fancy woman's house.

But this . . . this blood — because it looked like blood — and those shoes . . . They didn't belong to Eric. He was more of a boot person, and they appeared to be all different sizes. And why hadn't Ida asked what they were doing there? Why hadn't she mentioned the could-be-blood?

Quickly, and on tiptoe, as if moving like that would minimise her disturbing any evidence, Prudence pulled the washing from the machine and took the bundle upstairs. She plonked it in an empty basket and carried it outside.

Ida sat in the garden sunning herself in a deckchair, her eyes closed. Prudence ambled past her towards the washing line. She didn't stir. Either she was fully asleep or she plain couldn't hear Prudence's footsteps. That was a worry. Anyone could creep around her cottage when she was alone and she wouldn't have a clue.

And Eric could be doing God knows what in that cellar and she wouldn't have a clue there either.

Was that why he brought Rory here so often? To keep Ida occupied? But why would he want to do anything sinister to his old friends? Five had gone missing so far, and the rumours were rife that they'd been killed. If that was Eric — and it had to be, all that blood — then it didn't make sense. He'd never said a bad word about any of them to Prudence. If he held a grudge, then surely he'd have mentioned it, wouldn't he?

She finished hanging the washing and went to sit by Ida, who opened her eyes and gave a watery smile.

"I must have dropped off," Ida shouted.

"Does Eric usually help you with that?" Prudence shouted back, gesturing to the clothes, which hung static in the absence of wind.

117

Ida cupped one ear. *"What? I can't hear you."*

Prudence prepared to raise her voice even louder. *"Does Eric normally do your washing for you?"*

"Yes, he popped that load in earlier before he went out with Rory."

"Are you having trouble getting things done, then?"

"No, it's because of the mice."

"The mice?"

"They're everywhere in that cellar. He's worried I'll trip over them and hurt myself. Said I'm not to go down there. He's going to bring the machine up and put it in the kitchen one night next week, then I won't have any reason to go down there at all."

"Can't he just set traps?"

"I said that, but he's fretting about the stairs. They're slippery. He doesn't want me falling."

Prudence stared beyond the washing to the moors. Eric had grown up here, was used to the isolation, but it gave her the creeps. She preferred to have neighbours, someone on hand if the worst happened. Ida was here on her own, and it didn't sit well.

"Have you ever thought of moving to Marlford?" Prudence bellowed.

"What for?" Ida shook her head. *"This is my home. I like being by myself."*

"So Eric keeps bringing Rory here . . . isn't that annoying?"

"Oh, they're down in the cellar all the time, trying to catch the mice."

Prudence's stomach rolled over. *"Rory's down there with him?"*

"Well, not all the time. Sometimes he sits up here with me. What's wrong with that?"

Prudence swallowed the ball of fear in her throat. If what she suspected was true, her son may have witnessed things he shouldn't. Although she wasn't in any way fond of the boy, it wasn't right if Eric was . . . was killing people in front of him.

She laughed to herself, at how stupid that sounded. Eric, killing people. But she had to phone the police, do something about it. And if it amounted to nothing, if he had a shoe fetish or whatever and kept those pairs here, if that dark stuff on the floor wasn't blood but something else, then she could rest easier. She would still phone the station and say she was worried because her mother-in-law could hear noises in her cellar, then it wouldn't be like she was grassing on Eric.

She nodded and, although she was afraid, if the outcome proved he'd been up to no good, that people would look at her funny as if she must have known what he was doing, that was better than more men going missing, wasn't it? It wasn't just the shoes and the blood. There was the guinea pig fur, too. Those notes, sent on cream cards, like the ones she used to write thank-you messages for birthday gifts. Him lying to the police, saying he was here and not at the bookies. The lies about the cellar being overrun with mice.

She stood and entered the cottage, and poured them both a cloudy lemonade from the jug in the fridge. Ida made it herself from scratch; the same with bread. Prudence's eyes prickled at the thought of that lovely woman being duped. At herself being duped. And Rory, while a weird child, may well be an accomplice, even though he knew right from wrong. So did that mean Eric had threatened him to keep it quiet, their cellar shenanigans?

She returned outside and sat. Handed Ida her lemonade. "Whose are those shoes in the cellar?"

"What shoes?"

"There are a few pairs. They look like they cost a fair bit."

"I don't know owt about any shoes." Ida sipped her drink, then smacked her lips. "Ah, that's lovely, that is."

"Has something been spilled on the floor down there?"

"What?"

"On the floor. In the cellar. There's dark patches everywhere."

"That'll be the mice weeing all over the place. Dirty beggars."

Ida had well and truly been suckered in.

"Mice wouldn't wee that much," Prudence said, "and anyway, piddle would dry out. This stuff is still there."

"I bet the washing machine pipe has been leaking again."

"The floor's not wet."

Ida sighed. "I'll let Eric know. He'll fix whatever it is."

Prudence wasn't getting anywhere here, so she changed the subject. An hour later, she drove home, going over everything in her mind. She'd speak to Eric before she phoned the police. See if he thought she was as gullible as his mother. See what excuses he gave her.

"Lying bastard," she muttered.

***

Rory had gone to bed, exhausted after his day out. Prudence paced the kitchen, gearing herself up to confront Eric. He was watching telly in the living room, sprawled out on the sofa, and she'd been putting off going in there. It was going to sound so silly, what she had to say, especially as, other than the evidence she'd seen and heard, she didn't have any solid proof, just her gut telling her something wasn't right.

"Go and do it, get it over with," she whispered.

She straightened to her full height and walked down the hallway. It seemed so long, as if a terrible fate awaited her at the end of it, and her nerves twanged. She turned in to the living room and stopped short. Eric wasn't watching the TV but writing on a piece of cream card — with gloves on. Odd, when it was summer.

But not odd if he's hiding his fingerprints.

He looked up, his eyes wide, then he narrowed them and stuffed the card and pen behind him.

Prudence kept the door open in case she needed to escape. Eric was hard to read when it came to his temper. Sometimes he flared up with the least provocation, and other times he laughed off whatever she had to say. Going by his thunderous expression, she had to be careful this time.

Maybe I should leave it for tonight.

"What are you staring at, woman?"

She fiddled with her fingers. "I went to see your mum today."

He cocked his head, glaring at her. "What for?"

"I thought I'd help her with some housework, hanging out her washing, that sort of thing. Keep her company seeing as you and Rory weren't with her like you usually are on a Saturday."

"Right . . ."

"She said you'll be bringing her washing machine upstairs because of the mice, but I didn't see any while I was down there." She lowered herself into the armchair closest to the door. "But I did see some men's shoes, all different sizes, and what looked like dried blood on the floor." She paused. "And a knife on the workbench."

"You ought to mind your own business, that's what you should be doing. Don't go round my mum's again. She doesn't need you when she's got me."

"Whose shoes are they?"

"I got them at a second-hand stall on the market, if you must know. They're worth a fortune — the bloke selling them didn't have a clue. I haven't got round to flogging them on yet."

"What about the dark patches?"

"Oil. I was cleaning her generator one day, and it leaked everywhere."

"What's the knife for?"

"Fuck me, what is this, Twenty Questions? How should I know why it's there? Mum's losing her marbles, so she must have taken it down there for some reason."

"And the mice? Where are they?"

"There aren't any. I just don't want her in that cellar."

"Is that because those missing men were killed there?"

Oh, Jesus Christ, she'd said that out loud.

Eric shot up off the sofa and marched over to slam the door. Prudence winced and stood, wishing she'd kept her mouth shut. He was in one of those moods, where he'd fly into a blind rage and not remember that he'd hit her. He stalked towards her, gripped the front of her blouse and twisted it in his fist.

"What if I were to tell you that I killed all of them, eh? Would you believe that?"

"No," she whispered. Yes, I think you did.

"Well, it sounds like you do, else why have you been bugging me with questions?"

"I just . . . I don't know. I . . ."

"Do you know what it's like to be laughed at when you go to someone cap in hand? Do you? Eh? How humiliating it is when someone you thought was your mate tells you to fuck off? They deserved it, all of them, and now they're rotting, stinking up the air, going mouldy."

His eyes blazed, and she saw the truth in them, of what he'd just admitted to. He was so angry he might not have realised what he'd said, might not even remember when the haze of rage passed, but she'd heard it all right.

He **had** *killed those men. She wasn't going crazy.*

He twisted the fabric further, so one of the buttons dug into her throat.

"And do you know what it feels like to be forgotten, pushed aside as if you don't matter? To have people turn their backs on you because you asked for a loan?"

"A loan?" Why did he need money? She'd thought they were OK. The pet shop brought in more than enough for them to manage. "Why did you—?"

"Don't ask what I needed it for, it's none of your business. Just know that I couldn't ask you, else you'd be pecking at me about it. I can handle it, I've borrowed some off Mum, and when I sell the shoes in the Plough I'll have even more. But I can't yet, it's too soon."

His words didn't register— until they did. The wives and families of those men might recognise the shoes if Eric tried to sell them in the pub. But those types of people wouldn't even go in the Plough, they were too posh, so that didn't make sense.

"Where are they?" she whispered. "The men."

"Somewhere obvious. The fucking police are thick as pig shit. Can't even work out where they are from the notes. You'd think they'd have checked that area as a matter of course, but no."

A great wave of nausea threatened to send Prudence to her knees, but his grip on her kept her upright.

"You're hurting my neck," she croaked.

He tightened his hold further. "Not a word about this or you'll be next, got it?"

She stared at him, scared out of her mind. "You told the police you were with your mum, and you told me you were at the bookies. What if the police had asked me about it? They'd have picked up that you'd lied to one of us. Where were you really?" As if she needed the answer.

"Mum's. I had to take them somewhere, didn't I?"

"Why did you take them, though?"

"I was just supposed to scare Bryan, he was the first one. But it went too far. I got too angry. Then I couldn't stop. I wanted to kill all of them. They'd seen how desperate I was, they'd thought it was funny, and I couldn't handle the shame."

"The guinea pig fur taped to the notes. The police are going to realise I own a pet shop. They're going to ask questions."

He put his face right up to hers, his breath sour, vinegary. "You tell them nothing, understand? If you do, I'll fucking kill you." He raised his other hand and clamped it round her neck. Squeezed. "I swear to you, no one will ever find your body."

"But I . . . I can't just let you get away with this."

His nails dug into her skin through the glove material. "Didn't you hear what I said? I'll slit your bastard throat, so keep your gob shut."

The certainty behind his words finally sank in, that he meant it. This wasn't the Eric she knew talking, this was a new one, a stranger. Something had happened to him, warping his brain, and she needed to get away from him. Or had he always been like this but had hidden it from her? He'd shown her over the years how he could be cruel, and he liked to hit her, but this cruel? Saying he'd kill her?

"I want a divorce," she blurted. "I'll keep quiet, I won't breathe a bloody word, you know I won't, but I can't live with you anymore, not now you've done this."

"Fine by me, but I'm warning you . . ."

"Just go. Please, just get out."

He released her, and she staggered back with the force of it, landing lopsided on the armchair. He snatched up the card and pen, then went to the sideboard to take out the rest of the cards left in the pack. She stared, weirded out that he'd done it, that he was focused on making sure she couldn't give them to the police, who would match them to the ones he'd sent.

"Why guinea pig fur?" she managed to ask.

He sidled to the door and smirked. "You've always taken the piss out of me going to the library, reading all those books, but you learn a lot from them. They were the sacrificial animal of the Incas in Peru. Those men were my sacrifices, to show people not to ignore your friends in need."

Prudence frowned. He was off his sodding rocker.

"But no one will know that," she said. "What's the point if the police won't work that out?"

"I'll know," he said, poking a finger at his chest. "And that's all that matters." He sniffed in derision. "Remember, mouth shut, or else."

He walked out and his boots thumped on the stairs. She listened to him moving around above, likely filling a suitcase, and it hurt that he could leave her so easily, go without a fight. Didn't he love her anymore? As well as killing, was he having an affair? Did he have someone he could run off to? And it was a risk on his part, walking away when she could so easily pick up the phone on the coffee table and ring the police once he'd gone. But his threat — his promise — echoed in her head, and she knew he'd meant it.

He clattered back downstairs, and she got up. Followed him into the kitchen. He'd packed a suitcase and left it in front of the cooker. He stormed out the back to the shed, and she waited for him to return, biting all her nails off, her agitation levels rising. He walked in with a pile of shoeboxes. She thought of the shoes in the cellar and supposed he wanted his boxes for those, but a strange smell wafted in, like rotting meat, and she scrunched her nose up.

He plonked the boxes on the worktop and took the lid off one of them. "If what I said isn't enough to convince you I meant what I said, fucking look at that."

She stepped closer — the smell was stronger now — and peered into the box.

A hand, the severed end dried out, the nails lifting from their beds. She jumped back in shock, shrieking, her heart thumping so hard it hurt.

Eric grinned. "That's Bryan's, so that's why it's in such a state, but if you want to look at a fresher one be my guest."

She recoiled, stumbling backwards and banging into the fridge-freezer, pain slicing through her hip. "Out. Get the fuck out." She couldn't catch her breath, couldn't think, couldn't stand the sight of him.

He bent to take a roll of black bags from the cupboard under the sink. Placed the boxes inside, laughing all the while. Who the hell was he? Why hadn't she spotted that he was a freak?

There was nothing for it. She had to keep quiet.

Quite simply, because she didn't want to die.

* * *

124

Two nights later, Prudence woke to a hand round her throat. Breath on her face. Sour. Vinegary. She sucked air in, her chest tight with fear. In the darkness, she made out Eric's shape, one she'd learned from many years of being married to him.

"I could have killed you tonight," he whispered. "You didn't even know I was here until I pinched you awake. Remember this whenever you think about going to the police."

Although her mind was scrambled, she wasn't scared enough not to be able to think. His words were those of a desperate man — she had options.

They'll keep me safe until they find you. You won't be able to come here and strangle me.

"Or I could run you over," he said, bulldozing over her thoughts. "Stab you down an alley on your way home from the pet shop. Stage a mugging and murder you. I can get to you any time, shut you up whenever I want. Mum will say I was with her if the police come knocking."

The tendrils of hope withered. Unless she phoned the police as soon as he'd left, she wasn't safe from him. She shut her mind off from what he'd done, told herself this wasn't happening, that if she grassed him up she'd have to deal with Rory all by herself. If she remained silent, she'd barely see him, because he spent so much time with his father.

"You don't have to worry about me," she rasped. "Just stop what you're doing. Please, just stop."

"One more to go, then I will." He released her neck. Moved away, a nasty blob in the dark. "I'll take Rory with me now. You're not having him."

If he thought he was punishing her, he'd got it very wrong. Relief poured into her. No more creepy son. No more vile husband.

To her shame, she vowed to keep the secret. It was for the best.

125

CHAPTER SIXTEEN

Placket waited for Prudence to lock the shop door and flip the sign to "closed". She popped her head round the other door at the back and told whoever was there that they could take a longer break. She stood behind the counter, as if she needed the barrier between them, and Placket felt for her. He doubted many people would want to discuss their exes when they'd moved on years ago. Sadly, with no other family members available to question, ones who would clearly remember the past, she would have to do. Her son had been ten at the time and could have been shielded from the news.

He'd browsed the files before coming here. Prudence had divorced Eric in the nineties but still lived at the same address. Eric had moved to a cottage on the moors — which had alarmed Placket somewhat, considering the "more" angle in the notes. A suitable place to dump bodies during the night without being seen. At the time, the property had belonged to his mother, Ida McFadden. Her husband was deceased and both of them had been Scottish-born. Upon Ida's death, Eric had inherited the cottage. The son, Rory, had then inherited it two years ago. The current tenants were a Mrs and Mrs Euston.

"Sorry to trouble you enough to close the shop," he said. "We could chat out the back if you like?"

"No, it's fine. What do you need to know about Eric?"

"His name has cropped up owing to a recent death that has links to an old missing persons case. Six men, their bodies were never recovered, nor was any proof of life established. Do you remember it?"

"If you're talking about ninety-three, most of us around here will never forget it. A terrible time, men going missing one after the other. A woman who just left, she was telling me the police have been in her street today. Her camera caught someone delivering one of those notes through her neighbour's door."

Placket smiled despite his irritation. That was the trouble with some people. They used gossip to pass the time, spreading it all around. Eventually it would turn into Chinese whispers, the truth clouded by layer upon layer of added snippets until it didn't have a grain of truth to it.

"What, exactly, did she say?" he asked.

"That someone posted a note, and she went over to see . . . Donetta, is it? The woman whose husband was found in the Dobson warehouse?"

Placket cursed the customer. Cursed whoever had spoken to her — Ollie, he recalled — for not sufficiently warning her to keep things to herself. "I see. I wanted to pick your brains as to what you can remember from that time. Your husband was questioned — he was friends with every man who went missing, but he had alibis for each one. I noted you weren't his alibi at all, and you weren't even spoken to. He said he was at his mother's with your son. Did he spend a lot of time with her?"

"Yes, she went deaf towards the end, and I suppose he felt he had to make sure she was OK." Her top lip curled.

"You don't agree with that assessment?"

She shrugged.

Placket filed away her nonchalance. "May I ask why you divorced him?"

"A difference of opinion."

"Do you know if your son remembers anything about that time? The men going missing, not the divorce."

"It was on the news a lot, but I didn't let him watch it. Most of the kids were scared *their* dad would go missing, I know that much."

"Did Rory feel that way?"

"I don't know."

"Was he a child who didn't express his feelings, then?"

"Yes."

"Were Rory and Eric close?"

"Very." She shifted from foot to foot.

"I see you sell guinea pigs." Placket wandered over to the cages. Two were empty of animals. One had obviously been cleaned out recently as there was no hay and the wooden base was damp.

"Yes. Only three left now. We sold one today, actually."

His interest was piqued. "Who bought that?"

"I wasn't here, but my assistant said a woman and her daughter."

"There are two empty cages. Did both sell?"

"Um, no, only the one."

"What about the other?"

Prudence came from behind the counter and walked to the front door. She beckoned Placket over and spoke quietly. "This morning, that cage there didn't have a pig in it. It was locked, so the guinea pig couldn't have got out. I told my assistant — that's Cuddy — that it had died because I didn't want him worrying someone had stolen it on his watch yesterday and he hadn't seen. He's very diligent at his job and would be upset if he thought he hadn't kept an eye out properly."

"Do you believe someone stole it?"

"What other explanation is there? I searched the whole shop, and Copper isn't in here."

"Copper. The guinea pig?"

"Yes. She's ginger."

Placket held back his reaction. "Do you have CCTV?"

"Unfortunately not, and you've just reminded me that's on my list of things to sort out today. If people are stealing my animals, I want proof."

"Does anyone else have a key to the shop?"

"No, but I was going to give one to Cuddy later in case I get poorly and he needs to open up for me. I trust him."

"Does your son have a key?"

"No."

"Any signs of a break-in?"

"No."

"And Cuddy himself wouldn't have taken a guinea pig home?"

"God, no, he's as honest as the day is long. Besides, where would he have put it? He never has a bag with him, and I doubt very much he'd have stuffed it inside his coat. He'd panic about it suffocating."

"Did any of your animals go missing in ninety-three?"

"No, that was the first thing I thought of when it came on the news that the fur was from guinea pigs."

"Did you check your animals? Had any fur been cut or pulled out?"

"I did check, and as far as I could see everything was fine."

Placket sighed. "It's always puzzled me as to why guinea pig fur was used."

"Maybe it's online somewhere, the reason. Perhaps look up their history?"

"I'll get my team to poke into that. Is there anything else you can add? Did you also know the missing men?"

"Yes, but I didn't see them much. There were rumours that Lewis Winch had been questioned, too. Is he still in prison?"

129

"He is. Could I perhaps speak to Cuddy? I'll maintain your ruse that Copper died, if that helps."

"Of course. Go through to the back. My son might be there — he's the one who was here when you came in."

"Thank you."

Leaving Prudence to open the shop, Placket walked into what appeared to be a small staffroom. A young lad sat on a sofa nursing a cup in one hand and a phone in the other, using his thumb to scroll. No one else was there. Was the son in the toilet?

"Sorry to trouble you." Placket held up his ID as he shut the door. "Prudence said I could come and talk to you. I'm DCI Placket. Is her son not here?"

"Nah, he left a couple of minutes ago."

"What, through there?" Placket motioned to the back door.

"Yeah."

Placket eyed the glass and lock. It didn't seem as if anyone had broken anything in order to steal an animal. "I just want a word about the guinea pigs."

An expression of sadness cloaked Cuddy's face, not alarm or guilt. "Copper died this morning. Or maybe it was in the night. Prudence buried her in the yard."

"What about the one you sold today? What colour was it?"

"White and black."

"Do you know who bought it?"

Cuddy nodded. "Yeah, it was Alice Flowers and her kid, Natalie. They live in the street next to mine in Northgate. Nat was spending her Christmas money."

Placket doubted they had killed Martin. "What's Mr Flowers like?"

"There isn't a Mr. He buggered off after Nat was born."

"Is there another man in the household?"

Cuddy frowned, as if he wondered why Placket would need to know that. "Nah, Alice stayed a single parent. She's

130

nice, she is. How come you need to know about the guinea pig an' all that?"

"It's a line of enquiry I'm following. Did Rory say where he was going?"

"He had to take some dog treats to his next-door neighbour. Bob's well old so can't get out himself."

"OK, well, thanks for your time." Placket cursed himself for not taking enough notice of the man who'd been in the shop when he'd arrived. With a guinea pig being missing, it wasn't a stretch to imagine that the owner's son may have taken it. Couple that with Eric being questioned in the past and the crime appearing to have been committed by a copycat . . .

We'll have to speak to this Rory fella.

Placket returned to the shop, convinced Cuddy had told the truth. He made a mental note to get CCTV checked for someone entering the shop during the night.

He found Prudence stacking packets of sawdust on a shelf. "Is this shop alarmed?"

"No." She blushed. "I know, stupid of me. I'll be sorting it today, along with the cameras."

"Make sure you do. Thank you for your time today."

Placket walked out and the cold air slapped his face. High Street was set out as an elongated U, with Prudence's Pets at the base along with a few others, the rest up the sides. No CCTV cameras pointed this way so, if someone *had* broken in, they may not have been seen. Still, the camera operators would need to be spoken to anyway. Depending on what time the supposed robbery had occurred, there may have been people out in the pubs or the two nightclubs. Any altercations or groups of people outside would have been monitored closely, and the cameras may have been moved to track them. Would they get lucky and see someone entering Prudence's Pets? Or had the shop been accessed from the back? The back door had looked OK when he'd glanced at it, though.

He strode through an alleyway on the right-hand side to the parking area and got in his car, then phoned the team about looking into the CCTV. Prudence and Cuddy were firmly off his suspect list, but he'd add them to the board just the same.

He googled for other pet shops in the area. Only one other came up, based at the shopping outlet on the outskirts. He headed there, just so he'd checked all avenues, but sadly came up empty. Pet Town didn't sell guinea pigs, only hamsters, gerbils and fish.

Placket set off for the station. His phone rang, and he answered it on the hands-free. It was the prison where Lewis Winch resided.

A woman introduced herself as Shiloh Bennett. "Is there any way you can speak to him on a call rather than a visit? Only, Winch is a bit volatile these days, and his visitation rights have been revoked for the time being. He stabbed another prisoner over the differing sizes of their turkey slices on Christmas Day. Said inmate is in the hospital wing."

Placket thanked the Lord he didn't have anything to do with criminals once they'd left the station. Small things became huge in prison. "A call will be fine if my presence will be disruptive. I just want to ask him about a case from years back. He was questioned, and I need to know if he's remembered anything in the intervening years."

"If he had anything to do with it, he'd likely admit it. Bit of a Bernard Bragger. Bigging yourself up in here is a way to keep yourself safe. Keep people away from you. The more notorious you are, the better you'll be."

"I understand. When should I expect the call?"

"Give me half an hour to get him from solitary, all right?"

Conversation ended, Placket floored it to the station. He'd rather speak to Winch from the comfort of a desk chair with a coffee in front of him than out on the road. He hoped Shiloh was right and that Winch would confess to murdering the missing nineties men. It would certainly send the investigation in the right direction.

He pondered what Prudence had said, something the team had yet to discuss. Why guinea pigs? What on *earth* was the link there? And had she encouraged him to look up their history for a reason? Was it her way of letting him know the answer was in the species' past?

Does she know more than she let on?

CHAPTER SEVENTEEN

Rory had been at his happiest in life when he'd moved to Nan's with Dad. Sadly, his stay there hadn't lasted long, and Dad soon took him back to Mum's, saying it was harder to look after a kid than he'd thought. Number Six had been killed and dumped, and *Rory* had felt dumped, too. Dad had used him for those two short weeks, then shipped him back home when he didn't need him anymore. Not that he'd really needed him; he'd killed well enough by himself. In later years Rory had realised that Dad had allowed his son to witness what he was doing so he could control him, by constantly reminding him of their secret and what would happen if the truth ever came out.

It hadn't stopped Rory from idolising him, though.

During that fortnight at Nan's he'd met Billy, a kid his age who'd moved into the next cottage, a mile along the road. Rory had taken his fishing net to try to catch things in the stream that meandered through the moor. Billy had been standing on the little wooden bridge halfway between the cottages, throwing stones into the water.

At the tail end of the summer holidays, they had played together on the moors, mucked about in the water, though Rory was always careful to keep their treks to the other side so Billy didn't see the bodies. They had lunch sometimes at Billy's cottage. His mother, Deborah, was much younger than Mum and so pretty and kind. His dad was in the army and didn't come home much.

They'd remained friends right up until college. Such a shame they'd drifted apart. And now look, Billy was on the kill list through no fault of Rory's. He had gone and married the daughter of Number Five.

Billy leased a swanky floor of offices in Southgate, in a building called the Gear Hub. Rory had checked using the internet on his pay-as-you-go phone whether the business was open between Christmas and New Year. The Facebook page for the company stated that a skeleton staff would be on hand, so Rory reckoned Billy would be here. Sure enough, his car was parked nearby.

Rory wedged himself down a skinny alley opposite and, knowing the streets around here were quiet and he was unlikely to be seen, prepared for a long wait. Lucky for him, an hour later Billy came striding out of the building. Rory wanted to check whether his emotional attachment to him would cloud his judgement. If it did, there was always another son-in-law in that family he could murder instead.

With Martin's shoes pinching his toes because they were too small — the walk here had given him blisters on his heels — Rory stepped out of the alley and strode with his head down towards Billy, to engineer an impromptu meeting.

He purposefully bumped into his old friend and looked up. "Shit, sorry, I — Billy? Fuck me sideways! How *are* you?"

"Rory? Bloody hell. This is a blast from the past. What have you been up to?"

Rory laughed. "Got married, divorced, the usual."

Billy chuckled. "Who did you marry?"

"You'd know that if you'd stuck around." Rory nudged him with his elbow to pretend he was joking. "No, seriously, someone I should never have got involved with. We live and learn, eh? How's life treating you?"

"As well as it must be treating you, what with those shoes." Billy raised his eyebrows at them.

"Christmas present from Mum." Rory shrugged. "I mean, I can afford to buy my own — Dad died and left me a load of money and a cottage — but, you know, I prefer not to splash the cash on fashion. Never been my thing, has it?"

"I was going to say, they look weird with tracksuit bottoms, pal, but each to their own."

Rory didn't like that. How Billy had cut him down with so few words. Made it clear he thought Rory was crass, unrefined, whatever. Beneath him.

No, I won't have any trouble killing him. Not now.

"Anyway, I must get on," Rory said. "Nice seeing you."

"I was just on my way to the Jacobean round the corner. Fancy a few beers and a catch-up?"

"Can't at the minute. I said I'd help Mum out in the shop. How long will you be there for? I might be able to nip in later."

"I can wait. Say a couple of hours?" Billy grinned, resembling the freckled, carefree kid he used to be. "If we get leathered later, I could always get a taxi home. The wife won't mind. She's at her mum's until tomorrow."

"All right, then." Rory waved as he walked away. "Catch you later."

He had plans for where they'd meet later, no eye in the sky to clock them. For now, he'd play the game right. Go home and get these fucking shoes off.

Dad was wrong.

Walking in a rich man's shoes was worse than wearing your own.

CHAPTER EIGHTEEN

The working day was drawing to a close, but the team were still hard at it in the station. Anna's stomach rumbled and she forced herself to get up from the spare desk, where she'd been working closely with Peter. He'd been jumpy at first, being paired with her, but had soon settled down and had taken no breaks. Whatever had bothered him seemed to have disappeared once he'd dug in and concentrated. He was a bloody good copper, so it was a shame he was under covert investigation. What a waste of talent if he got caught still working for the Kings. What a waste of their friendship, their trust, loyalty.

Anna was surprised she trusted anyone now because of him.

She stood. Stretched. "Time for a chat, see where we're at, then we may as well go home."

Peter seemed relieved. Too relieved.

Placket sighed, pushed his chair back and lolled his legs out in front of him. He'd had the job of going through the history of guinea pigs, plus he'd gone off to help Ollie and the other PCs with the CCTV, among other things.

Warren had been adding to the interactive board as they'd all passed information to him, and as a favour to Anna he'd put abridged versions on the whiteboard, so she could glance across at it from time to time. She'd arranged for a copy of the note sent to Donetta to be put on the police social media pages with an appeal for help: *Does anyone recognise this handwriting?* On another post, the descriptions of the killer — or what little they had so far — and Martin Lowe: *Did anyone see these men in Aragon Park yesterday evening?*

As she was tired, she went with the interactive board as there was more information on it; it would save her scraping the barrel of her brain to recall all the data associated with the short snippets on the other board. Dare she admit she was warming to the new way of doing things?

Steady on . . .

Sally was distracted by something on her monitor. Normally, Anna would pull her up on it, but she was clearly engrossed in spotting clues in the old notes, and it was better that she continued with that if she was close to working them out.

Anna began. "Let's go from the top and work our way down. OK, Donetta said she doesn't know about any drugs or why Martin would be at Aragon. She didn't hear the letter-box — apparently, she and Ines finally fell asleep about three in the morning and didn't wake until six. Peter, elaborate on what else she told you."

He didn't appear to want to. A flicker of annoyance crossed his face, as though he had the urge to run off again. Why did he want to leave?

He cleared his throat. "She couldn't think of any reason he wouldn't have come home straight from work without saying why. No secrets between them, so she claims. The only interesting thing she *did* have to say, which may be relevant, is that Martin had this idea of being a property developer of sorts as a side hustle. The kind who buys houses, does them up, then leases them out. A rental business, focusing on Airbnb."

Anna thanked him. "Did anything come of you looking into the property market, Warren?"

He took charge of the board. "As you can imagine in a city, there are hundreds of homes for sale, so it's going to take a while to get through all the estate agents and private sellers to see if Martin visited any properties. I've got some PCs looking into that side of things for me — they're halfway through all the estate agents, but so far nothing."

"OK. Let's clear up the weirdness in the old notes. According to family members, number four didn't wear a pince-nez, and number five didn't have any condition that would result in shaky legs."

"I've got it!" Sally flapped a piece of paper in the air. "I'm going to have to write it down." She rose and walked to the whiteboard, picked up a marker, and wrote.

Coxcombry and folly. (BRYAN)
A couple of metres. (LEO)
To roam is to find. (TORO)
Pince-nez, radical. (EZRA)
Shaky legs. (KYLE)
The car lags. (CARL)

"Christ," Placket said. "The bloody victims' first names."

Everyone stared at the board for a moment. Now it was down in bright-red pen, it was obvious.

Sally sat back at her desk. "That's given me a headache."

"Worth it, though, eh?" Placket said. "Bloody well done, kiddo!"

Sally blushed. "I'm just annoyed it took me so long. Sorry."

"What, a couple of hours?" Anna shook her head. "That seems pretty quick to me. At the moment, we don't have a clue why each one was chosen when they were. Were they picked at random? I don't think so, as they were all friends. Before, the investigators went down the obvious route of looking at people the victims knew. As we now know, Eric McFadden is dead and Lewis Winch is in the nick. Do you want to talk us through that call you had with him, sir?"

Placket folded his hands over his belly. "Shiloh, the prison officer I spoke to, said he was in solitary for stabbing another inmate, so she'd prefer I didn't visit in person. That was fine by me, I hate those bloody places. She called him a bragger, reckoned he'd confess if asked whether he'd murdered the missing men. He didn't. He was a confident sort, seemed confused as to why I'd think he'd kill his old mates when they were so close as teenagers. He didn't think Eric had it in him either, although he mentioned the man had a temper that flared out of the blue, which was why he'd agreed to loan Eric some money — didn't fancy being punched for refusing. So I phoned Prudence to ask her about her husband's behaviour. She confirmed he was sometimes unstable, cited it as the reason they'd divorced, yet in person she'd said they'd had a difference of opinion. As we discussed, I've got our lot on the lookout for Rory McFadden, as he scarpered once he knew I was a copper. More than a little suspicious. So far, no news as to his whereabouts. If he's at home, he isn't answering the door, nor is he picking up his phone. His car hasn't been caught on camera yet." He sighed. "So that's where I'm at."

Anna turned to Warren. "What's what with the sons and sons-in-law of the men from the nineties?"

He clicked to a new page on the board. "PCs visited, warned them to be vigilant. There's not much else we can do really, we're too thin on the ground. Designating officers to watch them isn't an option unless we have definite proof they're on some kind of kill list. I *did* pass on that I thought they should all go and stay elsewhere, maybe take time off work until Martin's killer is caught, but that isn't feasible for most people, plus it could take months to find him. They promised to stay indoors as much as possible, not to go out alone, and that if anyone asks them to meet up, someone they don't know, to avoid it."

Anna nodded. "Good. OK, CCTV surrounding Donetta's street, the area around the train station, and the route Martin took from work — Landmere Road and Mile Street. Anything?"

Warren clicked again. "Martin's car was caught near the train station — or at least it's suspected to be his car." He brought up a still image. "As you can see, all we have is a side view of the vehicle in the dark. The front wing, wheel, and half the driver-side door. The window hasn't been captured fully, all that's on offer is gloved hands on the steering wheel. Given how far away this image was captured, the bigger I make the picture, the worse the clarity gets. It's being driven along the top of a T-junction, the road directly towards the station. No number plate visible. However, it looks like a Mondeo, the dark colour is in line with Martin's, and it matches the time or thereabouts that Martin's vehicle entered the PS car park. As for where it'd been before that, sod all so far, I'm afraid. ANPR was a bust."

Anna gritted her teeth. "Talk about frustrating."

"Oh," Sally said. "Listen to this." She had the station's Facebook page up on her screen. "Someone's commented about the park. She was walking her dog and saw two men by the bandstand — one was in dark clothing, the other a suit. She wasn't close enough to hear what they were saying, but they seemed to get on well enough. She changed her route to go out of the park at the nearest exit as she was naturally worried, what with it being two men and her a woman. I'll message her, shall I? Get her in to give a statement?"

"Please." Anna moved on. "Any news on the missing guinea pig?"

"Sadly not," Placket said. "Irritating as hell. The only odd thing that stood out to me in my research is they were used in sacrifices. Now, I looked at the images of Martin in the warehouse. That doesn't scream sacrifice to me. There's none of the usual hallmarks. He wasn't posed, et cetera. Mind you, as this may be a copycat, our killer might not know the significance of using guinea pig fur, he could just be imitating

141

the killer. Let's face it, it was all over the news, and the internet lives for ever. As we don't have any pictures of bodies from the nineties to go by, neither will the copycat — unless he knows the killer. *Those* men could have been posed in a sacrificial manner. Annoyingly, we may never know."

"Did you check with the super about sending K9s onto the moors?" Anna pressed.

"I did, and he's agreed to two dogs going out tomorrow. It surprised me, to be honest. I didn't think he'd go for it."

"Maybe he's thinking along the public relations lines. You know, bad press if it's later discovered the remains are out there and nothing was done sooner."

"Probably." Placket stood and flicked his hands to iron out the kinks. "We have to be seen to be *doing* something, in their eyes."

Which is one of the reasons why I pushed for it to be done in the first place. Anna smiled at everyone, proud of herself for not blurting that out. "So, what do we know, if anything, about Martin's friends and colleagues?"

Warren moved to another page. "I've had PCs on that all day. Colleagues say he was a lovely man — none of them seemed suspicious and all had alibis. I rang Donetta for a list of his friends, who are few and far between. Seems he distanced himself from them while he concentrated on his business. Whoever he hung around with before she came on the scene, she doesn't know them."

"How annoying." Anna loosened her ponytail. A headache was brewing. "OK, then, let's call it a day. Sally, is the witness coming in?"

"Yes, but she can't make it until tomorrow. She's been away for Christmas and isn't due back until then."

Anna collected the empty cups from the desks. "Go home. Get some rest."

Peter shot up immediately, powering down his computer. Anna watched him from the corner of her eye. He said goodbye and left at a trot.

Placket got up to shut the incident room door. He prodded his phone screen and spoke to whoever he'd rung. "Subject in a rush to leave. On his way out now. He's been antsy most of the day. Something might be going down. Yep. OK. Let me know, doesn't matter what time it is." He tucked his mobile in his trouser pocket. Glanced around at everyone. "What's got the wind up *his* arse?"

Sally drew her handbag towards her. "I might be able to help with that . . ."

"Oh God." Placket flopped back into his seat, hand to his forehead, dreading what she had to say. "What?"

She took out a recording device. "I know, I know, it's unethical, but it's done now."

"Why didn't you say anything about this earlier?" Anna asked, a little pissed off. "A quiet word would have been appreciated."

"We were all busy, when was I *supposed* to say anything?"

"I'll give you that one," Anna said. "Go on, press play, then."

"Wait." Placket got up and stood in front of the door. "In case he comes back."

Anna understood his paranoia about needing to keep what they were doing a secret. It played on her mind every day, that they were spying on a colleague, and Peter finding that out now, after he'd been under surveillance for so long, would cock the operation up.

"Ready?" Sally asked.

Placket nodded.

A conversation emerged out of the speaker. At the point when Sally had finished talking about her ex waiting outside her house, Placket held a hand up for her to hit pause.

"Have you done something about this?" he asked.

"As it happens, I asked Karen to send a car over tonight."

"Good. Carry on."

She pressed play. The chat continued with Sally saying she might have to move away from Marlford, then she swam

143

into darker waters by bringing up the Kings. Peter sounded either offended or annoyed, Anna couldn't work out which. As she expected, he made out he was the good guy and had left the Kings and became an obedient copper.

"I s'pose if you walked away before they got into the proper bad shit, you can't be held accountable for what they did after."

"And what they do is only speculation."

"Sounds like you're sticking up for them."

Sally stopped the recording. "Sorry, but I wanted to get him to open up — or fuck up. During this part, he was *not* happy, although he did his best to hide it." She resumed play.

They discussed the tattoo, then:

"What's going on up there, can you see?"

"Err, looks like someone's been knocked over. There's an ambulance."

"Poor sod. I hope they're all right."

"I doubt it."

"What makes you say that?"

"Nothing, it's just . . . doesn't matter."

"No, go on."

"Can you just shut up? You've done nothing but peck at me for the past few minutes."

Sally paused the tape again. "Arsey much?"

Peter was clearly on the edge. "He's under immense pressure. I don't know whether to feel sorry for him or not. Can you imagine being under the control of a gang, how it must affect your daily life, your mental health? On the other hand, if he's still with them out of choice he deserves all he gets."

"What's this in relation to?" Warren asked.

Sally toyed with a pen. "We'd stopped at a traffic jam in Warner Road. Police and an ambulance were there. He went bright red, and to me it looked like he'd said too much, something had slipped out. As in . . . well, it could be Kings business and he knew about it."

"Did you have to go down Warner Road to get to Parking Solutions?" Placket asked.

"No. There are other routes."

144

Anna scrubbed a hand down her face. "So Trigger could have told him to go that way, so he saw what was going on. What *was* happening?"

"I rang Karen," Sally said. "Fatal stabbing. In broad bloody daylight. Honestly, if he didn't know about it beforehand, he was super bothered about it in the traffic jam."

Warren blew out a breath. "Put yourself in his shoes. He was affiliated with the Kings, so anything they do now, he feels guilty, or maybe relieved that he got out and he isn't involved. On the flip side, if he's still in with them and was told to go to Warner Road, maybe he's had a warning from Trigger for some reason. Like, 'Look what we can do to you if you don't do what we want.' But what if he *did* leave them all those years ago and now they're asking him to be their mole?"

"That would *kind* of explain him getting into Trigger's car a few months back, I suppose," Placket said. "You know, outside the pub, when Trigger supposedly told him about Smithy and the drugs. He could have been asked back into the fold then. But then why didn't he come to me or Anna about it?"

"Maybe he was threatened," Sally suggested. "Listen to this bit." She forwarded the tape a little.

"No amount of wise words from you will fix what's going on with me."

"Maybe give it a try?"

"Please, just give it a rest. Listen, ignore me. I get that you've clocked I'm not myself, but honestly, there's nothing you can do. It's best I don't involve you."

"That doesn't sound ominous . . ."

Sally pressed stop. "I offered a helping hand, and he turned it down. I honestly think he was on the verge of spilling the beans, but something stopped him. He tried to leave earlier to go and phone Donetta, and he shot out of here just now, couldn't wait to leave. What if he's been desperate to get hold of Trigger all day about the Warner Road situation but couldn't because Anna made him stay here? He'd have been stuck between a rock and a hard place. He chose to remain here, be a copper, do his job, rather than nip out to use the loo and message Trigger. After that conversation earlier, I'm inclined to believe he *has* been playing both sides but no longer wants to. Plus he was weird after Jamal got stabbed. If you want my opinion, he's involved in that somehow, and he's now shitting himself. If I push a bit more, maybe he'll confess."

"Lots to think about," Anna said. "D'you know the worst bit about all this? He's a good bloke deep down. He's got caught up in God knows what and has found himself in a mess. Still, that doesn't change the fact he's dodgy. Nice Peter aside, he still chose to remain a King. I very much believe he's been snooping into police files on their behalf, no matter that we can't prove it." She sighed. "Right, that's enough for today. Sally, let me know if anything kicks off when the officers speak to Richard tonight."

Anna wanted nothing more than to go home and hide herself away from the world, but her working day wasn't over.

She had a date with Parole in York.

CHAPTER NINETEEN

This was perhaps one of the stupidest things Peter had done. He stood in the Kite, a pint of lager in hand, the coldness of the liquid seeping into his fingers. He shouldn't be there; it was a Kings pub, for God's sake. And especially as he'd clocked those two men tailing him all the way from the station. But he was sick and tired of Trigger playing games with him. All this subterfuge. He wanted answers. Tonight. An end to this bullshit.

He didn't intend to approach anyone he knew, and, if the surveillance men *were* police, he hadn't done anything to warrant being taken in. Just a man having a drink. But his presence would be enough to alert Trigger that they needed to talk. Face to face. Someone would have told him Peter was there. In the past, that was how it had worked. Peter arrived, and a little bird would twitter in Trigger's ear. And he'd come, wouldn't be able to resist it. Give him fifteen minutes, and he'd be waiting out the back in the yard.

Wheels had served Peter's pint as though they were strangers. It stung, the casual way the other man had treated him, like he didn't matter and never had. Like they didn't have a past together. Peter's thoughts were so contradictory.

One minute he wished they'd all forget him and let him go, then, when he was being pushed out, he sulked.

Grow up, dickhead.

He turned his back on the bar so Wheels couldn't make eye contact. He had been watching in the mirror behind the optics to see if his followers had come in, and they had. Coppers if ever he'd seen one. Yes, they had casual clothing on, but just by their bearing it was obvious who they worked for. The police had an air about them, including him, and it got Peter thinking about how Anna had wangled her way into going on dates with Parole when all the Kings knew she wasn't for turning, that she'd be no use to them. *She* had that air, yet there she was, getting an in.

It pissed him off that she hadn't told him what she was up to.

Again, he'd been left out. Excluded.

Why? Did the team know what he'd been doing all this time? That he was a snake in their nest? He'd grown to care about all of them, and they'd always had his back. What he'd done by playing both sides would upset them, especially Warren, as they'd been good mates.

Was Anna mucking about with Parole to find out if Peter was a King?

He should abandon his pint, forget asking Trigger what had gone down on Warner Road, and leave the city. What did *he* care what had happened? He'd intended to go and phone Donetta outside the incident room, then check the database in another area of the station to see what had gone down, but Anna had stopped him.

Why? If the Old Bill *were* after him, then Placket and at least Anna, if not the rest of the team, knew he was being watched. *They* were probably watching him, too.

Was that why she'd been so abrupt earlier when he'd made to leave? Had she been told to keep him close so they could monitor him? Maybe she *was* undercover after all, and not seeing Parole on the sly. Parole might have let something slip to her about Peter being with the Kings. She could have passed that on to Placket. But the timeline didn't fit. His followers had been outside the pub when he'd got into Trigger's car that time — that was when this had all started. Anna had only recently started going on dates with Parole. Or so Trigger had said.

Confused by the feelings that caroused inside him — he was neither a King nor a copper, neither one thing nor the other — Peter glanced over at his two shadows. One of them hadn't quite looked away in time, and their gazes locked. He had to give it to the bloke, he acted casual, as if their eye contact had been nothing out of the ordinary. The burly blond stared through the window into the dark night, the left side of his face lit up by the orange of the streetlamp oozing through the pane, turning his hair ginger. The brown-haired fella picked at his fingernails, seemingly oblivious to the exchange.

Peter swigged some of his lager. He felt the need to get steaming drunk so he could forget everything. Pass out and never wake up.

Enough. You're not a tree. If you don't like where your roots are, leave.

He put the glass on the bar and stalked to the door that led to the toilets. He'd fuck off this way, lose his tail. Go home and collect his holdall. Leave the city. Trigger wasn't here yet, so Peter would avoid having to speak to him. It had been a silly idea anyway. The way Trigger had acted lately, he'd only expect Peter to do something for him. He'd have a go at him, too, about not passing on any intel today. That wasn't Peter's fault. The whole team had been in the incident room when he'd arrived for work, so he hadn't had the chance to go snooping.

A fire exit stood at the end of the corridor, and he walked out into the yard. The security light snapped into action, startling him for a moment. The cold bite of winter wrapped around him, and he slipped his gloves on. He made it to the gate, then stopped at the voice, dread swirling in his gut.

"You took your time."

Trigger.

"Been freezing my nuts off out here, waiting for you. What's so important that you risked coming here of all places? I've been informed two little rats followed you into the pub. How thick are you, leading them here? What the fuck's your game? What do you *want*?"

Peter gritted his teeth, the sting of tears annoying him. Shaming him. He'd been reduced to feeling like a child caught in the act of sneaking out. "Warner Road."

"Ah, you heard about the outcome, then."

"I was in a traffic jam there."

"Did you see anything juicy?"

"No."

"Shame. It would have shown you what will happen if you even *think* about fucking me over. *Us* over. The Kings — your brothers from other mothers." Trigger chuckled. "The fella we sent there to do a loyalty kill is going to be caught, arrested and banged up for life, to prove to you that I can do whatever I want. He doesn't know that yet, though. He won't until you just happen to get a random text from an anonymous sender telling you who stabbed that innocent woman and her little boy to death."

Little boy? Jesus Christ, he's lost the plot.

This had gone too far. All because Peter had wanted to leave the Kings. Trigger had always been a controlling bastard, even as a kid, wanting everything his own way. Yes, Peter knew too much, he could tell Placket when he'd accessed the database and link it to unsolved crimes, but there wasn't any proof they'd done anything, otherwise they'd have all been arrested by now. The phone Trigger had used to film Peter killing Jamal would likely be stored somewhere safe, as would the clothing he'd had on. Trigger would have safeguarded himself from ever having anything pinned on him.

"Why would you chance him saying it was a Kings job?" Peter asked.

150

"Because everyone will assume it's bullshit, some no-mark scrote who wanted to be a King but wasn't allowed to join so he took matters into his own hands. We were in the Plough. Alibis as tight as a duck's arsehole. He can sing all he likes, and if he does he'll be offed in prison. You know how easily that's done. So let this be a warning to you. I could send that video in of you stabbing Jamal. Or I could send *Anna* an anonymous text about it. Or get Parole to whisper in her ear that her DC murdered a sixteen-year-old kid."

Cold fear pierced Peter, and the urge to turn round and kick the shit out of Trigger took hold. It gripped him so hard he couldn't shake it off. Didn't want to. Was this what it felt like to finally snap? To lose your ability to give a shit about the outcome? To have had enough? To want to murder someone?

He spun to face him, full attention on the man he'd once called a friend. The instinct to obliterate took over, and he understood now why offenders said they lost control, that they couldn't help it. Peter lunged forward, fists up and ready, and Trigger just stood there as if he'd expected this, as if he'd *wanted* to push Peter to the edge. From the smug smirk, he didn't believe Peter would go through with it, but fucking hell, he would.

The first punch connected with Trigger's nose, the crunch of bone and cartilage loud in the still night. Trigger bumbled back a step but maintained his upright position.

"I'll allow that one," he said, "but—"

The second punch cut off whatever else he was about to say. Peter punched and punched; all the anger, the unfairness, the fear, the insecurity, the *everything*, came out in the force of his clenched fists. Trigger threw a few right hooks of his own, but Peter's rage was so intensified that he was focused, dodging, weaving, only receiving a couple of clips to the face. One big, two-handed shove to Trigger's chest sent him toppling to the ground, and he quickly rolled over onto his front to get some purchase in order to stand.

"You *arsehole!*" he spat.

Once upon a time, Peter would have been scared of him. He'd have told himself he couldn't attack this bastard because of loyalty, misguided at that, but he'd seen the light.

Fuck that noise. I need him gone.

"You're going to regret this," Trigger warned, like he was some Mafia boss, someone to be feared.

Peter kicked him in the head to shut him up. To blot out that voice. And he kept kicking. Trigger's face bloated, skin splitting in places. His nose skewed. Peter struck out until Trigger slumped, unmoving, his features a bloodied mess. Swollen. Lips split. Some of the ire filtered out of Peter, and in its place came the whisper that he'd *really* fucked up now. Another nugget spoken by many an offender: *And when I realised what I'd done, I couldn't believe it was me.*

Wheels would be waiting for him to return to the bar, and when he didn't, and Wheels came out here to find him, he'd discover Trigger instead, that Peter had . . . had what, killed him? *Had* he?

He took a few seconds to process that. Found he didn't care. That eliminating the source of pressure meant more to him than anything. To be free of Trigger's voice. No more messages or calls. No more orders. Their friendship meant nothing to him now, not since he'd realised Trigger hadn't held it dear. How he'd enjoyed toying with him just to prove a point. How he'd let running the Kings go to his head, elevating him to some godlike status that Peter wasn't prepared to worship.

He crouched. Felt for a pulse in the neck. Nothing beat through the thickness of his gloves, so he tried again.

Still nothing.

No puffs of grey exited the mouth. No more words. Taunts.

Blessed silence.

Peter stood. Checked the windows of the flat above the Kite. Darkness. But that didn't mean he hadn't been observed. His detective mind kicked in, working out the steps he needed to take now, overriding those incessant whispers, and he fled the yard, rounding into the alley beside it and creeping into the car park. No CCTV cameras here; the Kings didn't want to advertise what they were up to, that they met in the pub from time to time, and, idly, Peter wondered whether Wheels would curse that fact once he found Trigger dead.

No proof who'd done it.

How ironic.

He walked along the darkest side, away from the windows, then glanced around for his followers' car. He spotted it parked in front of the pub. He slipped into his car and, when he drove away, navigated to the left, hoping they wouldn't clock him as the second exit was out of view.

On his way home, he cried. For the friend he'd thought Trigger had been. For the murders of him, Jamal, and that poor woman and her child in Warner Road. Why had Trigger ordered the killing of a little kid and his mum and not some irritating pleb who no one would miss? What had she done to the Kings to deserve that? Or was *innocent* the key word here? She hadn't done *anything*, Trigger had just been making a nasty point.

He parked outside his flat. Rushed inside and collected his prepacked holdall, the one he should have grabbed a long time ago. It had cash in there, lots of it from his many withdrawals, and he'd use it to live anonymously in some bed and breakfast that wasn't so hot on asking for identification, in an out-of-the-way town he'd chosen during one of the nights he'd made plans.

He left his place, still, even now, despite everything, feeling the confusing need to stay. To not leave Marlford, the only place he'd felt at home. To confess. Do his time. But like Trigger had said, people could be killed in prison, so Peter wouldn't even be safe there unless he convinced someone he had to be placed on a secure wing.

Was it even worth it, this need to escape? To be who he wanted to be? Free of his secret burden? He didn't know, so he walked up the street, not looking back at what could have been — his home, his car, his life — and concentrated on getting to the train station. Then he remembered there might still be police there, so he opted for a bus instead. He'd be seen on CCTV, but he'd think about that when he had to.

It had arrived, his time to start again elsewhere, and he already mourned what he was giving up. The team, his job, his need to make amends for the stuff he'd done for the Kings. To Jamal and his mother, the lad's whole family. And now to Trigger, who, despite being a complete wanker at times, had had Peter's back on more occasions than he could count.

Until it had mattered. Until he'd gone all weird and treated Peter as if he were the enemy, just because he'd asked for a break.

"I don't need friends like that," he whispered, eyes leaking. "Fuck the lot of them."

CHAPTER TWENTY

With her little boy fast asleep in bed, Sally stood at the living room window of her dark house. Richard sat out there in his car beneath a streetlamp, staring her way. Was he asking himself if she'd gone to bed at the same time as Ben? Or did he think she was waiting for her supposed fancy man to turn up? Was *that* why he was doing this, to check whether she was in a new relationship? What the hell did that have to do with him? He should know she'd never choose anyone who wouldn't love Ben like his own.

But you chose Richard once upon a time. You thought he *was OK, and now look. He's an outright nutter.*

For a moment she thought he could actually see her, but then she dismissed it as paranoia. She only had one eye peering round the edge of the closed curtains, in the middle, the gap just enough for her to make everything out. No, he couldn't see her.

He turned away, his loathsome profile clear in the lamplight.

Nervous in case Karen's note on the police system hadn't been seen yet, Sally prepared herself for a long wait. It was half past seven, so officers must be busy elsewhere if they hadn't arrived here by now. She was hardly a priority. She hadn't phoned in previous arguments with Peter, so there was no log of his behaviour, before or after the divorce. No reason for the police to rush here to see if she was OK. She'd been too ashamed to ask for help, to be pitied by her colleagues. She'd gone down the same route so many abused women did. The team would have understood, they wouldn't have thought badly of her, but embarrassment had ensured she'd kept it quiet. Until recently, when she'd allowed herself to reveal bits and bobs. And she'd found it wasn't as bad as she'd thought, admitting she'd married an abuser.

Whatever Richard was looking at on his phone lit his face up. He wasn't even trying to disguise the fact that he was there, which spoke of his arrogance — arrogance she'd failed to see at the beginning of their relationship.

No, don't do that. Not anymore.

Why did she always insist on talking herself out of blaming him?

Why did *she* always have to carry it?

"He hid who he is, so it's his fault," she whispered. "He tricked me into believing he's a good man." There, she'd said it out loud. Cemented it as the truth.

Memories of him came tumbling in. The dirty looks, the rolled eyes, the tutting, all things he'd denied doing. The hard shoves to get her to see his point, pushes he'd said were a joke but weren't. Him implying she was taking them the wrong way. The hand at her throat when he'd wanted her to stop talking, which he'd tried to turn into him messing around, *pretending* to throttle her. The violent sex that had developed gradually, a slap here, a hand over her mouth there, the sharp tug of her hair wrapped round his fist, all things he put down to wanting to introduce some excitement back into the bedroom. All things she'd hated and had said so. Him stropping off, saying she was no fun anymore. His sour beer breath when he'd staggered in after a night out with his friends. The scent of perfume he'd said was from a mate's wife who'd given him a hug. The gaslighting, saying what he'd said hadn't been what she'd heard, what she'd seen hadn't been what had happened. Moving things in the house, hiding them, then putting them back a day or so later, exactly where she'd looked in the first place.

She couldn't get over how she'd allowed him to convince her they had a ghost, that the house was haunted.

How dumb can you be, you stupid cow?

But she consoled herself that she'd been young, as in love as she imagined she could be; or perhaps she'd been infatuated with him, blinded by the *idea* of love but never really experiencing it.

Would she ever?

No, not as long as he lived.

If his version of love was controlling her, sending her crazy, all the while seeing other women behind her back, then she wanted no part of it. Yet there he was, outside, tormenting her. But not for much longer. She was finally doing something about it.

The rumble of an engine drew her focus; her memory-glazed eyes sharpened, her stomach somersaulted. A patrol car pulled up next to Richard's and both officers got out. She'd already cracked the window open for this part, so she strained an ear, waiting for the expected rubbish to come out of his mouth. One officer stood at the passenger door, the other at the driver's side but towards the rear, as if he expected Richard to get out to speak to him.

Instead, the window sailed down. Of course it did. He wouldn't want to do as he was told. He'd want all the control, even in the face of the police. That had been his favourite taunt, that he could do and say whatever he wanted to his wife, a *copper*, who should be able to do something about it but wouldn't.

But you're wrong. I have done something.

"Yes?" Richard said in his egotistical way.

God, she *hated* him. Again wished him dead. Gone. Out of her life.

"We've had a report from a neighbour down the way that you're here, sir, and have been for a fair few evenings lately."

"Was it Sally?" Richard asked. "Aww, diddums, did she get her pals to come and tell me off?"

"Sally?" the officer said. "Err, I don't know a Sally, and I won't divulge who did phone it in. You need to move on."

"But I'm not doing any harm. I'm just sitting here."

"What for?"

"My ex lives there with my son. I like to make sure they're OK."

"I expect they are. You being here is making another resident uncomfortable, so you have to leave. If you come back, I'll arrest you for loitering with intent."

Richard's laugh streamed out. "Intent to do what? Jesus, even I know that nothing will be done until I do something. That's what happens, isn't it? Stalkers are allowed to do whatever they like, scaring women, so long as they don't actually do anything? It's a joke."

"Are you saying you're a stalker?"

"No. It was just an example of how ridiculous you lot are. Did the little grass also tell you that I don't get out of my car? That I don't *do* sod all except read on my phone? Is that a crime now?"

"Creating unease isn't something a normal person would want to do, sir. Just go." The officer sounded tired of the conversation. Of Richard. Probably his smug, self-satisfied speech.

"Tell Sally she can fuck off with her games, I know it was her." Richard drove away, his red taillights growing smaller the farther he went.

Sally breathed a sigh of relief, then stiffened at the thought of the coppers coming to her door. She didn't want Richard to see them there if he came back; he'd know for sure she'd grassed on him then. But they got in their car and followed him. She shut the window and remained there for five minutes, then sat in the dark, contemplating what he'd do next.

He'll come back.

Or he'd wait, pick Ben up on Friday evening, and likely mention tonight. Accuse her of setting her friends on him. Warn her that *he* had new friends who'd *really* scare her if she reported him again; then he'd make out he was messing about or he hadn't even said it.

Christ, she was so *weary* of him.

A tapping coming from the back of the house had her bolting to her feet, her heart rate losing its rhythm. Her first instinct as a mother was to go up to Ben, but her police training reminded her he'd be safer if she investigated the noise, then called it in. She felt around on the coffee table for her phone and brought up the keypad, ready to dial 999 if Richard had returned and was opting to speak to her from the back garden instead of being seen out the front.

Cunning bastard.

She walked down the hallway and into the kitchen, anger fuelling her courage. Jumped at the sight that met her. Stifled a scream. A face pressed to the glass, hot breath creating a ragged island of condensation; but it wasn't Richard who stared in at her.

It was Peter.

What the hell did *he* want?

CHAPTER TWENTY-ONE

Anna sat in the posh comfort of a hotel in York. Parole had nipped to the toilet, and she took the opportunity to check her work phone. No messages had come in, so she looked through her emails. Nothing she couldn't leave until tomorrow. Herman hadn't sent the highlights of Martin's post-mortem report through, so she assumed he hadn't got round to it yet. Toxicology would be a while.

Parole returned, and her stomach flipped at his charming grin. Over the course of their times together, she'd grown to like him as a person, the one he was deep inside. The more she saw him, the more she wished she wasn't who she was and he wasn't who he was. Life could be cruel when it came to affairs of the heart. What if he was her soulmate? The only one destined for her? Not that she believed in such things, but still, she'd been dealt a shitty hand if that were the case. She'd always known nothing could come of this, despite the chemistry that drew her to him.

He sat, and she wanted to ask him if he'd ever killed for the Kings, find out what his role was, whether he deserved to go to prison. What if he was just a foot soldier who passed messages along or did a bit of menacing? Could she tell Placket he wasn't a main player so he should walk free?

No. Whatever he's done, he has to face the punishment.

"Why couldn't we have met years ago before you got involved with the Kings? You might not have gone down the criminal route then, and we could have been together." She hadn't meant to let her thoughts spill from her mouth, but they had, so she'd just have to deal with it.

"Believe me, I've thought the same. But we didn't, so we have to work with the hand we've been dealt."

Odd, that he'd echoed her thoughts about dealt hands. She dismissed it as just a coincidence. Something most people would say or think in this situation. It wasn't that they were connected in any telepathic way.

She studied him. Wished he wasn't so bloody good-looking. "So, are you saying you're happy to see me on the side, no one knowing?"

His usual confident air vanished, and he squirmed. "Um, about that . . ."

Her guts sank. "Don't tell me you've told someone. Bloody hell!"

"Only Trigger. He won't say anything."

"Seriously? Isn't Wheels right up his arse? Best buddies an' all that? He'll have told him, surely."

"Hmm, maybe I didn't think it through."

She launched herself into manipulation mode. "You could have really fucked this up, d'you know that? If I'm going to be a mole for you lot, we have to keep our relationship a secret. We discussed this. You promised. Now I don't know whether I can trust you or not."

"So you've thought more about my proposal, have you? Becoming a proper mole? Not just giving us a few snippets?"

"I said I'd consider it."

"Sounds to me like you've made up your mind. Then I'd have to tell Trigger anyway. I couldn't keep something like that from him."

161

"But you could have said you had a secret mole or something."

He laughed. "Yeah, I'd like to see how he'd take that. Not very well, I can assure you."

"I'll do this on one condition. I give you lot information, you give me some in return. For every snoop job I do for you, you do me the courtesy of helping me out. I've helped you out three times already, so you owe *me* snippets."

"I might have to run it past Trigger first, what I can tell you."

"For fuck's sake, seriously? You let him rule everything you do? I didn't take you for an arse-licker." She prayed for her goading to bear the fruit she intended to pick.

"It's not that I'm an arse-licker, more that we all agree the Kings have a certain way of doing things, and I can't fuck that up. What do you want to know?"

She *could* ask who was supplying spice in Marlford, it would take the Kings down if he admitted it was them, but her instinct prodded at her to ask something else first. She was Aladdin, Parole the genie, and she didn't want to waste one of her three wishes. She reminded herself that she wasn't meant to lead when it came to getting information, she couldn't plant stuff in his head. It was supposed to come from him first.

But she was going to throw that rule out of the window.

"Now, you're likely going to deny this, but I need you to promise me you won't say anything. To *anyone*."

"Can't guarantee that, but go on."

She could balls everything up, but she had a plan to get round that. She just had to hope it worked. That she could talk him into believing her. "Is Peter Dove your bent copper?"

"No."

"You're lying. Maybe he isn't a full grass at the minute, but he *has* been one and will probably resume duties when it's deemed that he's safe."

"Safe from what?"

Oh, he was good at hiding things. Very good.

162

She scoffed. "Even *I've* noticed he's being followed. Probably something to do with Trigger. Keeping a beady eye on him for whatever reason."

Parole sighed. "He *is* being tailed, but not by us. We thought it was your lot."

Anna frowned. "Why the fuck would the police be following him?"

"Probably for the same reason you've asked if he's our mole. He hasn't been as diligent as he should have been and someone noticed. Got suspicious."

"You do realise you just admitted he's your inside man, don't you?"

Parole closed his eyes for a moment. "Fuck. That's your fault. You make me forget who I am sometimes."

"Err, that's not nice, telling me it's my fault. You can pack that right in and own what you said. Don't blame me."

"Sorry."

She hid her surprise that he seemed to mean his apology. Christ, he liked her more than she'd thought. "So, moving on from your mistake . . . It was the day Jamal Jenkins got stabbed that Peter fucked up."

"Jesus Christ. What did he do?"

"He was acting shifty, jumpy, and kept getting messages, maybe phone calls. He spent more time out of the incident room than in it. I put two and two together, that he was being told what to do. For days after, he wasn't himself, and he hasn't been since, not really. I've kept it to myself, been watching him as much as I can, but, if someone else at the station has cottoned on to what he's doing, I know nothing about it."

"Sounds to me like he's panicking. Fucking up because of it. Trigger's not going to like it."

She went in for the kill. "I think Peter stabbed Jamal."

"Please don't ask me to confirm that."

His answer was confirmation in itself.

She ploughed on so he didn't have time to get his wits about him and close himself off. "Listen, just so it's clear, the reason I've brought this up is not to get info out of you about him but for you to let Trigger know that the police are onto Peter."

"He knows that already."

"Then he has to stop using him. Use me for now, until Peter starts behaving like his old self. Don't let Trigger know this came from me, though. We don't want to mess things up so he goes off half-cocked and has a go at him. I can't have him telling anyone I'm seeing you. For me to work for the Kings, maybe alongside Peter farther down the line, everything has to remain as normal. I can't be seen as dodgy. Do you think you can pull that off? Just you and me, working together on this for now?"

Parole smiled. "Yep. I've just got to work out how to phrase it to Trigger, that's all. For the record, I didn't agree with the Jamal thing. That was Trigger's and Wheels's idea. A loyalty job."

Anna shook her head as if she felt sorry for Peter's predicament. "Why the hell would he need to prove his loyalty? If he's been working for both sides since he joined the force, isn't he doing enough to prove he's trustworthy? Bloody hell, how much does Trigger expect a King to do?"

"It's complicated. How was Peter today?"

Here we go. I might find out the real reason behind the Warner Road incident. "Something weird came up. A member of my team was with him in a traffic jam. Something had happened, police and an ambulance were there, and he acted as if he knew what it was about. It was enough for said team member to tell me about it on the quiet. So now *two* of us have noticed Peter's being weird. How long will it be before someone else at the station does?"

"Sounds to me like they know already. The tail they've got on him. What are you referring to anyway?"

"Warner Road."

Parole knocked back his whisky. "Ah. Trigger will go mental if he finds out I told you anything about that."

"Who's going to tell him? I certainly won't. I'm more concerned about Peter being erratic, going off the rails because of the pressure he's under. Trigger needs to back off. From my observations, Peter isn't firing on all cylinders. It's a concern. I can't have him acting off while working cases."

Parole sighed. "It was a warning to him, all right? Don't ask me to elaborate."

"If I did, that would be another question." She smiled. Reckoned she'd got more than enough out of him for tonight regarding their mutual acquaintance. "OK, next question. Who's the main supplier of spice?"

His eyebrows shot up. "It isn't us. Trigger wants the lion's share, but he hasn't got enough guts to topple the outfit who are bringing it in. They're . . . well, they're the big guns. Nutters. Come from London. That's all I'm prepared to give you. Last question."

She'd dreaded this one, but in order to make him believe she was on his side, in this with him for the long haul, she had to say it. Maybe even go through with it. To bring the Kings down. To get justice for Jamal and whoever else the gang had targeted.

Shit.

She smiled again. "It can't be tonight, because I need to get back soon, but when are you going to take me to bed?"

165

CHAPTER TWENTY-TWO

Well away from Southgate or his usual haunts, in case the cell mast indicated where he was at the time of the call, Rory used the burner to phone the Jacobean and asked them to speak to Billy. To tell him to meet at a car park that wasn't spied on by cameras — none that he could see anyway. And to bring his car. There was an emergency, and he needed Billy's help.

All he could do was wait and hope the message got through and Billy turned up. Rory stood behind a border of bushes. Refreshed his memory about his old friend. He drove a dark-grey BMW, had a wife, no kids, and fitted Bryan's mould — coxcombry and folly. Add a dash of self-assurance, another of arrogance, and that pretty much summed him up.

How had he changed so much since they were kids?

A car swung into the area, and Rory smiled. Billy parked close by, a nice little coincidence, and Rory stepped out from his hiding place. Head down, just in case, he approached the vehicle and reached out for the passenger-side door handle, his palms sweating from his gloves. He bent to check Billy's reaction to the face paint. Billy started, clearly alarmed, then recognition hit.

Rory opened the door and got in.

"What the fuck?" Billy stared across at him. "I didn't know you were in the army. Taking it a bit too seriously with that face paint, aren't you?"

The laughter in Billy's tone got on Rory's wick. "This is serious. Drive away, exactly where I tell you to."

"What's going on?"

"I've been sent to watch a target, but my car won't start." That was sort of true, the watching bit. Dad's voice had been waffling in his earhole on and off for days. "I just need you to drop me off at his house."

"Why couldn't you get a bloody taxi?"

"Just drive, will you?"

Billy did as he'd been told, and Rory issued directions. As far as he was aware, there were no cameras on this route, but he wasn't one hundred per cent on that. Those bloody things were everywhere, hidden too well sometimes. Still, he was in disguise.

"Who's the target?" Billy sounded nervous.

"Someone in a sleeper cell."

"Oh, fuck me, pal. Are you serious? Why the hell are you involving me in that? And do the army even send soldiers out on their own for that sort of thing?"

"I'm a colonel," Rory lied. "I get the covert jobs. The target is at a house, so I need to go and observe, see what happens."

How gullible is he going to be? When will he realise this is a load of old cobblers?

"What, with no backup? Do you think I'm stupid?"

"This is how we work sometimes. You can just drop me off round the back. But then again, I might need your help if I have to go inside. If it looks like something's going down. You can do it for king and country."

"No." Billy pulled over. "I'm not having anything to do with it."

Rory burst out laughing. "Your face! I was *joking!*"

"What?" Billy gaped at him. Then he chuckled. "You fucking bastard. You got me."

"It was my turn," Rory said, recalling how they'd played tricks on each other as kids. Sometimes days would pass before either of them showed their hand. "Jesus Christ, I can't believe you thought I was a colonel, let alone that I'd take a civilian to a dodgy house. God, that was funny."

"So where *are* we going, then?"

"May as well go to my place now, seeing as we're nearly there."

Billy shook his head in amusement, smiling, and drove off again. "I'll get you back, you just wait."

"Yeah, yeah." Rory told him the name of the street behind his house. "We have to go in round the back, else we'll be seen."

"What's the problem with being seen?"

"It's for sale. I'm not meant to be living there — that's the terms of the divorce. While it's up for sale, I can't use it. My neighbours are that nosy, they'd tell the ex."

"Are you mucking me about again?"

Of course I bloody am. "Sadly not."

"I've never heard of that, you know, not being able to live in your own house."

"It's complicated. Park just there, look."

Billy slid the BMW between a couple of cars. They got out and Billy blipped the locks. Rory led the way. Near his rear gate, a noise came from Bob's garden.

"Shit," Rory whispered. "Shh."

Billy froze.

A dog barked.

"Be quiet, Izzy," Bob said. "Noisy little tart."

The shuffle of Izzy scampering over Bob's pea gravel sounded so loud. A door closed, and the lock clicked.

Rory glanced at Billy in the darkness. "Should be OK to go in now."

He entered the garden, then the house. Billy closed the door. Rory turned the key in the lock and switched the light on.

Billy gazed around. "Blimey, there's sod all in here."

"I told you, it's up for sale. The ex-bitch cleared me out. Took everything. I was staying at Mum's, but she still does my head in, so I had to get out. I kip here on the quiet."

It seemed this place was beneath Billy. His sneer said it all. "Couldn't you have just gone to the pub and met me there like we agreed?"

"Nah, it's cheaper to drink here. Then you don't have to get a taxi home. You can sleep here."

"Thought you said she cleared you out? I'm not sleeping on the floor."

Rory smiled. "Got blow-up beds, haven't I?"

"Christ, and you're *proud* of that?"

Once again, Billy had shown how much he'd changed. How life's lefts and rights had morphed him into someone else. Or the money had.

Despising his tone, Rory nipped over to the worktop. "I'd say take a seat, but there isn't one."

Billy sighed. "Come on, back to the Jacobean. I don't slum it these days."

"No, you lord it about, don't you? I've seen you."

Billy frowned. Glanced at the back door, then to Rory. "What's with the attitude?"

"I could ask you the same thing."

"What are you on about? Fuck this, I'm off." Billy reached out to turn the key.

Rory opened the drawer and took the knife out. "I wouldn't if I were you."

Billy stared over, his eyes widening. "What the hell? Is this another joke?" He laughed unsteadily. "Because it's my turn now, don't forget, and, to be fair, that kind of joke isn't funny." He nodded to the knife.

"Remember those blokes who went missing that summer?"

169

"Of course I do. One of them was my wife's father."

Rory took a few steps towards Billy. "That was my dad. He killed them all."

"Stop pissing about now. That's enough. Pack it in."

Another couple of steps closer. "And that man found in the warehouse today. Heard about that?"

"Yeah, but—"

"That was *me*."

On the last word, Rory raised the knife and slashed it across Billy's face. A screech, even wider eyes, and Billy stumbled backwards in shock and pain. His hand automatically came up and he touched the wound. One finger poked into the slit. The strike had been so quick, so unplanned, that the blade had gone through the cheek instead of just scoring the pork rind pattern.

Billy lowered his hand and stared at the blood. Breathing erratically, he fumbled in his pocket, likely for his phone. Funny how that was his first port of call when the door was *right there*, the key just a twist away. Funny how the mind didn't work logically in times of distress.

He's panicking, son.

Rory took the chance to stab Billy again while he was distracted. A plunge to the stomach. Blade withdrawn. A plunge to the thigh. Blade withdrawn. Then, as Billy retreated to the wall, plastering himself to it, more plunges, deep, so piercing.

All the while, Rory stared into his eyes. It only took one unfortunate decision in life to put him on the list. One wrong turn had come to this.

"I bet you wish you didn't choose her now," he said, knife held by his side.

Billy clutched at his stomach, frantically trying to stop the blood flow. "W-w-what? What have I ever done to you?"

"Nothing except speaking to me with derision a couple of times. This isn't about what you have or haven't done. It's not personal. It's not about *you* specifically. Dad always said men with money couldn't help themselves, that they thought they were superior. I've proved him wrong, because *I* don't go around acting like that."

A flash of memory took him back to the pet shop, the way he'd spoken to Mum when he'd nicked her cup of tea. No, it wasn't money that had made him do that, it was her treatment of him, how she'd never loved him.

Rory studied how the blood bloomed on Billy's shirt, tainting it. The fabric seemed to swell with liquid, then it slapped against the skin beneath. Did it feel cold, like Rory's pants had that time when he'd pissed himself in Nan's cellar?

"I need an ambulance," Billy pleaded. "Please . . ."

Rory shook his head. "The only vehicle you're getting in is your own."

"OK, OK, I'll go. I won't tell anyone what you did."

Rory smiled. Drew the knife back, ready for another stab. "I know you won't. Because you'll be dead in the back seat."

CHAPTER TWENTY-THREE

Peter sat at Sally's kitchen table, thankful that the standard lamp in the corner opposite left him less exposed than he would be if the main light was on. Less seen. He'd be telling her things soon, and he didn't want her to spot the shame on his face in stark brightness. The bulb must be a low wattage; it gave the dining area of the kitchen a gentle glow. Ambient, the magazines would call it. Whatever, he was glad of it.

He was going to tell her the lot. Halfway to the bus station, the copper in him had insisted on it. Swamped him with guilt that he'd abused the team's faith. The way he'd acted with Trigger had scared him, that he was capable of losing it like that. He couldn't trust that it wouldn't happen again one day. What if, in the new life he'd been desperate to run to, someone else pissed him off to such a degree? He couldn't allow himself to run, to put someone else in danger.

No, Trigger was a one-off. He pushed you to do it. Pecked and pecked.

But what if that wasn't the case? What if there were more "one-offs" in his future?

Everything he'd been taught in the job meant he deserved to be punished for his part in Kings business. Filtering

172

information back to them. Ensuring they got away with crap. And Jamal, that hideous, *hideous* loyalty job that had been the beginning of the end. The proper end. Now. Tonight. The end of life as he'd known it.

Trigger's murder had sealed Peter's fate. He couldn't walk away and continue his life as if nothing had happened. If he'd run, the Kings would be gunning for him. The police would. He'd be prey, legging it from creatures who wanted to catch him, rip him to shreds. All right, that might still happen in prison, but he had no fucks left to give. If he got shanked in the shower, then that would be a blessing. No more tormenting thoughts. No more guilt.

He acknowledged that he was taking the coward's way out. Hoping someone took control of his destiny and snuffed him out so he wouldn't have to face it on the daily.

He thought about the broken chain tattoo on his arm. The flying eagle on his wrist. Both of them had signified freedom to him, although he hadn't expected he'd take *this* path to liberty, where it would be taken away from him behind bars anyway, just in a different way.

What a mess. But it felt right, being here. The best thing to do, no matter what that meant for him. How weird would it be to find himself on the other side of the fence, where *he* was the one being handcuffed, not the one doing the cuffing? Where Sally would read him his rights — which she would, she wouldn't let him walk out of here without arresting him — when usually it was him saying it? Being booked in. Going into a cell. The questioning. The charge. Placed on remand. The sentencing, because he'd admit he was guilty. Wouldn't insult the Crown or the taxpayer by saying he wasn't.

He stared at the table while Sally waited expectantly for him to speak. Cups of tea sat on coasters she must have had made of Ben's artwork. A house, a woman and child in front of it. A park, with swings and a slide, a little stick figure standing at the top of it. Both images created from an innocent mind, for whom the most pressing thing was whether Daddy was going to be mean to Mummy today. Although that was pressing enough for a kid. Too much for a kid like Ben to handle. But it wasn't in Peter's league. Deception and murder. Bringing shame down on his family. Hurting those he worked with. Jamal's mother.

"I've killed someone," he said. "Two someones."

She didn't gasp, didn't narrow her eyes, just nodded, as if she'd expected this all along. Then stated, "You're still a King. It was inevitable."

So she knew, then.

"I didn't mean to do the first one, I was forced, but I knew exactly what I was doing with the second."

"The first was Jamal, wasn't it?"

He nodded. "Poor bastard. He didn't deserve it. All he was doing was what Trigger told him, selling drugs. They used him to prove a point. To remind me they have something on me. I asked Trigger if I could leave, see. Didn't want the pressure of being a King anymore. He filmed it, what I did, and he had the clothes I was wearing. Jamal's blood will be on them. My DNA. I'm fucked if they're ever found."

"Was killing Jamal easier than telling one of us — your *friends* — that you were in deeper than you wanted to be with the gang? If it were me, I'd have said Trigger forced me to poke into the police database. Yes, you'd have lost your job, maybe spent a bit of time in the nick, but it wouldn't have been as bad as now."

"So you know I've been snooping."

She nodded. "Talk it through. Explain your reasoning."

He shrugged. Couldn't explain it if he tried. "You wouldn't understand. No one would unless they were a King. All I did as an officer was funnel information to them, like whether the police would be in certain places when Kings planned to get up to stuff. And I nosed into files to make sure none of them were being looked at for anything. Altered a few things."

"Do you realise there's a dedicated team now who are *only* looking at the Kings?" she asked gently.

It shouldn't surprise him, but it did. "How come I didn't know about it?"

"Because you've been suspected of belonging to them for a while. We all know. We've been keeping tabs on you." She sipped some tea. "You can't blame us. Your crown tattoo tipped us off."

He closed his eyes. Opened them to stare at an iron stopper propping open the interior door into the hallway. Shaped like an old-fashioned kettle, the spout long. Pointed at the end. Sharp. "I told Trigger I shouldn't get one, but he insisted."

"You should have put it on your arse." She smiled.

He huffed out a laugh. "Yeah, that would have worked better."

"I know you — well, the part you've always shown us — and I don't believe you're a bad person underneath it all. Things just went a bit wrong, didn't they?"

"You could say that. Like I said, I wanted out, I told Trigger, but he said I couldn't leave. He gave me six months off instead, but he kept moving the goalposts, asking me to look shit up at work. Then there was the Jamal thing. Then tonight . . ."

"I can tell something bad happened. You've got a black eye."

"I kicked Trigger to death."

Sally hid her shock well, as she'd been trained to do. She always had been good when it came to interviewing suspects. Calm. Controlled. Kind, as if she didn't think you were the scum of the earth. The thought that she might well be thinking that about *him* hurt more than he thought it would.

"I didn't want to be this person," he said. "I swear to fucking God. It all got out of control."

"I know. But this is where you are, and we need to deal with it."

"Something happened with Trigger. It's like a part of me is broken now. I don't particularly care what happens to me. Don't even care whether I get done over in prison. It'd be best for everyone if I was."

"Why did you kill him?"

"To make it stop. To stop *him*. But as I was leaving, you know, to get the bus out of here, something told me to tell someone. To actually admit my part in it. I can't hack the fact I killed Jamal. He was a *kid*, Sal, a bloody *kid*."

"If you grass on them, it'll go in your favour."

"I can grass, but it won't get them sent down. Trigger was too clever."

"But maybe someone lower down the ranks will break under questioning."

He laughed. "You have no idea, do you? There's a code. *No one* will break, even with Trigger dead."

"I won't kid you, we both know you'll serve concurrent sentences for the murders, but maybe the judge will be lenient because you realised the law was the best way forward in the end."

"I always knew it was, I just . . ."

"I get it, and I'm not just saying that. All of us have bad thoughts, no matter that we're coppers. We're human. I've thought about Richard being killed, just so he's out of my life. I'm a good officer, yet I've imagined it, how I'd be free, how I wouldn't have to live with the anxiety he creates. Sometimes, our thoughts come without us consciously drawing them out. They're just there. It's what you do about them that matters. Whether you act on them."

"I acted on the one for Trigger. I *wanted* to kill him, plain and simple."

"Where is he now?"

"In the yard behind the Kite, unless someone's found him."

"If they haven't, it won't be long before they do." She sighed, eyes bright with unshed tears. "I told myself you were a

176

bastard for being a mole. That you deserve everything coming your way, but now . . . Christ, this is hard. We're mates, despite it all. I don't want to nick you, but I'm going to have to."

"I know."

She took a deep, juddering breath. "Peter Dove, I am arresting you for the murders of Jamal Jenkins and—" Her mouth dropped open. She stared behind Peter to the back door.

"What's the matter?" he asked, alarmed in case Wheels stood on the other side of the glass. He couldn't trust himself not to kick *him* to death, too. *Jesus, what's wrong with me?*

"It's Richard. Coppers sent him away earlier, but . . . I knew he'd come back. It just pissed him off. He'll want to have a go at me about it."

Peter didn't turn round. "Don't let him in, for fuck's sake."

"Bit of a problem there. I forgot to lock the door when I let you in."

"Then I'll get rid of him." Peter stood and faced the door.

It opened slowly. Richard stepped over the threshold, his stare latched onto Sally. He closed the door behind him. Leaned on it. "Of all the people I thought you were shagging, this is the most surprising."

"Hang on a minute, pal," Peter said.

Richard glared at him. "Don't fucking *pal* me. This is between me and her."

"Not anymore, it isn't." Peter veered towards his police training instead of his instincts to batter the crap out of this bloke for everything he'd put Sally through. Was this how serial killers felt, the ones who confessed they had the urge to murder everyone who caused pain? The insight into their minds, that *he* now felt the same, disturbed the shit out of him. "You've come in uninvited. Richard Wiggins, I am arresting you for trespassing—"

"Fuck off!" Richard shouted. "Piss off and mind your own business."

Sally stood, her chair scraping back. "Get out or *I'll* arrest you."

They stared at each other for ages, two people who had once been happy together, the sourness of their broken relationship tainting the air. A challenge lingered. It seemed Richard couldn't work out whether Sally would go through with her threat or not. A slight smirk appeared, like he really didn't believe her, but Sally glared, and it was obvious Richard now had doubts. What the hell had gone on between them? How had he been able to manipulate Sally when she was a copper and knew better?

The same way Trigger could manipulate me.

Peter assessed the situation. Sally was in work mode, ready to take down a suspect, and Richard had no clue what his ex was like in that type of scenario. Fearless. Brilliant. Full of courage. Considering how she must have acted at home with him, he wouldn't realise she had a steely side to her.

"If you don't leave in the next few seconds," she said, "I promise you, I won't think twice about nicking you."

Richard's hand shot out, and he pushed Peter out of the way so he could get to Sally. Peter pushed back, aiming to make the man stumble, but Richard was as rigid as a tree, his back still against the door. Sally stepped forward and took hold of his upper arm, and Peter did the same with the other. They'd done this before out in the field and knew the drill, how the other would think and act. God, he'd miss this. Both of them wrenched Richard forward at the same time, Peter diving into the space behind him, gripping his wrists and holding them together with both hands at the small of his back.

Sally read him his full rights.

Richard laughed. "You're joking, right? You've arrested your son's father?"

"I don't care who you are." She made eye contact with Peter. "Hold him steady while I get my cuffs."

178

Peter nodded over the man's shoulder and prepared to keep his grip tight. As expected, Richard struggled. He managed to yank one arm free, punched upwards and back, aiming for Peter's face. Peter ducked his head to the other side, grappling with Richard's flailing arm. The man was too fast. He tugged his clasped wrist free and spun to face Peter, who, mirroring his earlier actions in the yard with Trigger, shoved Richard's chest.

Oh fuck . . .

It all happened as if in slow motion. Richard staggering in reverse, his top half leaning backwards. Sally appearing in the kitchen doorway, cuffs in hand, staring at her ex barrelling towards her. Richard losing his footing, his head smacking into the edge of the door.

Time sped up.

He went down, the side of his neck landing on the spout of the iron kettle stopper. Most of it slid into his flesh. Sally stared down at him, as if she couldn't believe her earlier confession about wanting him dead was coming true right in front of her. Richard cried out in agony, blood spurting from his mouth and seeping around the spout.

Peter looked at it. "If that gets pulled out, he's dead."

"Oh God, oh shit, oh fuck." Now that this situation had become too personal, Sally dithered in place, then glanced at her phone on the table. She composed herself. "Ring it in. For God's sake, ring it in."

Peter remained where he was. Sally stared at him, and so many silent words passed from her to him, him to her. She contemplated what he'd said, what that could mean for her, for Ben. This secret exchange, one he'd never admit to, would remain between them so long as she didn't crack under the pressure. She would have to carry the burden of it.

Do you want me to do it?

He swore she gave him a slight nod as confirmation.

"You weren't here until it was over," he said. "You didn't see me push him. You couldn't find your cuffs and, when you walked in here, he was dead."

"Peter, I . . ."

"It'll be all right, I promise. I've got you, OK?"

"Oh God . . ."

"Shh."

Peter stepped forward. Bent over. Pulled the spout from Richard's neck.

Blood gushed. And gushed.

He stood upright. "I'm going down for two others, so I may as well make it three."

"You . . . Jesus fucking Christ, Peter, this isn't something to joke about! You didn't kill him. You *didn't*, do you understand? He pulled the spout out himself. I came in here and found him like this, got it?"

"All right, if that's the way you want to play it." He smiled; he'd done the right thing at last, killed someone for a good reason. "Now put those bloody cuffs on me and ring for an ambulance. Best for you to follow protocol, eh?"

He laughed, a tad maniacally, but it felt good.

It was over. For him and Sally.

Bar the guilt.

CHAPTER TWENTY-FOUR

The two men who'd followed Peter into the pub still sat there. Trigger must have turned up if Peter wasn't back by now. Or maybe Peter had been sent away on some Kings job or other and Trigger had gone home. Either way, Wheels wanted that pair of coppers out of here. They weren't good for business, stinking up the air. Some of his regular customers appeared uncomfortable — many could smell a pig a mile away — and they'd soon take their custom elsewhere if the bacon rashers didn't make themselves scarce soon.

He left the bar in the capable hands of his assistant and walked down the corridor. The fire exit stood ajar, which wasn't unusual as Peter would likely have left it open so he could come back and finish his pint. But maybe they were still talking.

Blimey, they've been ages. What the hell takes that long to sort out?

He opened the door and stood on the threshold, expecting the security light to be on and Trigger and Peter to be hashing things out. Instead, darkness. Silence.

"Fuck's sake. If they've both gone off and left this door unlocked . . ."

He stepped into the yard a few paces to set the motion sensor off. The light splashed on, showcasing the plastic crates of empty bottles, the metal barrels.

Showcasing Trigger.

"Oh, *fuck* no."

He had enough sense not to approach the body. To know his old pal was dead. To retreat into his office and phone the police. To tell them that someone was dead in his yard, and no, he didn't know who it was — too much blood, the face too swollen for him to be recognisable. He'd do all that in a minute.

Thank God most people around here thought he'd retired from the Kings. Anna and Lenny knew he hadn't, because he'd helped them out on a case a while back, but they couldn't prove it.

If Peter had killed Trigger, it meant he'd wanted the bloke silenced, that something was happening behind the scenes. The police were coming for the Kings.

Wheels wanted no part of that.

As a courtesy to the only King other than Trigger he really liked, he quickly prepared himself to phone Parole on a burner he'd throw away as soon as possible. Then ring the police.

Then that was it. He was done.

A King no more.

He had to pray his fake early retirement saved him.

CHAPTER TWENTY-FIVE

Anna didn't enjoy being the sober one. Parole had sunk a few whiskies and was on his way to being more than three sheets to the wind. The alcohol she'd plied him with and the promise of sex in the future had loosened his tongue. He'd spoken a lot about how the Kings worked, the levels of hierarchy, the things they were involved in. How Trigger was so anal about things that it was unlikely any of them would ever be caught. Anna wasn't surprised by any of it. A gang like that was bound to have fingers in a lot of pies. He'd claimed he didn't do an awful lot, mainly acted as muscle to scare people, but since his grandfather had asked him to go on the straight and narrow, bribing him to do so with a posh penthouse beside Jubilee Lake, Parole had been careful not to get involved in the heavy stuff.

He'd admitted he'd kill if he had to, though, and that had burst Anna's bubble of hope that he had turned a corner. It confused her, because one minute she wanted him sent down, the next she didn't.

He wasn't the only one affected by their chemistry.

Once she cut him off, once he wasn't anywhere near her, she could think clearly. While she was with him, though, that changed.

She had to end this soon. Go home and ring Placket. Tell him Peter was definitely the mole. Get him arrested, questioned, persuade him to spill the beans on the gang.

"When can you manage to get away for a whole night?" Parole asked.

So we're back to the sex again. "Not at the moment. I've got a murder case on the go."

"Another one? My, my, what is Marlford coming to . . ."

"I'd better make a move." As she stood, her work phone rang, so she plopped back down to answer it. Sally's name sat on the notification bar. Shit, had things kicked off with Richard? She swiped to answer. "Are you OK?"

"No, I . . . Oh God, Anna, Richard's dead."

Anna shot to her feet again and walked away from Parole into a corridor where no one else was around. She had a clear view into the bar, though, so she could keep an eye on him in case he had a mind to come out here. "*What?*"

"Peter came here, he confessed to killing Jamal and Trigger and—"

What the hell? Anna felt sick. And sad. So sad that their suspicions had been right regarding Jamal, that it had been confirmed for a second time tonight. Maybe a small part of her had thought Parole was feeding her a line about Peter to see what she did with the information, checking if she was safe to become a King. But this?

"Bloody hell. Slow down. First and foremost, where are you?"

"Out the front of my house in my car. Ben's asleep on the back seat."

"OK, and you're safe?"

"Yes."

"Right. Carry on."

"Peter was sent on a loyalty job to kill Jamal, he had no choice. Well, he did, but you know what I mean. Then, to try and stop things from getting worse, he killed Trigger tonight.

184

He wanted to admit it all, he'd had enough, so he came to me. And then Richard turned up."

"So he wasn't outside your house earlier?"

"Yes, about half seven. Officers sent him away, but he came back. I bloody *knew* he would. He thought I was having it away with Peter, of all people. We asked him to leave, but he wouldn't go. I arrested him for trespassing and went off to get my cuffs. By the time I got back, Richard was on the floor. You know that doorstopper I've got, the one my nan gave me?"

"The kettle?" Anna imagined all sorts. That spout was lethal, and she'd worried Ben would fall and hurt himself on it.

"Yes. It went through his neck. Richard pulled it out, such a stupid thing to do, and the blood . . ."

"How did he end up on the floor, though?"

"When I arrested him, Peter had hold of Richard's wrists. I can only assume Richard got away from him, tripped and landed on the kettle."

Anna had interviewed enough people to spot when a story sounded like the truth but laced with a trim of fabrication. She sighed, disappointed that she was being lied to when she'd thought Sally would trust her. "That's bloody unfortunate. Did you ask Peter what happened?"

"I was too panicked at the time, so I just phoned it in, but when the PCs arrived Peter told them Richard had gone for him, and to defend himself he'd pushed him away."

"He's been taken in, yes?"

"Yes."

"Good. Parole came up trumps. Confirmed Peter is a mole and he killed Jamal on a loyalty job, like we thought. Thank God Peter confessed to you; it means I don't have to do this anymore." A pinch of sadness hit her, but she'd allowed herself to live in fantasy land while with Parole, to pretend, and she should never have entertained anything other than bringing him down.

She glanced into the bar at him.

He was on his phone. Was someone telling him Trigger was dead?

"What am I going to tell Ben?" Sally said. "How do I explain it to him?"

"Go into work mode, use your training. It'll get you through. Where are you going to go? Your house is a bloody crime scene."

"I can't face my parents at the minute, so no clue. The Premier Inn?"

"No. You'll be going down the station first anyway, won't you? In my office, top drawer, at the back, keys to my place in case I lose my other set. Once you've given your statement, take Ben to mine."

"Bloody hell, I don't deserve you being nice to me. Not after . . ."

Anna hated being right. She'd push a little, see if Sally trusted her enough to open up. "What do you mean by that?"

"N-nothing."

"Sally . . . what *really* happened?"

"Oh God, I can't tell you . . ."

The good Peter was the type to want to make Sally's life better. Everything slotted into place, and Anna had to ask herself what to do now. Keep quiet or stick to the rules? God knew she'd learned a lot about herself while undercover. She wasn't white as snow; she'd thought things, hoped for things she shouldn't. And Richard had been a bastard. All right, he hadn't deserved to die, but whatever had gone on between Sally and Peter, in that moment Sally had wanted a final solution. Only now she'd realised the ramifications of that. Having to lie. Having to live with whatever had occurred.

Can I carry this secret? Really? Who am I if I do?

Who have I become?

"Peter pulled the spout out," Sally blabbed.

Anna took a deep breath. "Don't tell anyone, do you understand me?"

"What?"

186

"You heard. Stick to the other story."

"But—"

"I mean it. Peter did you a bloody favour. But I'm telling you, this part of our conversation didn't happen, right? I'll deny ever being told."

"Right. I . . . Thank you."

Parole stood, slipping his phone away.

"I have to go. Parole's coming. Remember, stick to the story." Anna ended the call, telling herself that Richard's death had been an accident, that he'd pulled the spout from his own neck, not Peter.

Whatever, she'd chosen her road, and so she'd walk it. For Sally.

She grimaced to let Parole think she wasn't happy about the news she'd just received. He came to a stop in front of her, his poker face giving nothing away.

"I've got something to tell you," she said. "Best we talk about it in the car."

She led the way outside and, once they'd settled into their seats, she pulled up her last reserves, her last bit of acting for this job. She looked at him. "Peter's confessed to everything." She slammed her palm on the steering wheel. "Of all the fucking idiotic things he could have done. What are we going to do now?"

He ran a hand over his face. "Trigger's dead. Peter killed him."

"I know, I've just been informed. What the hell was going through his head? Who told you?"

"Wheels. He's retired — well, you know he hasn't, but he really has now, if you catch my drift. He wants nothing to do with this. He's had enough. He phoned me in case I wanted to distance myself, too. With Trigger gone, Wheels was next in line to take over. With Wheels stepping away, it's me."

"Don't do it," she blurted.

He frowned at her. "Do you know something I don't?"

"Take it from me, you don't want to be a King right now. You'd better hope you've told me the truth about your involvement with them, because with Peter singing, you could go down for a bloody long stretch if you've done worse." She'd given him hope that he might be able to walk away from this, but Anna would have to file a report about tonight, the same as she had for all the other nights she'd been with him. Her undercover role might be coming to an end, but she still had to continue as a copper, and bring him down along with all the others.

But it would be her word against his. Parole admitting he'd kill for the Kings could be brushed aside as her making it up in order to frame him.

And he'd perhaps know soon that this had been nothing but a sting operation. The police would speak to him, maybe tell him.

"I'm going to have to stop seeing you, you know that, don't you? I can't risk being drawn into this, not while Peter's shone a bloody great light on himself and the Kings."

She paused. Contemplated saying something that wouldn't go into a report, something she could deny if he repeated it during questioning. Still, she'd say it anyway. Because it was true. "I actually really like you. I want you to know that. Whatever happens, whatever comes out, I was starting to care more than I should."

"I know, and it kills you, doesn't it? Falling for a King."

"I wouldn't go *that* far."

He laughed, then sobered. "Seems like we're destined not to be together."

"We were stupid to think we could be."

That eye contact. That chemistry.

He leaned over and kissed her. She kissed him back, wishing it could have been different, all of it. She eased away before she did something stupid. Reined in her emotions and tucked them away, although a corner of them poked out and probably would for a while. Their opposing paths aside, she now knew what it felt like to be with someone you really connected with, to think about them in *that* way, to fantasise about a future if they'd met in another time, another place.

She sighed. "Like I said to you before, I'm a copper, you're a criminal. It could never work."

"I'll miss you, Anna."

She hated herself for thinking it, but she'd miss him, too. "We'd better go."

He nodded. "Sod's law that I was on a promise and I've had a bucket of cold water thrown over me."

She laughed, then drove away, relieved he hadn't pushed it, asked her to keep seeing him. He had enough sense to know they couldn't be caught together, not now. Not ever.

No more beating myself up for how he makes me feel. No more dates. Nothing. Clean slate, like this never happened.

She swallowed the lump in her throat and concentrated on the road. That was better than pretending she could've had the world with him.

In a different lifetime, maybe, but not this one.

CHAPTER TWENTY-SIX

What a rush, taking a risk like that. Bringing Billy to Southgate where there were so many cameras. He'd waited until the Jacobean had shut, of course, and turned its lights off, leaving that area of town nice and quiet now all the revellers had gone home. He'd left Billy's BMW in the corner of the car park. Carried him, fireman style, round the back to the yard where the smokers got their nicotine fixes. No security light had come on. He'd sat Billy at a wooden bench table, resting his chest and head on the top as if he'd had one too many beers and had fallen asleep. Arms laid on the surface, his remaining hand curled into a half fist. The other lay in a shoebox at home.

Prior to leaving the house, Rory had recalled Dad's teachings, how much time he had before rigor really set in. There had been plenty to spare. He'd placed Billy on the back seat, then returned to the house. Changed his clothes, showered, put on clean fatigues. Billy's shoes were the same size as Rory's and as comfortable as anything, although they still rubbed the blisters he'd got from Martin's. He'd painted his face again. Set off to the pub, whistling.

He backed away from the body. Whispered, "Will she cry, your wife? Or will she be glad she doesn't have to put up with your arrogance anymore?"

Rory left via the back fence, climbing on a beer barrel and hoisting himself over. He was a tad clumsy and made a fair bit of noise, catching his foot on the wooden slats, and on the other side he paused, waiting for lights to go on in the flat above the pub. The landlord must be a heavy sleeper, though, as the place remained in darkness.

Rory made his escape through the cobbled backstreet area, where more rich people slept on their stupidly expensive mattresses, likely under high-thread-count duvet covers. Egyptian cotton or some bollocks like that.

You're not being as careful as you should be, son. Stop letting your mind wander.

Rory acknowledged that. But how brilliant would it be tomorrow, when he read the news and saw Billy had been found? How amazing that, if he got lucky, no one would know it had been him.

"Camouflage, Dad. God."

That won't save you.

"It'll be fine. Stop worrying."

Did you bring the note?

"Yeah."

Rory walked on, towards Billy's house. Brought the note to mind: *He's in a **public** place. James was the king.*

Would they find Billy before his wife read the note?

He said his wife's away, don't forget.

Rory's face flamed hot. He *had* forgotten.

Maybe Dad was right, he wasn't being as careful as he should be.

191

CHAPTER TWENTY-SEVEN

Anna got up at half past six to find a happy little boy sitting at her kitchen table with a plate of jam on toast in front of him. Sally poured coffee from the carafe, dressed as if she planned to go to work, although she looked shattered. As Sally's clothes would have been kept as evidence, Anna had left her a note to help herself to anything hanging in the spare bedroom that she used as part wardrobe, part crash pad for when Lenny had too much to drink at the village pub and couldn't drive home. *New packet of knickers in the top drawer*, she'd added. Had Sally spotted some of Lenny's stuff in there? The bugger had conveniently left a spare outfit, a toothbrush and some toiletries.

Sally had chosen one of Anna's old suits, a grey one, and a light-pink blouse. Ben had his uniform on. He must have slept OK at the station, if Sally thought he'd be OK to go to school.

Anna had deliberately turned her phone off when she'd dropped Parole at Jubilee Lake. She'd wanted to be selfish for a while and ignore work, tend to her confused heart and mind, accept things could never be, then close off the chapter. She'd yet to switch it back on, and anticipated many missed calls from the DCI, maybe a few messages, too.

She was only thinking of herself, she realised. Placket might have worried about her going dark, seeing as he'd known she was out with Parole, but perhaps Sally had told him, when she'd arrived at the station, that she'd spoken to her and all was well.

"What time did you two get in?" Anna asked.

"About one."

"Not too bad, then. You're taking Ben to school?" Anna took one of the coffees. She sat opposite the lad and ruffled his hair. "Do you want to go and eat that in the living room? You can stick the telly on if you like."

He grinned at her and trotted off.

Sally smiled after him. "Believe it or not, he slept like a log all night. Didn't even know we weren't at home until he woke up here."

"Oh, to be a child," Anna said. "Have you told him yet?"

Sally sat opposite. "No. Can't face it. Not at the minute."

"In your statement, did you say what I told you to? Last night?"

"Yes. What I don't understand is why—"

"I've realised things aren't always black and white. Life has some seriously grey area — and if it makes you feel better, I can trade secrets with you, then we'll be even."

Sally eyed her. "Do I want to hear this?"

"Probably not, no more than I wanted to hear yours, but I'm telling you anyway so you don't beat yourself up about lying. So you know that even I walked in the grey area and likely always will when it comes to a certain person and my feelings about him. What I mean is, regardless of whether I like it or not, there will always be a little space in my heart for him."

"Parole?"

"Hmm. I fancied him back. I wanted us to be together. Now, I can't work out whether that's because he seemed to put a ruddy great spell on me whenever we were together, or because for the first time I actually wanted to know

193

what having a serious relationship was like. But whatever, I dreamed. I wished. For one tiny, tiny moment, I imagined actually being a mole for the Kings just so I could please him."

Sally gaped at her. "I don't believe you. You're just saying that so I don't feel bad for my thoughts about Richard. When I nodded to Peter and—"

"When you *didn't* nod to Peter."

"Right."

"But I'm not lying. It's a mess up here regarding him." Anna tapped her head. "I want him to be able to walk away from this — how mad is that?"

"You've never felt like this about anyone before, have you?"

"No."

"First love is always a kicker. Take me and Richard. I remember feeling like that. I'd have done anything for him. And I understand how you could want Parole to get away with whatever he's done. Kind of like how I feel about Peter now, although he won't get away with sod all. I remembered our friendship when I *didn't* nod." She gave a sad smile. "All the times we'd had a laugh and whatnot, the trust between the team, all of it, and he just knew what to do. He wanted to make everything all right for me, maybe to make amends for lying to us, and I let him do it. I'm a horrible person, because there's been many a time I've wished that man dead. Richard, I mean."

"I know who you meant. I'd have wished him dead an' all."

"How do we move on from this?"

"We pretend. We lie through our teeth."

"But we're coppers. We're supposed—"

"I know what we're *supposed* to do, but it's happened, we can't change it, and whenever you think about confessing, think of that little boy in there. He needs you. He can now grow up without that bastard's influence. Peter was right on the money."

"We're not meant to condone murder."

Anna smiled. "Like I'm not meant to condone Parole and what he's done. But just this once for each of us, eh?"

Sally nodded. "You've changed."

"I know."

Sally sighed. "Me, too."

"I know. It's called life, I suppose."

* * *

The mood in the incident room? Sombre.

Anna handed out cups of tea in the bristling, spiky silence. No one had spoken since she and Sally had arrived. Anna had followed her to the school to drop Ben off for breakfast club, and when they'd got here Placket, Warren and Lenny were waiting. Sally sat at her desk, staring into space. Placket paced in front of the whiteboard, gaze on the floor. Warren sat at his desk, his forehead in his hands. And Lenny? He appeared fit to burst, standing by Anna's office, desperate to speak to her privately.

She felt bad that the person she'd opened up to about Parole was Sally. It should have been Lenny, they were good mates, but maybe it was best he didn't know. Probably because she didn't want him to see a different side to her. He flitted from woman to woman, going on dates, never picking one to settle down with, never giving himself a chance to feel what love was — similar to how Anna had been, except she hadn't even dated anyone for a long time before Parole. He probably wouldn't understand how she could have feelings for a man who did bad things. Lenny didn't see grey areas if it didn't suit him.

The silence seemed to strengthen. It was to be expected, considering they'd all had such a heavy blow. No matter that they'd anticipated this, it still hurt. A member of their team had confessed to murder, among other things, and would be interrogated today by another team. No words seemed necessary — or else they *couldn't* be spoken, not yet. Because if

195

they were, all that raw sewage would come out, spewed into the open, everyone revealing just how upset they *really* were.

It was like Warren had said, a bereavement.

Anna took her tea into her office. She shut the door. Checked her emails. Tried to get her head in the game by going over the current case to see if they'd missed anything, but after half an hour it was clear she had to be the one to prod everyone's open, festering wounds. They'd have to discuss it at some point, so it may as well be now, and, so the elephant didn't lurk in the corner all day, clouding their work, she took charge and returned to the incident room.

"Look, we knew he was up to shit, just not how much. We toyed with the fact he'd killed Jamal, and I understand that finding out for sure is a massive blow to us all, but we have to move on. We've got a case to solve."

Warren lifted his head. "I was angry before, when I thought he'd only been filtering information out, but all this? Killing Jamal? Trigger? It's knocked me for six. I didn't really believe he had it in him to stab a kid or kick a man to death."

"Me neither," Placket said. "It just goes to show what a hold Trigger had over him. Imagine the influence he had over people who are weaker than Peter? The man we knew wouldn't have voluntarily gone off to knife a young lad. We should have known he'd been forced."

"If he's telling the truth about that," Lenny said.

"And it still doesn't change the fact he did it," Anna reminded them. "He made a conscious decision there." She glanced knowingly at Sally. "No matter that Peter had been told to do it, he could have said no. He was the one who took the final plunge. He's the one responsible."

Another quick glance at Sally. Her shoulders relaxed as the crux of it sank in. Yes, she'd given Peter the green light to take that spout from Richard's neck, but Peter could have said no. Instead, he'd decided to save her from a life of misery. As far as anyone else was concerned, Richard killed himself accidentally.

"I'm going to nip down and see him," Anna said.

She left the room, leaving her tea behind. Downstairs, she asked Karen to make one for Peter in the safe cups they provided for offenders. In the kitchen beside the booking-in desk, they stood side by side with the door closed.

"Bloody awful about Peter," Karen said while sorting the tea.

"We knew he was up to something, so it wasn't a shock to us like it must be for you and everyone else."

"How the hell did you keep it quiet that you were watching him? I mean, I get it, but I thought you'd have at least told me."

"Sorry, it had to remain completely covert. I'd have told you if I could."

Karen poured milk into the cup. "But Peter, though. We all believed him when he said he'd left the Kings as a kid. I feel so stupid now. Don't know who to trust anymore. He lied to us all for *years*."

That touched a nerve. From now on, Anna and Sally would be lying, keeping secrets, pretending they were someone they weren't.

"He had no choice," Anna said, as if to confirm to herself that she and Sally didn't either. When they did. *Don't think about it. Move on.* "The Kings had him wrapped around their fingers."

"I suppose I can feel sorry for him. A little bit." Karen handed Anna the cup. "It's got to be hard for you. He was a big part of your team."

"We'll manage. Someone else will take his place. Anyway, cheers for making this. I'm popping in to see him now."

Anna left. Her stomach churned on the walk to the holding cells. She caught the attention of a nearby officer, who let her into Peter's room. Peter glanced up at her, his face flaming, and tears dripped down her face. She hadn't expected to want to hug him, but she did.

"Here. Thought you might like a cuppa." She gave it to him and sat on the bed. "How are you?"

"I've been better." He sniffed. "I'm sorry. For everything."

"You did the right thing." She meant about Richard, but to anyone watching through the camera in the corner, listening, it would seem she'd referred to the confession.

She looked up at the camera.

He did, too. Then stared at her. Caught on to her meaning. "Is Sally OK?" he asked.

"She will be."

"Wheels will take over."

He won't. "I have no idea whether he's even been brought in. Depends whether you've mentioned his name or not."

"I haven't gone into all the details yet. I'm being questioned this morning."

"Depending on what he's done, whether proof will be found, he might not walk back out of here. Same with other members." *Parole.* "I assume you're grassing on the lot of them."

"Do you want me to?"

No. "Any King who has done anything illegal needs to pay for it."

"Some didn't do anything that would warrant them spending time inside, and there isn't any proof they did stuff anyway."

"I see." *He's telling me Parole will walk.*

"I understand why you went undercover."

She smiled. "Ah, someone's been talking, then."

"Trigger told me."

"And how do you feel about that?"

Peter shrugged. "You were doing your job, like I should have. Jamal . . . I should never have done it. But they were in my gaff, Trigger and Wheels, and they'd have hurt me if I refused."

"Don't tell me anything else. Save it for the other officers during the interview. It's best you do this with a solicitor present. You know that."

He sighed. "I wish I could turn back the clock."

"Don't we all." She laid an arm across his shoulders. "Remember that you did a good thing near the end."

"Right."

She stood. "I'd better go. The case, still got to find that bloody killer."

"Good luck."

She couldn't look at him. Funny how her anger towards him had all but dried up. How his lies didn't burn her so much now she had some of her own tucked inside her. "I hope . . . I hope you can find some kind of peace eventually. No one hands us an instruction manual on how to feel, we just have to muddle through. You can beat yourself up all you like, but in the end, so long as you can forgive yourself, maybe it'll all turn out right."

Was she talking to him or herself? She didn't know.

She walked out, a range of emotions flickering through her.

Life really was hard sometimes.

* * *

Just as she was about to go upstairs, Karen came running towards her.

"What's up?" Anna asked.

"There's another body."

"Bloody hell."

Karen handed her a piece of paper. "All the details are on there."

"Thanks. I'd better go." Anna rushed upstairs to the incident room. "OK, enough of being maudlin. There's been a second murder. Can you arrange for another DC to join us now Peter's not here, sir? Or do you think we can handle this without one?"

"I'll dig in as much as I can," Placket said. "We'll sort a new DC after this case. When the dust's settled."

Anna walked to the whiteboard and wrote down the details from Karen's note. "Male, possibly in his forties. Both shoes are missing, as is the right hand, so it's our man up to his tricks again. Location of the body is in the yard behind the Jacobean in Southgate. Lots of cameras there, so we might get lucky."

"Trigger was offed in a pub yard as well," Warren said.

"A coincidence," Lenny muttered. "Unless Peter confesses to killing this bloke an' all."

No one responded.

"That's all we've got so far," Anna said, sweeping away the awkwardness. "So, get on CCTV around the Jacobean. I'll let you know the ID of the victim once it's been established so you can poke into him."

She glanced at Lenny, who still looked like he wanted that private word.

"In the car," she said to him. Then to everyone else, "Chin up, eh? At least this will take our mind off things."

"Never thought I'd see murder as a silver lining," Warren said, "but I get what you mean."

At last, someone laughed, breaking the tension. Placket.

"Jesus Christ," he said. "Come on, everyone to it. Life goes on."

"Or not, for the victim," Warren quipped.

Anna smiled. The dark humour was back.

Maybe they were going to come out of this OK after all.

CHAPTER TWENTY-EIGHT

"Spit it out," Anna said.

Lenny, in the passenger seat, folded his arms. "What the hell were you thinking, turning your phones off? You were with that bloody lunatic, and no one could get hold of you. Placket rang me to come in last night because of Peter, seeing as you were unobtainable, and if it wasn't for Sally telling us you were OK the boss was going to send local officers to that bloody hotel in York."

Anna winced. When Sally had taken Ben into school, she'd finally switched on her phone. Lenny had left a frantic voicemail message, convinced Parole had tied her up somewhere.

She swerved down a side road. "Sorry, but I had a lot to process and needed to go into my shell. I chose the wrong time to do that."

"Too right you did. We all know you're an introvert and need space, but seriously, last night was not the moment to go off and hide. I even checked ANPR to make sure you drove home from York. That's how paranoid I was." He paused to take a breath. "Do you know what I thought? That Parole had twigged that you were undercover, that he'd found out somehow and he'd been ordered to get rid of you. I even imagined Peter had found out, he'd told Trigger, and Trigger had said you needed to be shut up, then Peter had killed him to save you."

"I really am sorry."

"Yeah, well, don't scare me like that again. I bloody love you to bits and don't want to have to scrape your body up off the floor because some maniac has seen fit to hurt you."

"He wouldn't hurt me."

"Don't kid yourself. He might fancy you but, when it comes to the Kings, you can bet he'd choose them over you. The lot of them are weird, like a cult, all sticking together. You've already told me he makes you uneasy, which didn't help when I was panicking. Anyway, that's not an issue anymore because Placket said you won't have to go under-cover now Peter's ready to tell all. And thank God for that, because—"

"All *right!* I get it. You were worried, and thank you, but I'm fine, it all worked out."

"Promise me you won't go near him again unless it's to question him and someone else is with you. And how can you be so sure he wouldn't hurt you?"

"Like I said in one of the debriefs, I've seen a different side to him. He isn't as hard and scary as he makes out. I really appreciate how much you care about me, but drop it now. We're here."

She stopped behind a short snake of patrol cars. Officers spoke to rubberneckers who were out bright and early. Some turned people away. Drivers drew up in cars, eager to snatch the free parking spaces along the road. Having two cordons up, sectioning the pub off, had created a miniature world of chaos — ants, so used to their routine, thrown off course by the strips of tape.

Anna and Lenny got out. She found some protective clothing in the boot and handed Lenny a set. They togged up, leaving the booties off for now; they drew too many gazes

202

in their direction. She supposed that seeing this many officers, the patrol cars, and the general buzz of activity was a huge shock. It was obvious something big had happened. She'd be curious if she wasn't in the know, too — but, when someone produced a phone, she held her hand up.

"Err, no way. Go home, please."

The man holding the mobile backed off, but she'd bet he'd get it out again once her back was turned. Before long, pictures and videos would make their way onto social media, luring more people to the area.

At the cordon, she signed the scene log and smiled at PC Parvati Jahinda. "Bet it's been a nightmare keeping the nosy parkers at bay."

"I didn't realise anyone would be out so early," Parvati said. "But there's Brunch round the corner, so people have been trying to park here so they can go and get their breakfast. That's their excuse anyway."

Anna's mind lingered on their sausage rolls. As she'd followed Sally into work today, she hadn't stopped off at Brunch to get her usual rocket-fuel takeaway coffee. Maybe she'd nip round there after they'd seen the body and fill up on caffeine.

Lenny signed the log. "That's made me want a sausage cob. Can we . . . ?" He glanced at Anna to check if she was on the same wavelength.

"Yep, I thought exactly the same, but first things first." Parvati laughed. "Bring me one while you're at it."

Lenny winked. "Crime scene contamination, young lady, what with you dropping crumbs, so no chance."

"Excuses, excuses." Parvati smiled.

Anna and Lenny ducked under the cordon, then through an open gateway at the side of the pub. She paused to put her booties on, imagining the killer taking this route to escape. Or hoping, because it meant he'd be caught on camera somewhere in Southgate. She came out into a yard full of forensic techs collecting bits and bobs off the ground. Herman stood beside a picnic table, staring down at someone slumped over it. The victim had one hand missing. Anna looked down. He didn't have shoes on. Definitely the same killer.

She took a deep breath and moved closer. "Morning, Herman."

His eyes crinkled above his mask. "Morning."

Steven popped his head up from the end of the table where he was crouching. "Morning."

"Feeling better today?" she asked him.

"In some ways. It was nice and quiet at home last night, for a start. No one nagging." He laughed, probably to hide the hurt.

"Always a bright side to everything." Anna focused on the victim's face. "That's a deep slash on the cheek compared to the rest of the face. Is it me, or do the slices look like the fat on roasted gammon? Or the diamonds of a pineapple?"

Herman nodded. "Someone took their time to carve that. It's been done precisely, apart from that deeper cut."

"So wherever he was murdered, his killer wasn't worried about being discovered." Anna compared this location to the warehouse. "At Dobsons, if it wasn't for the Kent boys finding Martin, the body may have gone undiscovered for a while. Yet this time, he's out in the open. It's obvious he'd be found quicker. Who rang it in, by the way? The landlord?"

"No, he's away for the Christmas break. His manager was the unfortunate one," Steven said.

"Where is he?"

"Inside with Ollie."

"We'll go and speak to him now. What's his name?"

"Keiron Jones," Steve said.

Anna jerked her head at Lenny. He followed her to the back door. She knocked, and Ollie opened it. She peered inside at what amounted to a staffroom. A man in his thirties sat at a table, both hands round a mug. Shaved head. Gaunt. A neck tattoo. If she went by appearances, if a person's looks alone told you they were evil, she'd believe he was the killer.

Good job she knew killers could appear absolutely normal, although she disliked that word.

"DI Anna James," she said to him. "Sorry, I know you've probably been through this already, but I need to ask a couple of questions."

"No problem." He stared beyond her, his blue eyes bright, perhaps with unshed tears.

"When you arrived, was the BMW already here?"

"Yeah. I didn't take any notice, though. Some people leave their cars if they've had too much to drink. I can't remember if it was there when I got a taxi home after closing."

"Talk me through what you did prior to finding the body."

"Not a lot. I used the front door, turned the alarm off. Came straight in here, put the kettle on. While it was boiling, I nipped out for a smoke. Saw him. Rang the police."

A man of few words. "So you didn't approach him to see if he was OK? That isn't me picking fault, I want to rule out your DNA if you touched him."

"No, I kept well back. His face . . . It was obvious he was dead. Plus it shit me up, know what I mean?"

To take his mind away from whatever was playing out in it, she asked, "Do the cameras work or are they dummies?"

"The ones out the front are functional, but the back ones are only deterrents."

Ollie caught Anna's attention. "We've already sent the CCTV in. Keiron found the relevant section for me. Around 3 a.m. Man in dark clothing, matching the previous description."

"Right." Anna returned her focus to Keiron. "Have you been told you won't be able to open up today?"

"Yeah."

"OK, I'll leave you with Ollie."

She turned and left, snicking the door shut behind her, and faced the scene again.

Wayne, the photographer, dipped in to take close-ups of the face. "All done here until he's moved."

Herman slid a gloved hand behind one front of the suit jacket. He pulled out a wallet. "Again, the killer didn't feel the need to hide the identity." He opened it. A driver's licence sat behind a transparent panel. "William Faulkner."

"Shit," Lenny said. "He's one of the sons-in-law on our list. Married to the daughter of Bryan Liedson."

Anna tutted. "Yet he was warned about being careful. Bloody hell. OK, as we already have details on him, I'll ring Sally, get her to contact the other men and reiterate that they *really* need to be careful."

"I expect they'll listen now two people have died," Lenny said.

Anna sighed and phoned Sally. "Hi. It's one of the sons-in-law. William Faulkner. Can you give me some details on him, please?"

"Aww, poor sod. Fifty-two Portland Road. Wife, Gina. He's got a business suite in the Gear Hub. Architect. No priors."

"Thanks. We'll nip round to the house now. Can you get hold of street CCTV, please? There's cameras all over the place here, so hopefully we'll get something useful."

"Will do."

"Ollie's sent in the footage from the front of the pub, so look out for that. Has William been reported missing?"

"Hang on." Sally tapped on her keyboard, the clicks loud. "No."

"OK. Find out if he went to work yesterday, what his movements were."

Anna ended the call. As he hadn't been reported missing, had he arranged to stay out overnight? If so, why had he disregarded the advice he'd been given by the PCs to tread carefully?

She'd soon find out, but she didn't relish speaking to yet another wife who'd have her world turned upside down, her husband's death linked to her father's.

"Come on, Lenny," she called. "Time to do some dirty work."

CHAPTER TWENTY-NINE

Rory hadn't slept very well. Dad's whispers had got to him, and he worried he'd get caught before he'd completed the list. Was he prepared to go to prison? No. But it might end up that way. Even more alarming than that thought, someone had knocked on the front door around half past eight this morning. Rory had peeked out of a gap in the living room curtains and seen an older man in a suit. He'd looked official, and it had scared him. More so when the visitor had written something on a card and the letterbox had clattered. The irony of that wasn't lost on him. Rory had gone out to see what the bloke had posted and had found a business card on the mat, a note on the back: *Can you give me a call, please? Just need to ask a couple of questions.*

He hadn't liked the sound of that. It couldn't be about anything other than the murders, could it? He must have been caught on CCTV in town last night. Or the police had followed the guinea pig angle. What if they'd been to see Mum? Would she have mentioned her precious Copper going missing? Had that prompted the man to come and speak with him? Typical that she hadn't warned Rory. She wouldn't care if he got arrested.

So here he was, in Southgate, preparing himself to go into the pet shop and see if she told him anything. A lot of police officers stood around in High Street, six that he'd counted. Rory hoped he could dodge being questioned, especially since he had Billy's shoes on. Bloody hell, he hadn't thought that through, had he?

He strode along the pavement, browsing shop windows as he passed, going for a casual air. He caught sight of himself in the glass. His reflection showed that he didn't look casual at all. More like panicked. Uneasy. Trapped.

"Shit," he muttered, and stopped to stare at the display inside Superdrug. To get his bearings, centre himself. Oil of evening primrose was on a three-for-two offer. Multivitamins had forty per cent extra in the tubs.

Shoppers darted about behind him, their movements playing out on the pane as cinefilm flickers. Someone in dark clothing approached. They had the word POLICE on their vest. Rory kept his attention lower than the man's eyes, in case the officer was checking to see if Rory had seen him.

"Can I have a quick word, sir?"

Rory spun round, a hand to his chest. "Oh, you gave me the fright of my life!" He chuckled.

The PC smiled. "Sorry. Shouldn't have snuck up on you. Have you seen anyone this morning who may have acted suspiciously? Hanging around?"

Rory shook his head. "I haven't been taking any notice, to be fair. Why, has someone been shoplifting or something?"

"There's been an incident at the Jacobean. Did you come to town that way?"

"No, I came from up there." Rory pointed to the top end of High Street. "I'm just going to my mum's shop to help her out." *Why did I say that?*

"Which shop is that?"

"Prudence's Pets."

"And your name is?"

Look at the hole you've dug for yourself, son. Didn't you pay attention when I was teaching you?

Fuck it. "Rory McFadden."

"OK, sir. Thanks for your time."

Relieved, Rory strode off, wishing he had eyes in the back of his head. He couldn't resist peering over his shoulder — stupid of him, Dad was quick to say, but it was done now. The officer spoke into either a radio or a phone, he couldn't make out which, and it bothered him. What with that copper leaving the business card this morning, it seemed the police were onto him. But if they were, why had that plod let him walk away?

Rory continued on, heading for the row of shops at the bottom of the U. His heels were so sore, he reckoned the blisters had popped. He got closer, safety only a few steps away.

He caught the reflection of the officer in Mum's window.

The fucker was following him.

Shit. Shit!

Rory wanted to run, but he had to maintain his cool. He pushed the door open, holding it wide for a customer to go out, then he shut it, locked it and grasped the blind cord. Through the glass he could see the copper frowning and speaking into that phone or radio again.

Rory tugged, and the blind blocked the view. The barrier created the illusion that Rory would be OK now, but the front window was still exposed, and he glanced that way. The policeman stared inside, his face visible between two hamster cages in the display.

"What are you doing?" Mum asked.

He spun to face her, jumpy as hell. "Is the back door locked?"

"Yes, but—"

"Where's Cuddy?"

"Having a cuppa. Why?"

"Tell him to stay there. Do it."

Mum eyed him funny. "You're worrying me. What's going on?"

"Just do what I fucking said, you silly cow, all right?"

Mum gave him such a nasty glare he thought she'd bite back at him.

Instead, she turned to the door behind the counter, opened it and poked her head round the edge. "I just need a little word with Rory, so can you stay out of the way?"

"Everything all right?" Cuddy asked.

"Yes, yes, don't worry." She closed the door and leaned on it. Stared at Rory. "Why have you shut the shop?"

"A copper followed me here."

"So?" One of her snide expressions twisted her face. "Ah, maybe you fit the description of that man who's killing people."

He narrowed his eyes. Was she accusing him? In his panic, he couldn't be sure. He'd play innocent for now, like he didn't know about the second murder. "People?"

"Yes, another man was found this morning. Behind the Jacobean. But I'd have thought you'd know about it already."

She's messing with me, isn't she? She can't know anything. "What do you mean by that?"

"It's you, isn't it? Doing whatever it was your father did?"

The shock left him speechless for a moment. "How . . . ?"

"How did I know?" She lowered her voice. "Because he bloody *told* me, that's how. Why do you think I divorced him, you thick little shit?"

Confusion coiled through him, and anger that she'd called him a name. He wasn't a child anymore, he didn't have to put up with it.

Don't let her derail you, kid. Keep focused.

Rory shook his head. "He never said you knew."

"Why would he?"

"Because we shared the secrets."

210

Hurt lanced his chest. Dad had said Mum mustn't know, that she'd tell the police on them if she did, and Dad would go to prison. Yet she had known. He'd told her.

"Why did he lie to me?" he whispered.

Mum chucked a laugh at him, the bitterness of it taking another vicious swipe at his emotions. "Why did he lie full stop? Because he could. It's what he did best."

"Why didn't you grass him up?"

"Because he'd have killed me." She glared at him. "Where's my guinea pig?"

What was the point in pretending anymore? "In a shoebox."

Her love for animals far outweighed any love she had for him, and her face crumpled. "Oh God, you've even done that, have you? Got a couple of hands in boxes an' all?"

Dad told her about that, too? Wasn't anything sacred? "You're not supposed to know that."

"Well, I do. Now get out. Let that policeman deal with you. Face up to what you've done. You're on your own."

"I've always been on my own when it comes to you. You don't give a shit about me, never have."

"Is it any wonder, you weird little *freak*?" The last word came out as a shriek.

Rory acted before he could think it through. He rushed at her with his fist raised, and launched it at her spiteful face.

* * *

Cuddy eased his ear away from the door and crept into the yard. He took his phone out of his pocket, guilt pricking at his nerve endings because of what he was about to do. He was fond of Prudence, but wrong was wrong and, no matter that she'd been good to him, he had to tell the police.

He dialled 999.

CHAPTER THIRTY

Anna drove towards Gina Faulkner's address. In the cup holder, her phone rang. "Can you answer that for me and put it on speaker?"

Lenny picked it up. "It's Karen."

"Bugger, something must have happened."

He did the necessary. "Hi, Lenny here. You're on speaker because Anna's driving."

"OK. You might want to get yourselves down to Prudence's Pets in town. We've had a call from a Jacky Cud, who's locked himself in the yard out the back. He's overheard Rory and Prudence McFadden discussing the murders, both now and then."

"What? His mother knew about it all along? Are other officers there?" Anna asked.

"Yes, PC Franks spotted Rory in High Street and called it in. Then he saw Rory hitting Prudence and kicked the door in. Thought you'd want to know the suspect has been apprehended. At least you can tell the latest next of kin."

Anna itched to go to the shop, to speak to Rory, leave the dreaded death knock to uniforms, but what was the point when everything was in hand? There was time enough for her to talk to him later at the station.

"Right, we really need to see Gina first, so we'll go to the station afterwards."

"Tarra!"

Lenny ended the call. "That's a turn-up, the mum knowing."

"Hmm. Wonder why she kept it quiet all these years? Was she in on it, d'you reckon?"

"God knows, but I suppose we'll find out."

Anna drew up outside the Faulkner house and approached the front door. She knocked, taking her ID out of her pocket. Lenny did the same with his. Then the growl of an engine close by had her turning. A woman drove onto the driveway, her frown severe.

She parked and walked over to them. "Can I help you?"

"Gina Faulkner?"

Anna inhaled. Let it out. Held her ID up. "Can we come in for a chat?"

CHAPTER THIRTY-ONE

In interview room one, Prudence shook in her seat. When that policeman had burst into the shop, she'd never been so relieved. Her face pounded with pain from where Rory had landed several punches, and her stomach felt sore from a nasty thump that had winded her. She'd seen a station doctor, who'd informed her she'd have nothing except a black eye and a few other facial bruises, and declared her fit for questioning.

She didn't want to go to prison but had a feeling that her part in this may well send her down that awful road. She'd known about it all and hadn't said a word.

A woman who'd introduced herself as Anna James sat opposite, someone called Lenny beside her. A solicitor by the name of Gideon Hemmings lounged next to Prudence, quite unprofessionally, she thought. His advice swirled in her mind.

"None of this 'no comment' business in this instance. Because Eric and his mother aren't here to refute it, you must say you were so scared of him that you'd remained silent. It's already noted in the ninety-three file that he had a temper, so this should be plain sailing."

Would that fly, though? She supposed he knew what he was doing. He'd told her about all the cases he'd worked on, that his success rate was ninety-five per cent, so that was promising.

"But what about these murders?" she'd asked, picking at a hangnail. "As soon as Copper went missing, I should have phoned it in."

"You didn't realise. You thought a customer had stolen her."

"But Cuddy heard what I said to Rory."

"That's fine, you only twigged what had been going on this morning. Have you heard of selective memory?"

"No."

"Then I'll explain it to you . . ."

She blinked. Focused on the here and now. The recording had been set up, and this . . . this official behaviour abraded her nerves, brought on another wave of the shakes. Would they think she was guilty? She tried to stop trembling, but maybe she shouldn't. It could go in her favour.

Anna smiled at her. "Tell me about your part in the disappearances of those men — the suspected murders of those men — in ninety-three, plus the two men killed this week."

Prudence launched into her tale, and after a while it wasn't so difficult. All the memories came back, and the night she'd accused Eric flooded in, bringing all the emotions associated with it. She sob-stuttered through the telling as the horror of it smacked her full force, and what Hemmings had said about selective memory made sense. She *had* blocked a lot of it out.

"How come you never came forward at the time?" Anna asked.

Hemmings cleared his throat. "My client suffered with selective memory. For the tape, I'll explain that it's a trauma response, a way for the mind to keep the person safe from the debilitating experience of a harrowing event. It helps the person to cope in day-to-day life, to function. As you can imagine, a husband admitting that he was responsible for abducting then murdering his friends is right up there as one of the most shocking things you can be told. Her instinct

215

was to get away from him, hence the fact that she wanted a divorce. From the state of my client now, you can see that having to remember it has caused tremendous stress. I feel she would benefit from a break."

Prudence didn't want to go back to that holding cell. "No, I'll be OK." She hiccupped another sob. "I want to help."

Anna frowned. "Are you sure you want to proceed?"

"Yes."

"You said you didn't put two and two together about Rory until today. That even your missing guinea pig didn't trigger memories from the past, yet you took the shop key from him in order for Jacky Cud to have it instead."

Hemmings had warned Prudence that the police would try every which way to get her to admit whatever they wanted her to, that there were so many miscarriages of justice because they put all their eggs in one basket and gunned for the person they suspected rather than taking a broader view and looking for others to blame.

"It has to be Rory and Eric who are pinned down for this," he'd said. "You going to prison won't be happening on my watch."

She now understood how guilty people walked free if they had a solicitor like Hemmings. How manipulative he was. How good at his job. She felt bad for thinking him unprofessional because of the way he sat.

Hemmings sat up straighter to answer that question. "My client may have subconsciously taken the key, the recesses of her mind knowing she should but not alerting her as to why. Look it up. It's a known thing. As soon as she did remember everything, when Rory came into the shop this morning, she accused him of taking the guinea pig and murdering Martin Lowe and William Faulkner. Before she could telephone the police, he attacked her. My client has since done everything she can to assist you. I suggest she's given a mental health assessment in order to prove selective memory."

216

Prudence worried that she wouldn't pass whatever test she'd be put through, but she had pushed it so much to the back of her mind over the years, so perhaps she'd be OK.

All she could do was hope.

CHAPTER THIRTY-TWO

Rory glared at the man in front of him. The same one who'd come to his door this morning and posted the business card. Placket. Rory switched his attention to the woman beside him, Sally someone or other, who stared at him so hard he had to look at the tabletop instead. A police-appointed solicitor sat ramrod straight beside him, tapping a pen on his notebook. The noise boiled Rory's nerves.

"Tell us your story," Placket said.

Tell them fuck all, son. It's none of their business why we did what we did.

Rory smiled. "No comment."

"Why did you target the sons-in-law of Toro Munoz and Bryan Liedson?"

"No comment."

"Were you aware that your father may have killed those men as well as four others? Leo Holt, Ezra Noakes, Kyle Minton and Carl Price?"

"No comment."

"What part, if any, did you play in ninety-three, when those six men went missing?"

Rory sighed. Didn't bother repeating his answer, even though his solicitor had advised him to do so after every question.

"Of course, you may not have had anything to do with it," Placket went on, "but it's in your best interests to let us know if you were coerced, as a ten-year-old child, into aiding Eric McFadden in murder. Your mother has told us her version of events as she recalls them, by the way."

"Don't fucking listen to her. She's a lying bitch. She'll do anything to get me in the shit, out of her life. She hates me."

The solicitor kicked Rory's foot under the table.

The Sally woman smiled, a gentle smile that reminded Rory of Kirsty when he'd first met her.

"If you *were* coerced," she said, "then that was a terrible injustice. You were a boy, you didn't deserve what is alleged to have happened. We can help you."

What was this, a tactic? Placket wasn't getting anywhere so Sally was playing the good cop? Rory laughed, couldn't stop himself, and folded his arms.

"Martin's and William's cars have been brought in," she said. "Can you explain why there's face paint inside them? Smeared on the upholstery?"

I said you weren't being as careful as you should, didn't I, son?

Rory swallowed, his stupidity burning him.

The interview continued, the pigs trying to trip him up, get him to confess, but he wasn't listening to anyone except Dad.

Silence from now on, lad. Silence.

CHAPTER THIRTY-THREE

While Prudence was being seen by a mental health professional, and Rory was still in his interview with Placket and Sally, Anna and Lenny joined SOCO at Rory's house. Mr and Mrs Euston were understandably shocked that they had to leave their home and wouldn't be able to go back to the little cottage on the moors for quite some time.

Prudence had mentioned what she'd thought was blood on the floor of the cellar, a large knife on a workbench, and a row of different-sized shoes that didn't belong to Eric. She'd also mentioned a story about mice and a conversation she'd had with Ida McFadden about them peeing everywhere. It had all sounded so ridiculous that it could be true. Eric had clearly been spinning yarns to hide what he'd been doing.

News from Steven's third team at the cottage had come through. The cellar floor had what appeared to be a recent layer of concrete, meaning that the blood would be underneath it. The workbench was still there, but the shoes weren't.

Anna, in protective clothing, stood in one of the bedrooms at Rory's oddly empty house. The wall was covered in newspaper clippings, scrawled handwriting and lines of red wool attached to nails, joining certain information together.

Photos of the men from the nineties had data beneath them on notepaper in the same writing as Donetta's and Gina's notes. The latter had been discovered when William's wife had checked her post while Anna and Lenny had been there.

*He's in a **public** place. James was the king.*

King James obviously pointed to the Jacobean era, and the bolded "public" indicated that the location was a pub. Again, had Anna not known where William had been dumped, she may not have worked it out to begin with.

Also on the wall were other pieces of notepaper held up with drawing pins, a few pages for each man. They listed stages of decomposition, using the same terminology as the likes of Herman. Different writing. Eric's? So he'd been au fait with pathology. Prudence had said he'd spent a lot of time at the library, so perhaps he'd studied it. He clearly had an obsession with how a body deteriorated after death.

Did Rory? Likely not, as he'd left the bodies where they could be found, so perhaps he hadn't wanted to go back and view them as they'd rotted. Going by these notes, Eric had visited the dump sites most days, and he'd written an explanation as to why he'd killed the victims.

Because the men wouldn't lend him money.

Such a *daft* reason to murder.

Anna turned to Lenny. "Bloody hell . . ."

"I know. Rory may not be talking, but this wall is."

"He was stupid enough to put William's shoes on today, so talking himself out of it, if he ever tries to, might be a tad difficult."

"He could say they were friends and they were loaned to him."

"Hmm." Anna glanced over at the corner where a tech, Debbie Short, crouched, having opened a row of shoeboxes. "What's in them?"

Debbie stood. "Six contain what are clearly old hands — the state of them indicates they've been there for a long time. Two have fresher ones in them. All right hands."

"Going by the notes on the wall," Lenny said, "the hands were taken to study decomposition. How sick is that?"

Debbie opened the last box. "A knife. A big one."

Anna gestured to the long row of shoes lined up against the wall beneath the window, each toe butting against the skirting board. "Seven pairs. Six from the nineties, one belonging to Martin, I should imagine, and William's are at the station. At least we aren't looking for a ninth body. We should hear something soon about the dogs going to the moors. Actually, I'm going to check those batches of notes to see if their locations are listed."

Debbie handed Anna a baton-type tool. Anna approached the wall and lifted the first page of one sheaf. More decomposition notes. The last page gave her what she'd hoped would be there. A crude map, drawn with a pen, not pencil. A house, with *Mum's* at the top, some trees dotted about, a stream, and then a cross to mark the spot. She checked all the other sheafs and found the same sort of maps, the crosses in different places.

"Can you take pictures of all these for me, Lenny?"

Anna held up the papers so he could photograph each map. He sent them to her, then she forwarded them to Warren and instructed him to find out who the relevant lead K9 officer was on the moors today.

"That should save them some time," she said.

She wandered out and into another room. Two techs, kneeling on evidence steps, collected small bits off the floor. Another nosed inside an open briefcase. A blow-up bed with a coverless duvet and pillows on top spoke of this being a place Rory had only used to camp out — and commit murder. She'd yet to view the kitchen as it had been filled with SOCOs earlier, but Rory hadn't cleaned up in there. There was blood all over the place, plus a knife on the worktop, so the blade in the other bedroom may well be the one Eric had used.

Prudence had said Rory stayed with her for a good while after he'd split from his ex-wife — someone else they needed to speak to — but that he'd returned here the past few nights.

PCs had spoken to the neighbours, and none of them had seen Rory entering via the front, although they'd noted seeing the lights on sometimes from around the closed curtains. They hadn't thought anything of it because he'd told them he'd be redecorating. Bob Fish, who lived directly next door, hadn't seen or heard a thing either, although he'd said his dog had been distressed in the back garden last night.

With Warren and other PCs still looking into CCTV, hoping to cobble together the string of events that had led to William being brought here — Billy, Gina had said he'd preferred to be called — Anna and Lenny could afford to leave this house and visit Kirsty McFadden. Had she divorced Rory for the same reason Prudence had ended her marriage to Eric? Would *she* conveniently have selective memory?

There was also the witness at the park who was coming in to give a statement. Maybe she'd remember something else once she put her mind to it.

Anna turned to find Lenny on the landing, waiting for her. "Let's go and speak to Rory's ex. I need to get the hell out of this place."

*   *   *

Kirsty had been shocked by the news. Anna didn't believe she'd known anything about Rory's summer spent with his father, but the snippets of conversation she'd overheard while she was married to him had been interesting. Her reasoning behind not thinking too deeply into it was plausible, and Anna doubted the woman would be arrested for hiding anything.

In the incident room, everyone gathered to add to the boards and discuss Rory, who had answered "no comment" all the way apart from blurting a scathing sentence or two about his mother. Despite all the evidence against him, he was going down the "not guilty" route, so a trial was on the cards. No jury would let him walk free, so it was a waste of time and money, but there was nothing Anna could do about that.

"So, we do the laborious work of tying everything up and getting our files shipshape," she said.

Ollie's eyes were glued to a monitor showing CCTV from near the Jacobean, and, at the sight of him occupying Peter's desk, Anna sighed. Would she ever get over her DC's betrayal? She'd been so angry at him before he'd been caught, yet knowing he'd killed Richard for Sally had changed things and she now felt grateful to him. Would keeping that secret prove too much for her in the end? Or would she and Sally eventually slip into the same state as Prudence, their minds wiping out the facts in order to protect them and their careers?

Are we any better than Peter?

"What I don't get is why Billy's face was carved like that," she said to take her mind off the wrongs she'd committed.

Placket drummed his fingers on the desk he sat at. "With Rory not being forthcoming on anything, we'll likely never know."

"That goes for so many things," Lenny said, "but at least we have Eric's written ramblings to go on. Did Prudence confirm that's his handwriting?"

"Yes," Sally said. "With regards to her and whether she gets charged with anything, it's down to the CPS now."

"There's sod all we can do about it if they say she has to walk," Anna said. "Kirsty said she can imagine Eric was a mean bastard, going by the way he used to talk about Prudence. And Jacky Cud remembered something that goes in her favour. A year before Eric died, he went into the pet shop and had a go at her. Gripped her by the throat. Sounds like he was a right charmer."

"The whole thing is bloody twisted," Placket said.

The team phone rang, and Sally picked it up. Listened. Nodded. "Right, thanks." She put the handset in the cradle. "The first body's been scented on the moors."

Anna took a moment to send up a prayer for whoever that man was. "At least we know why they were killed now." She scanned the interactive board, where the photographed

224

page from the murder wall at Rory's explained Eric's reasoning. "Shame we have no idea why Rory targeted Martin and Billy, other than they were linked to the original deaths."

"Sorry, but Eric wasn't all there in the head," Lenny said. "Killing people because they wouldn't lend him money is so off."

"It's more about the emotions he experienced because of it," Sally said. "Rejection, embarrassment, hurt because they didn't have his back."

"Hmm. Any word on the witness at the park?" Anna asked.

Sally shook her head. "She said nothing different to what she wrote on Facebook."

Anna sighed. "Sod it. Shall we sack today off and go for an early dinner? You're welcome to join us, too, Ollie."

No one needed telling twice. Everyone saved files, switched off their computers and gathered their things. Anna led the way out of the station to the pub down the road. The Horse's Hoof bustled with customers, mainly of the police variety, and they grabbed a table in the corner. Placket announced that this was his shout, and nobody put up a protest. Food and drinks ordered, they settled back to relax, talking about anything except the case. For now, they could put it to one side and give themselves a break.

It had only been two days, but so much had been packed into that length of time that it felt more like a week. Exhausted, Anna glanced around at everyone. She was sad that Peter wasn't with them. Then the anger returned; the choices he'd made meant he wasn't a part of the team anymore. Her feelings on that subject would remain topsy-turvy for a while, until the dust had settled, as Placket had put it.

Until she could pretend it had never happened. Hopefully, the same could be said about Parole, who, she'd heard, had been questioned but released due to lack of evidence. Every King had been pulled in, and all of them were closing ranks and refusing to grass each other up. Wheels included.

Would the gang disband now they'd had such a close shave? Or would one of the lower-ranking members take it upon him- or herself to lead them, seeing as Wheels and Parole weren't prepared to do it? Earlier, when she'd spoken to the DI in charge of bringing the Kings down, she'd been surprised to find that a woman called Jane Drummond, Parole's next-door neighbour, was also linked to the Kings. It made sense now, why Jane had backed up Parole's story in the Martin Brignell case a little while ago. He hadn't had to threaten her to comply, she would have been willing. Anything to protect a fellow King.

Anna leaned back. Let out a long sigh. For now, she'd join in the laughter with her team. Kick back and relax. Time enough to worry about the job tomorrow, when a new DC would be appointed and life would move on, as it was wont to do. An ever-flowing river, floating over the stumbling blocks beneath the surface, heading towards an estuary where she might well be able to forget she wasn't a law-abiding copper anymore.

Given time.

CHAPTER THIRTY-FOUR

After the pointless chat with Rory, Sally had popped in to see Peter while he was on an interview break. They hadn't said much because of the camera, but just sitting there, holding hands, they had said everything they'd wanted to say.

As she looked around the table at the remaining members of the team, she pushed down the guilt associated with Richard's death. She'd rather concentrate on what she had to do after she'd eaten — take care of her son. They'd left the station at four o'clock, so she had an hour and a half until she had to collect Ben from after-school club. She'd have to tell him about his father, then deal with Richard's parents, who'd been blowing her personal phone up all day since they'd been told about his death with calls and texts that she'd ignored. They'd also want an explanation as to how on earth she could have gone to work when their precious son had lost his life.

John and Sheila had never accepted his behaviour, and instead had blamed Sally for all of it. They'd been just as narcissistic and gaslighting as him when Sally had kicked him out. Thankfully she hadn't had to deal with them during the divorce or ever since, as Richard had always taken Ben to see them. Now, it would be her job to ensure he got to see his grandparents, and she didn't want to have that responsibility. To see them.

She'd been thinking about that conversation she'd had with Peter in the traffic jam in Warner Road. How, to stop Richard from being in her life every day, she'd have to leave Marlford. Seemed she'd have to do it now anyway if she wanted to protect Ben from the poison John and Sheila would try to infect him with. If she moved far enough away, so they couldn't be bothered to visit him, it would be all right, wouldn't it? Or would they apply to the courts to see him?

Another hassle she didn't need.

Her decision to leave, to distance herself not only from them but Richard's murder and everything associated with it, had cemented itself after she'd walked out of Peter's holding cell earlier. She'd whispered to him, "I'm going to run," and he'd nodded in response.

"At least one of us has the balls to do it," he'd said.

Now, she opened her mouth to announce her intentions to her colleagues, then snapped it shut again. It wasn't the right time. And she owed it to Anna to tell her first. Sally being gone would also mean Anna wouldn't have to see her every day, wouldn't be reminded of the secrets they shared.

The food arrived. Despite the turmoil roiling inside her, Sally was hungry, so she ate, joined in the banter, and pretended.

Something she'd be doing for the rest of her life.

EPILOGUE

A month had passed. Anna, still getting used to having two new DCs on the team, had had a bellyful of today. Louise Golding wasn't a patch on Sally when it came to rooting out information — her research skills were lacking in certain areas — and Rupert Cotter didn't quite fit, wasn't quite right. She acknowledged that her resistance to their presence was because of her wishing things had been different, but they hadn't, and she ought to accept that and stop being so mardy. Placket had not long pulled her up on it, so, if he'd noticed her somewhat distant attitude towards the newcomers, they'd probably noticed it, too.

It wasn't *their* fault everything had gone so tits-up.

She wandered down the pasta aisle in Tesco, stopping to compare the prices of spaghetti. Her hips wouldn't thank her for eating carbs, but she fancied a spaghetti Bolognese for dinner. It was quick and easy, and if she made enough it could last her all weekend. She planned to lie on the sofa this evening watching telly. Friday night, when she wasn't steeped in a big case, was the best. She had the promise of a whole two days

229

off ahead of her, relaxation, pottering around, then the weekly call to her parents on Sunday.

She had a nice surprise for them. She'd booked time off work, starting the week after next, and she was going down south to spend some time with them. They'd ground her, get her head out of her arse with regards to keeping that secret — not that she'd be telling them about it. She couldn't bear their disappointment. She could hardly bear the scorn she poured on herself, regularly thinking she was a hypocrite, a woman who'd promised to uphold the law yet had broken it.

She reached out for a mid-priced packet of spaghetti.

"There's a nice Italian that's opened up in Southgate. They do a mean carbonara. It'd save you slaving over a hot stove."

She froze at that voice, didn't want to turn to look up at who'd spoken. Yet she did it anyway. And wished she hadn't.

"Maybe I want to slave over a hot stove," she said, her voice steely when all she wanted to do was make it soft.

Parole smiled. "How have you been?"

She shrugged. "So-so."

"I miss you."

She swallowed, her outstretched hand dropping to her side. "Don't."

"The Kings have disbanded, just in case you wanted to know."

She snorted. "That sounds like a very King thing to say. Tell a copper they no longer operate, and said copper tells her colleagues, so they back off. They won't stop, you know. The team dedicated to the Kings will keep going until they find something. You're all free for now, but that could change. I don't believe you, that they've disbanded. You're just covering everyone's arses."

"It's true. Without Trigger, it all went to shit."

"You can't expect me to accept that all those drug pushers have stopped selling. That the big guns you told me about, the main spice sellers, haven't snapped them up as runners."

230

"I never said that wasn't happening."

"Right." She snatched up the spaghetti. Dropped it into her basket. "Well, I'd better go." She had to get away from him. Being close to him was dangerous.

"Do you really think they'll catch us in the end?" he asked. "Have they got loads of files on us all? On me?"

She stared at the shelves instead of him. "I couldn't pass on that information even if I wanted to."

"I know you were undercover, but I don't believe you didn't feel anything for me."

"Stop it."

"You did, didn't you? You wished things were different."

"I told you that on the last date."

"Yeah, it makes sense now, what you were trying to say. That despite making out you were fit to be turned, all the lies you told me to get me to talk, you still gave a shit about me. You didn't want me to take over the Kings — you *warned* me not to, in so many words."

She recalled her other words, ones she'd never forget.

I actually really like you. I want you to know that. Whatever happens, whatever comes out, I was starting to care more than I should.

"So?" she said. "There's nothing we can do about it. We can't have a relationship."

"I'll always wish we could, though."

Me too. "Yes, well, I must get on. I've got a date with the telly."

She walked away, hating the tears that stung her eyes, the swell of unfairness that whispered that she could be leaving the potential love of her life. The secret she kept for Sally was enough. She couldn't add more to it. Wouldn't.

But she'd keep another secret, that if she wasn't a copper she'd let herself fall. Annoyed at that thought, she rounded the end of the aisle and gave in to the tug, although she wouldn't act on it.

231

She allowed herself to have feelings for him. Ones she'd keep locked up inside and bring out every now and then on the nights she couldn't sleep.

Grey areas, remember.

THE END

THE JOFFE BOOKS STORY

We began in 2014 when Jasper agreed to publish his mum's much-rejected romance novel and it became a bestseller.

Since then we've grown into the largest independent publisher in the UK. We're extremely proud to publish some of the very best writers in the world, including Joy Ellis, Faith Martin, Caro Ramsay, Helen Forrester, Simon Brett and Robert Goddard. Everyone at Joffe Books loves reading and we never forget that it all begins with the magic of an author telling a story.

We are proud to publish talented first-time authors, as well as established writers whose books we love introducing to a new generation of readers.

We won Trade Publisher of the Year at the Independent Publishing Awards in 2023. We have been shortlisted for Independent Publisher of the Year at the British Book Awards for the last four years, and were shortlisted for the Diversity and Inclusivity Award at the 2022 Independent Publishing Awards. In 2023 we were shortlisted for Publisher of the Year at the RNA Industry Awards.

We built this company with your help, and we love to hear from you, so please email us about absolutely anything bookish at: feedback@joffebooks.com.

If you want to receive free books every Friday and hear about all our new releases, join our mailing list: www.joffebooks.com/contact

And when you tell your friends about us, just remember: it's pronounced Joffe as in coffee or toffee!